A Man Who Rides

Stefani Wilder

Tipped Z: Book 1

Stefani Wilder is a pen name for Robin Stephen

text copyright © 2013 by Robin Theodora Stephen Deutschendorf

stefaniwilder.com
robinstephen.com

Cover photography by Ashley Rose Williams (Phillips), Rocking Lazy A Photography ©2018. All rights reserved.

Cover design by Robin Deutschendorf.

PRINT ISBN: 978-0-9844912-4-7
EBOOK ISBN: 978-0-9844912-3-0

Brown Wing Press
Iowa City, IA
brownwingpress.com

First Brown Wing Press Print Edition

BOOKS BY STEFANI WILDER

A Man Who Rides
A Man Who Starts
A Man Who Heals

Vaquera's Haven
Vaquera's Bronc

for my husband

Chapter 1

You know how sometimes time seems to freeze for a moment, and the scene you're in stays with you forever?

I'm not talking about your iPhone, I'm talking about your mind. And I'm talking about those rare instants that are too perfect for photography.

I guess we're more likely to miss them now that our lives are digitized, but they still happen. They feel like they belong to another world. You forget to fish in your purse for your phone. You forget to try to save something for later. Time freezes, and you watch. Later you find the memory alone is more than enough.

I had a moment like that, and it changed my life.

It happened on the way to work one day. It was a Monday morning and I'd stayed the night at my parents' house. (Yes, I still do that sometimes, even though I'm almost 30. We'll explore the pathetic state of my social life later.) It was early because I had to get home and shower and change and head to work. It was summer though, and the sun was already rising. It wasn't brutally hot yet, but the flat, clear sky held that promise.

I had crossed the narrow bridge that spanned the Rio Oro wash, made my way through the subdivision that abutted my parents' small neighborhood, and was about to pull onto the road that would take me to the state highway. I'd stopped at the stop sign and looked left at an empty road. Then I looked right.

And that's when I saw him for the first time. At first, I thought I was seeing things.

He was sitting on a horse right in the middle of the road, and he had a flag in his hand. It wasn't the kind of patriotic flag they carry in a Fourth of July parade. This was a long, skinny stick with an orange flap on the end, almost like you see cops using to direct traffic, but not quite. I looked at him and he held up the flag at me to say, 'Stop.'

I stared, foot on the brake. There was a cloud of dust behind him and he was backlit by the sun. He was silhouette more than anything. His horse had its head up and a little to the side. I could see both of them in profile. The dust looked like glowing mist. Behind them, the foothills and mountains were lit in pink and gold.

That's the moment that stuck with me, that is etched in my mind forever. I remember thinking, *Who is this guy?* He seemed like something out of a myth: a modern Zorro caught out in his morning commute before he could round the ridge and disappear.

I sat for a moment, waiting, and rolled my window down in case the man wanted to say something. He didn't. He seemed to have forgotten me. He was looking a little over one shoulder. I heard a shout and the jingle of tack.

Another guy trotted his horse past the first one. He was moving on the shoulder of the road. Behind him were about a dozen other horses without riders. They trotted with their heads high, their eyes wide and dark in the weak morning light. They followed the lead horse in a jostle of heads and haunches.

The lead horse went through the intersection where I sat in my car as I gaped through the windshield. The horse and rider turned right and continued into the neighborhood across the road. All the horses followed. Another rider appeared midway back in the group. This one was a woman, a long braid hanging out from below her flat-brimmed hat.

There were not that many horses, really. Soon they had all passed. I lost sight of their hind feet in the dust. I looked back at the single rider, who still sat his horse in the road. He lowered his flag and gave it a little flick, indicating I was free to go on my way.

I took my foot off the brake, turned on my blinker, and turned left. In my rear-view mirror, I saw the man's horse walk out of the road to follow the herd, moving into a smooth canter when it reached the dirt shoulder and disappearing into the dust that still looked like mist or fog.

Two hours later, I heard the back door of the gallery open and close. I looked up from the book I was reading. August was always dead. There was literally nothing to do. But still I felt guilty when Anne came in and found me reading. I put my bookmark between the pages and closed the book, stowing it beneath the counter next to the stack of old-fashioned receipts for imprinting credit cards that had been sitting there since before I'd started here five years earlier, but weren't ever used.

I sat and waited, listening to the sound of Anne dumping her purse and keys in the office and the click of her heels crossing the tile floor of the back hallway that led to the service entrance and the bathroom. It was a small gallery: part of a strip mall that sat across from an upscale shopping center. On one side we had a pet store that specialized in exotic birds and small animals. On the other was a graphic designer. There was a central area between the three stores, with a fountain and an excessive amount of vegetation that our landlord spent an excessive amount of time keeping green and happy this time of year. But he was retired and had nothing to do other than maintain this little strip mall to excess. He was dapper and sweet and didn't talk your ear off. Anne said the patio was one of the reasons she'd decided to take this location. Walking through all those plants got people in the mood to buy art. Or so she said.

This time of year, people didn't seem to buy art no matter how many blooming bushes they'd walked by in the recent past. Some of them wandered through, small groups a couple times a day, but you could tell they weren't going to buy. It was in their body-language, the way they drifted from piece to piece, avoiding eye contact when they turned in your direction. I always left those people alone, either staying in the work room in back if I had something to frame, or looking at the computer if I didn't. Anne used to tell me I should engage everyone in conversation, that you didn't sell things by sitting all still and quiet like a cottontail trying to avoid the notice of a coyote. That was fine for her to say. Anne was the kind of person who could get fifteen minutes of good conversational mileage out of, "Fine, thanks." After she watched me trip over myself a few times trying to talk to the drifters (as I took to calling them), she stopped pushing me to do it.

Anne came clicking into the room, gave me a look, and turned on the radio. It was my other mild insubordination. When the gallery was dead, I tended to leave it quiet. Anne never liked anything quiet. But I'd been working for her for five years. I knew the gallery like she did. The regular customers trusted me, were comfortable with me, and some of them even preferred to deal with me. So there was no way my little trick with the radio was going to hurt my ability to retain the job. Anne thought it was funny.

"Good morning, Erin," she said, walking to the front door and checking to make sure I'd unlocked it. Which I had, of course. At first it had offended me when she'd done things like that. Now I knew it was her way of keeping moving, of using up nervous energy. "Any action today?"

The gallery opened at 9:00 all week, but it was rare for Anne to arrive before 10:30.

I adjusted a stack of business cards that lived on the counter, squaring the edge. "I saw the nuttiest thing on my way to work this morning." I told her about the guy on the horse, and the small herd moving up the side of the deserted little road in the glowing dust.

Anne did a circuit of the room, straightening frames that were already straight and dusting invisible dust off surfaces. She looked at me when I was done talking, amused. "Maybe you should track this guy down. It sounds like you're half in love with him already."

I stared at her.

"I mean, he must live around that area, right? How far can you drive a herd of horses in suburban Arizona?"

The land around my parents' house was a patchwork of small acreages and subdivisions, with the subdivisions gaining more ground every year. Many of the acreages had horse property. "I always wanted my own horse," I said. "I took riding lessons for years. I had to stop when I went to college."

Anne walked over to one of the potted plants we kept around. This was a colossal spidery thing that was always dropping long, skinny leaves. She stooped to pick up one that must have fallen since I'd come in that morning. "There's no time like the present."

It was Anne's mantra. She said it all the time, to clients and customers. And me, of course. But for some reason it sank in that time. I sat there, looking at Anne but seeing that guy on the horse, sitting in the cloud of dust.

Anne tossed the dried leaf into the trash can and clicked her way back towards her office. "I'll be in the back if anyone needs me."

I pulled my book out again but gazed at the page for a long time without actually reading. I glanced behind me to make sure Anne wasn't coming back, pulled out the pad of paper we kept next to the computer, and began to write down some numbers.

I looked at my watch. It was 5:45. I'd arrived five minutes early, which meant I'd been sitting here for twenty minutes. I looked towards the door again. There was no sign of Trace. I considered leaving. I always considered it—leaving her in the lurch for once. But I never did.

Because there she was, walking past the hostess. Julio's Mexican Cantina was midway between my apartment and her house. We met here for drinks once a week. Trace was dressed in nice jeans, a black top, and some sort of heeled boot. When she saw me, she smiled, waved, and hurried over to the table. She pulled out a chair and hung her purse on the back. "Ugh. I'm so sorry I'm late. Kylie got a flat tire on her way over."

I wanted to say, "And you can't leave your daughter in your husband's care for fifteen minutes?" But I didn't. Instead I said, "It's okay." Trace had been my best friend since middle school. Even if she could be a tad unreliable about punctuality since she'd become a mother, she was always there for me when push came to shove.

A server came over and we ordered drinks, G & T for Trace, a pale ale for me. Trace crinkled her nose at my choice. "I still don't know how you drink that stuff."

I took a sip of my water. "I think I'm going to get back to riding horses."

Trace looked up from her drink, her expression curious. We'd taken lessons together for a few years, before high school. "What brought that on?"

I felt myself start to blush. Suddenly I didn't want to tell her about the cowboy. It was one thing to tell Anne. Anne was great. She was a friend by now, but she was also my boss and she wasn't connected to my life beyond the gallery. We didn't hang out socially. Our families didn't get together for holidays. There was no chance of her passing my strange story on to anyone else who knew me.

I shrugged and wiped up the puddle forming around the bottom of my water glass. "I can afford it," I said. "I budgeted the whole thing out this afternoon."

Trace was giving me that suspicious look of hers, that one she gets when she's sure there's something I'm not telling her. Then a tone sounded and she turned to paw through her purse. She pulled out her iPhone and looked at it, her face softening into a smile. "Aw," she said, and handed me the phone.

It was a picture of her daughter, Olivia, who was sitting on a bright green and orange pad on the floor with a rubber ducky half in her mouth. I looked at it and made the obligatory noise to express how cute it was. I handed the phone back as it gave off another tone. Trace read for a moment. "Kylie says they're having a good time."

"Good," I said. Our drinks arrived. I took a few sips of my beer. It was cold and hoppy. Just what I needed. Trace drew some of her G & T through a straw, slouched in her seat, and let out a big sigh. "It's so great to get out of the house."

I knew this was the part where I was supposed to ask her how Olivia was, express interest in her latest baby milestones, and coo over the latest round of retro-style photos I'd already seen because I followed Trace on Instagram. I knew because that's what we did every week.

I tried not to be resentful. Babies were a big deal and Trace's husband, Andrew, was the creative director at this tech startup developing some top secret app. He had an unpredictable schedule and a lot of stress. He was not around enough to have gotten into the swing of taking care of the baby. Monday nights out with me were Trace's break, her one chance to unwind a little. Except all we ever seemed to talk about was Olivia.

I thought again of the cowboy sitting in the road. I couldn't seem to get the image out of my head. Before Trace could say something about Olivia's latest teething toy, I said, "So yeah, I could afford lessons for sure, and maybe even the cost of boarding my own horse."

Trace sipped on her straw again. "Maybe you'll meet a hot cowboy."

I gave her a gentle kick under the table. "Trace, I don't need to meet a hot cowboy. I'm with Ben."

Trace gave me a wicked grin. "I'll believe that when I see some evidence of his existence." She flipped open the menu as I resisted the urge to point out she would have met him already if she hadn't been busy making me sit alone at this very table the day he came over, asked if he could buy me a drink, and settled for taking my number when I explained I was waiting for my chronically late friend. She kept talking. "And anyway, hot cowboys are excellent as far as scenery goes, even if you're a married mom." She waved her left hand to display the glittering rock there. "I'm starving," she went on. "What are you going to order?"

I looked at her for a moment. She'd always been the pretty one of the two of us. Even now that she was married and had a kid, she was slender, wore just the right amount of makeup, and had a way of breezing into a room and striking up a conversation with the most interesting person there. I noticed two guys sitting at a table behind us. The one facing us said something to the other, who turned a little to look over his shoulder, then turned back around quickly. I knew they weren't looking at me. I felt a strange, bitter wave of something strangely close to jealousy. I tamped it down. We devolved into talking about the relative merits of red and green sauce on enchiladas.

I rode my bike home. There was a wide, paved path half a block behind Julio's that wound along the edge of a wash and past my apartment complex. I always liked to ride along there at night, although my mother worried it wasn't safe and gave me a can of mace approximately every six weeks. I asked her once if she'd prefer I drive drunk. She gave me her steely 'I am not amused' stare and pointed out I could always take a cab.

But taking a cab to go half a mile seemed ridiculous. Plus, I liked riding my bike. When we'd been in college, Trace and I had biked everywhere: to class, to work, downtown. I had a mixte single speed one of her pre-Andrew boyfriends who'd been into the bike scene had helped me acquire and fix up. It had a big wicker basket on the front and an old-fashioned bell. I adored the thing.

I pedaled along the path, looking past the railing into the sandy bottom of the wash. Small footpaths left by dog-walkers and joggers left traceries among the sprouted sagebrush. Out of nowhere, I thought of my cowboy. I imagined him, loping his horse along below, turning his head to look at me, matching my pace, spurting ahead to run up the bank and ... then what? There was a railing separating the wash from the path. Could ranch horses jump?

This was my problem with fantasies. I always got hung up on practicalities.

I pedaled the rest of the way back to my apartment, locked up my bike, and trudged up the stairs. I flipped on a light and hung up my keys and purse, checking my phone in case Ben had texted me. He hadn't.

My mom was always telling me I should get a cat, or one of those small dogs, or a Great Dane, which was supposedly an awesome breed to have in an apartment. Mostly the thought of having a pet seemed like too much trouble. But at the odd moment, coming home to an empty apartment with a fading buzz, I thought she might have a point.

I pulled off the deserted neighborhood street and squinted down at my phone. It said, unhelpfully, "You have arrived."

I looked around. In front of me there was a white house with a fenced yard where two large German Shepherds were watching me with interest but not barking. Behind me was a red house with a small shed in the back and a fence made of rusted piping. Two donkeys wearing fly masks were dozing in the shade, but it didn't look like a ranch, per say, or the type of place where someone would give horseback riding lessons.

On the other side of the street stood a row of smaller houses with smaller yards. The road was narrow, the pavement cracked, and it was a one way only loop. You drove up one side, it swung you around past the two big houses and took you straight back to the intersection where I'd seen the guy on the horse with the flag.

It was Tuesday afternoon. Tuesdays, I didn't go in to the gallery. It was the deadest day of the week and Anne opened late and closed early. My promise to myself was to use my Tuesdays for writing. Usually, I was pretty good about that. Except today I was stuck on this weird little road beginning to wonder if I'd made up the whole thing about seeing a herd of horses at dawn.

But I hadn't, because I'd found a reference to the ranch on the internet. It was called the Tipped Z, it was a historic ranch, and according to Google Maps it was right exactly where I sat in my car.

Except it wasn't.

The dogs had come all the way up to the fence and were sitting, their big ears pricked in my direction as if they were either expecting me to scale the fence and try to rob the place, or give them a treat. I tapped a couple of icons on my phone, got a message that said, 'Recalculating," and then the same unhelpful comment: "You have arrived." I resisted the urge to hurl the thing out the window.

I saw a movement in my rear-view mirror. A truck pulled around the corner behind me, rolled up next to my car, and slowed down. It was a battered thing with visible rust on the body and an engine that rumbled like a freight train. I felt my face flush as it rolled even with my window and rocked to a stop. There was a girl inside, wearing a flat-brimmed cowboy hat and sunglasses. She had to lean all the way across the front seat to roll the window down and must have let her foot slip off the clutch. The truck engine shuddered to a halt as I rolled my window down too, just in time to hear the girl say, "Damn." But then she looked at me. A smile split her face as she said, "You okay?" She was maybe half a dozen years younger than I was, with a pretty face and smooth complexion.

I gave a helpless gesture at the street. "I was trying to find the Tipped Z Ranch."

"Oh," she said. "You can follow me."

Before I could say anything else, the truck roared back to life. She didn't bother with rolling up the window.

Mystified, I waited for her to drive forward. She passed the yard with the German Shepherds and started around the bend that would bring us back to the stop sign. Then she turned right, disappearing behind a high screen of bougainvillea hedges. It was as if she'd driven her truck straight off the road and through a portal to Narnia.

I got to where she'd turned and craned my neck to the side, finally seeing a wide, dirt driveway that was more than a 90 degree turn off the road. The fence of the next house ran along one side, the bougainvillea hedges on the other. I turned hard to the right and bounced onto the dirt track. When I cleared the hedge, I saw the old truck chugging along in the distance, following a long driveway that looped back past the house where the German Shepherds lived.

No wonder I hadn't seen it. It was like they were going out of their way to make the place hard to find.

I hung back behind the plume of dust the truck was kicking up. We drove for a few minutes, the driveway continuing its slanted course. Finally, it bent and headed towards the foothills. A moment later we passed a large sign that said, "Tours by appointment only." Then there was a gate with a sign over the top that said, "The Tipped Z." There was a brand below: a Z nearly upended, balanced on one point on a line bent in an arc.

The gate was closed. The girl in the truck slowed down to punch in a gate code, motioning me to follow her through as the gate opened and she rolled forward again. There was another sign above the gate controller. This one said, "Gate code is 1234. <u>ALL</u> visitors <u>MUST</u> have an appointment. <u>NO EXCEPTIONS</u>." That made me feel self-conscious. I, after all, did not have an appointment. But I appeared to have been invited in, so I rolled through the gate after the truck and watched in my rear-view mirror as the gate swung closed behind me.

The driveway continued between two fences and ended at a long, low barn structure. The truck pulled up and parked slant-wise in front of a ramada that jutted off the side of the barn. Three dogs came trotting out, first running up to greet the girl. They shifted their attention to me as I parked my Hyundai Elantra next to the formidable pick-up and stepped out. The dogs were all the same breed, but it wasn't any breed I'd seen before. They had mid-length wiry coats, with patches of an assortment of browns and blacks and whites and grays all over their bodies. They came trotting up to me, ears forward, tails not wagging. One of them gave a short, sharp bark that sounded alarmingly business-like. I felt a moment of trepidation.

The girl said, "Dogs. Barn."

She didn't yell it, or even raise her voice. But the dogs all froze at the words, turned as one, and trotted back through the open door from which they'd emerged.

The girl was out of the truck now. She walked around the front of her vehicle, hand extended. "I'm Nora." We shook. "Sorry about all the smoke and mirrors and signs and everything. Mom spent like three years applying for historic ranch status and then we got it and all these people just started showing up here. It was the strangest thing. They'd come in busses and all unload and there'd be like 20 people wandering through the pastures trying to feed the horses carrots."

I looked around the vast dirt parking area. "You should put in a taco stand or something, charge for tours and lunch."

She stared at me for a moment. She had wide blue eyes and a dusting of freckles across her cheekbones. Her pale brown hair was pulled into a single long braid that hung down her back. She looked so shocked I thought back on my comment, trying to figure out how it might have offended her. Then she burst out laughing. At first, I wasn't sure if she was laughing at me or what I'd said. But she laughed so openly, I found myself smiling. "You obviously haven't met my dad. Or my brother, for that matter."

I felt self-conscious then, thinking she'd ask me why I was there. Instead she went on as if I'd never said anything. "It turned out a magazine ran this whole story that was totally wrong. Somehow they thought being a historic landmark meant being open to the public. They wrote this whole piece about the ranch's history, most of which was wrong, and put in all this stuff about visitors being welcome to drop by any time. It was a total train wreck. And the worst thing was it was one of those fancy southwestern lifestyle type magazines that salons and massage therapists put out around their waiting rooms, so even though they published a retraction when my dad called to complain, there are still copies sitting around. You never know when a convoy of sunburned tourists is going to turn up." She gave me this huge grin, like we were sharing some kind of inside joke. "Dad says watering the bougainvillea is going to bankrupt him, but it's worth it for his sanity."

I found myself at an utter loss for words after this outpouring. I stared at her in silence, feeling like a nosy trespasser, and trying to think of something to say in response to her story.

There was a movement in the doorway. I thought the dogs had come back. But when I turned my head, I saw him.

It was my cowboy. The one I'd seen by the stop sign. Even though he wasn't riding a horse or carrying a flag, even though that day he'd been half hidden by the weak light and a cloud of dust, I knew it was the same man. It was as if every cell in my body gave a little tug towards him, like iron filings lining up to point at a magnet.

He wore a hat like Nora's, with a flat brim and top, but it was pushed back on his forehead. I could see his face. He had smooth, classic features and was clean-shaven. He was slim-hipped, and wore a pair of leather leggings over his jeans. They had fringe on the edges. They would have looked ridiculous in about any other context. But on him they were nothing but sexy.

"Nora?" he said. "Who's here."

I felt even more ridiculous. I hadn't even had a chance to introduce myself. "I'm Erin."

Nora didn't even look over her shoulder. "She's with me, Clint." Her tone was impatient but not defensive.

Clint, my cowboy, didn't give me a second look. He disappeared, stepping back into the darkness of the barn. The leather leggings were open in the back. I looked away before his sister could notice me noticing the attractive way they framed his backside.

"My brother," Nora said. "You see what I mean?" She gave a comical roll of her eyes. I'd known her for all of five minutes and yet it felt like we'd been friends for ten years and were the best of co-conspirators. I couldn't help it. I laughed, finding it impossible not to like this girl who was as open and transparent as her brother was opaque and mysterious.

By the time I got home, the heat of the day had swelled to its full crescendo. I drank several large glasses of iced tea while I stood in my kitchen and stared out the window, trying to process the morning's events. My shirt was soaked with sweat and my shoes were dusty. After a tour of the barn and one of the pastures, I had finally managed to ask about horseback riding lessons. Nora had said, sure, she could give me lessons. Her offhand manner had surprised me. So I'd asked if it was something she did a lot. She'd said not a lot, that they didn't go out of their way to have horses around that were good for beginners, but she'd taught plenty of people to ride. That had made me feel a little better.

We'd agreed on Tuesday mornings at 5:30 as our lesson time. Then Nora had shown me a litter of wire-haired puppies and I'd forgotten to ask how much she charged.

I hadn't caught so much as another glimpse of Clint.

I was setting my iced tea glass in the sink and trying to decide whether to take a shower or try to get some writing done when my phone buzzed. I picked it up and saw a text from Ben. "Drinks tonite?"

I frowned at the little screen. Ben and I had been dating for about three months. We'd never had a talk about how serious we were, or if either of us was seeing other people. That didn't bother me. What annoyed me was his habit of going off the radar, totally disappearing for four or five days sometimes, not answering phone calls or texts. Then he'd pop back up with this kind of invitation, leaving me to wonder if all the cell phone towers in the greater Tucson area had been malfunctioning.

I resisted the urge to reply and got in the shower. I took a long, cool soak, washing the dust from my skin and thinking about the Tipped Z and Nora and Clint. And not Ben.

When I got out of the shower the LED light on my phone was blinking. I picked it up and saw another text, also from Ben. "Graze at 6:30. See you."

That annoyed me too. I stood in my bedroom, wrapped in a towel, my wet hair stuck to my neck, torn between the impulse to text him back with some snide remark about being otherwise occupied tonight and the tug to go straight to my closet to start trying to decide what to wear.

I had a bad habit of showing up early to everything. This was fine, most of the time. I even considered it sort of a virtue. I liked to be the person friends could rely on—the one who ensured the party wouldn't start an hour late.

But with dating, it was horrible. I hated being the first to arrive. I hated sitting there looking like I was waiting for someone who hadn't bothered to get there on time to meet me.

So I'd developed strategies. If I was driving, I'd often park a few blocks short of my destination and walk the rest of the way. If it was too crushingly hot for that, I'd sit in my car with the AC on and read a book. This could be risky though, because if your date arrived and saw you sitting in the car, you looked like a weirdo.

With biking, it was harder. When I left my apartment and settled onto my bike to head for Graze, I saw I had more than enough time to get where I needed to go without hurrying. I proceeded to make my way towards the restaurant as slowly as allowable by gravity without putting me in danger of toppling off my two wheels.

Graze was a few blocks further up the bike path than Julio's. It was a ritzy cocktail bar. Ben liked it. I was not a huge fan. Their beers were uninteresting, so I tended to let Ben order me froofroo drinks I would live to regret.

As I pedaled, I let my mind drift back to that morning. In my mind's eye, I saw Clint step out of the doorway wearing those leggings. He seemed to have this way of appearing, always on the edge of things, always partly out of sight. When we'd gone into the barn later, there'd been no sign of him. If Nora hadn't spoken to him, I'd have been doubting I'd seen him at all.

There had been no horses in the barn, either. The inside of the old structure had turned out to house nothing but dogs, tack, and hay. There were some empty stalls. But Nora said they kept the horses outside. They were happier out there, even in the summer.

I saw Ben as soon as I walked in. He was sitting at a table for two near the back, looking at his phone. As I stepped through the swinging doors into the cool blast of conditioned air, I felt goose-bumps rise on my arms. Graze was one of those places that seemed to assume that because it was hot outside everyone would prefer to be blasted with AC to within a few degrees of hypothermia. I could feel the sweat start drying on my forehead and wondered if I could sneak past Ben and get to the ladies to freshen up.

But he looked up, saw me, and waved. As I approached, he shifted in his seat to slip his phone into his pocket. I will say one thing for Ben: when he gave you his attention, he gave it all the way. I don't remember him ever sending or receiving a text on a date. Maybe that's why he dropped off the map when I wasn't with him—he was busy giving his undivided attention to other people.

He was also undeniably good-looking. I wasn't sure whether or not I'd ever get around to introducing him to Trace. But if I ever did, it would be satisfying to see her reaction. Ben was attractive in the effortless manner of an Abercrombie & Fitch model. His blond hair was always gel-free but somehow fell just so. He tended to wear simple clothes, but they looked fabulous on him because he was ripped. He'd also had the benefit of extensive childhood orthodontia. He flashed me his perfect smile as I walked towards the table. He rose to kiss me on the cheek and said, "I'm glad you could make it."

We sat, me trying not to wonder if the heat and sweat had done something lurid to my appearance.

"So what's new?" Ben said after the server had taken our drink orders and retired. "You look good," he added, trotting out the gorgeous smile again while reaching across the table to tuck a stray strand of hair behind my ear.

He was good with compliments, dropping them in like that at odd moments, making them feel genuine. I was not so good at receiving them. They made me flounder like a large fish in a shallow puddle of water. I felt myself start to blush and looked down at the menu. "Thanks. I'm good. I just signed up to take horseback riding lessons today. How about you? What have you been up to? I guess you've been busy?"

If Ben guessed my last comment was a subtle allusion to the fact I hadn't heard from him in almost a week, he didn't give any indication. He smiled at the server when she came back with two ice-filled glasses of water. "Horseback riding lessons?"

I squeezed my lemon into my water and poked it down past the ice with my straw. Now that I'd brought it up, I found I didn't want to discuss my cowboy, or anything connected to him, with Ben. I gave a light laugh. "It's something I did when I was younger and always wanted to get back to."

Ben fixed me with his direct gaze. "Good for you." He said this with a level of gravity that might have been more appropriate if I'd announced I was giving away all my belongings and moving to Southeast Asia. "So many people always wait for tomorrow."

"How about you?" I said again.

Ben sipped his water. "The usual. Work and work." Ben worked for company that consulted for the US Department of Transportation. In spite of having asked quite a few specific questions, I had only the haziest conception of what he did for a living. I knew it had something to do with developing marketing strategies based on the data received from road repair and construction equipment. But that was about all I could gather. I knew sometimes he got on a private plane and flew off to present his findings to small groups of middle-aged men in suits. Whenever I pressed him for details, for anything more specific, he would turn the subject or say he didn't want to talk about work.

So far I couldn't even figure out if he liked his job or not. Ben had a total knack for not answering direct questions. It was one of the things that was starting to get to me about him. I couldn't figure out if he did it out of a deep-seated sense of modesty, or if he was being deliberately slippery.

"Where are you taking lessons?" He looked up to thank the server as our drinks arrived. I asked about the artichoke dip. By the time the server left, I could pretend I'd forgotten all about Ben's question.

I set my water and abused lemon slice to the side in favor of the pink monstrosity Ben had acquired for me. With another guy, I might take the froofroo drinks as a veiled insult—a snide remark on the feminine palette. I don't think I could stand to date a guy who ordered me a fuzzy navel while he sipped whisky on the rocks. But Ben drank them too. When I ordered beer, he always seemed a little disappointed.

I'd hung my purse on the back of my chair. Now I heard my phone give off a notification, letting me know I had a new text. I felt gauche for forgetting to silence it, while immediately starting to wonder who it was from. It was probably Trace sending me yet another photo of Olivia in the bathtub. But I'd given Nora my phone number that morning. What if it was her? Or what if it was Clint? Maybe he was the shy type, and he'd wanted to speak to me today, but hadn't been able to find the nerve. Maybe he'd snuck a look at his sister's phone, figured out which number was mine, and sent me a message.

"Did you want to check that?" Ben had an amused look on his face, as if he'd been able to follow the gist of my internal dialogue.

I took a big swallow of my pink drink. It had a slab of grapefruit skewered on the rim, which I should have removed before sipping. It bumped into my eyelash and made me blink. I set the drink down. "I'm sure it's nothing important."

Chapter 2

It was dark and considerably cooler out by the time we left the restaurant. It was a relief to leave the sterile AC air behind and step into the warm desert night. Graze was the sort of place that got more crowded as the night went on. The parking lot was quiet by comparison.

Ben walked with me to the bike rack, his expression dubious as he watched me paw through my purse for my keys. I'd had three of the gigantic pink drinks, and my physical coordination was not at its best. Ben had only had two, because he had to drive home. Also, he weighed a good deal more than I did. He watched me find my key-ring, select my bike lock key, fit it into the lock, and unlatch the U-lock at about one-eighth the speed of a normal, non-geriatric human being, but without fumbling at all. He said, "Can I walk you home?"

I wasn't sure where Ben lived. I knew he had a house in one of the nearby subdivisions. He'd told me which one on one of our first dates, but I'd forgotten. We never went there. He'd been up to my apartment once, only because we'd stopped off between a restaurant and a bar so I could change my shirt, which had gotten an entire bowl of salsa flipped onto it when a server had walked around a corner too quickly and run headlong into me as we'd been making our way for the door.

We were still in the 'arm's length' phase of our relationship. For my part, I wasn't sure if I wanted to go much past that. Mostly, I could admit, this was because I couldn't gauge how interested Ben was. I had a huge aversion to being the one who cared more.

I set my lock in my basket and rolled my bike free of the rack. "It takes a lot longer to walk home than it does to bike."

Ben looked at the bike and glanced towards the parking lot. "I have a truck."

I hesitated. Ben put a gentle hand on my arm and steered me away from the bike path. He loaded my bike into his truck's bed without apparent effort and drove to my apartment without having to ask for directions, which impressed me because he'd only been there once and that had been weeks ago.

My apartment complex was quiet. There was a guest parking spot open near the covered parking where my Hyundai spent most of its life. I slid out of the truck and walked around to the tailgate, saying thanks as Ben lifted my mixte down from the bed of his truck like a gentleman from the 20's handing his lady off a train. I made to take the handlebars, but he said, "Where's your rack?"

I immediately thought of how this comment could be misinterpreted. I had to stifle a giggle while simultaneously realizing my sober self would not find that funny. I led Ben to the bike rack and he watched me execute my careful maneuver with the key and U-lock again. When I turned around, he was standing there like a (clothed) underwear model, lit by the soft glow of the yellowish lamps that were dotted around my apartment complex to keep the walkways from becoming too dim and shadowy. He said, "I had a nice time tonight."

I had just enough time to drop my keys back into my purse. He took a step forward and slipped his arm around my waist. He was not overly tall, and I didn't have to do more than tip my chin up to put myself in optimal kissing position. He smelled of aftershave and tasted like grapefruit.

Ben and I were in the phase where our good-bye kisses tended to get a little steamy but so far had never lead to anything more. He was a good kisser. I closed my eyes and leaned in.

Then, quite suddenly, I saw Clint. Ben and my apartment faded as my imagination took me somewhere else entirely.

Clint was wearing his snug jeans and flat-brimmed hat, walking into the dim, dusty aisle between the empty stalls, surprising me. Before I could say anything, do anything other than turn toward him with a start, he wrapped me in his arms and pressed his mouth to mine with no preamble, no explanation. His kiss was a thing of need, a searching thing, a question and answer in one. I gave in to it, feeling his hand pressing the small of my back and the way my heart had begun to race. I kissed him back, letting my desire for him grow and expand, letting it race up my spine and take me over. I kissed him and forgot to think about anything else.

Ben pulled away and looked at me. I came back to reality: the bike rack, the lamps, my apartment complex. A car door slammed in the distance, someone laughed, and an engine revved. Ben was staring at me with large, startled eyes. He said, "Erin." His voice was low and intent.

I'd never kissed him like that before. I'd never kissed *anyone* like that before. My blood was still singing in my veins. Even though I knew I was looking at Ben and not Clint, I was high, both on the pink grapefruit drinks and something even more intoxicating. "Do you want to come up?"

"You look tired," Anne said the moment she saw me the next morning. "Is everything okay?"

I wasn't so much tired as hung over. Ben had declined my invitation, kissing me again and saying he'd love to come up, but he had to get up early for work. I'd barely gotten myself upstairs and into bed before collapsing into an undignified, drunken slumber. I'd woken up with a sense of relief roughly proportional to my headache. The headache was from the grapefruit drinks. The relief was from knowing that if Ben had come up, I'd have done exactly the same thing. Inviting a guy into your apartment for the first time and passing out five minutes later had to be the worst sort of bad form.

"Hung over." I was squinting as I looked at her because she was standing in front of one of the side windows, and it was really bright out. "Ben was feeding me these pink froofroo drinks all night, which turned out to be surprisingly strong."

Anne gave me a measuring look. "That sounds fun."

"It was great until this morning."

"And how are things going with Ben?" Anne said it casually, moving around to my side of the counter to sort a stack of mail. Anne had a way of engaging you without seeming overly interested. Women who wandered in off the street would start spilling confidences almost upon meeting her, and men would be confessing their insecurities a few minutes into a conversation.

I sipped water from my Nalgene bottle. "They're fine."

Anne gave me a look over her shoulder. "Fine never means fine."

I stared down at the countertop, running my fingernail along a deep scratch that had been there since before I got my job. "He's really great. We always have fun. It just doesn't seem like it's going anywhere."

I hadn't confessed this to Trace, hadn't admitted it even to myself. "We had a fun time last night. And now I probably won't hear from him for another four or five days."

Anne tossed a stack of promotional mailings into the recycle bin and turned to face me, crossing her arms. "Is that so bad? It seems like you're the kind of person who might enjoy that. You dumped the last guy because he was stifling you. He was texting you about 50 times a day, as I recall, and it creeped you out."

She was right, of course. "Is a happy medium too much to ask?" My voice sounded a bit more plaintive than I meant it.

There was a jingle of the door's bell and we both looked up.

It was Ben, looking fresh and perky, carrying a slender glass vase that held a single orange daisy. He smiled as he strode across the room, said good morning to me, and set the vase on the counter. He was done introducing himself to Anne by the time I recovered from the surprise of seeing him. I'd told him where I worked during one of our first dates. But he'd never stopped by before.

He turned away from the countertop and looked around the gallery, treating Anne to a look at his excellent profile and biceps. "This is a great little place," he said. "I must have driven past a million times without ever realizing it was an art gallery."

"I thought you had to work this morning." I said this without thinking, before even thanking him for the flower. It came out sounding exceptionally ungracious. I felt bad before I even finished the sentence.

Anne gave me a quick, startled look. Always tactful, she excused herself. "It was nice meeting you, Ben," she said as she stepped around the counter. "I'll let you two chat." She headed for her office.

Before she was out of earshot Ben said, "I did. I had a 4:30 am conference call with some of our guys on the east coast. Now I'm on an early lunch break."

I looked at the clock. It was 11:12.

I tried to think of something to say, something friendlier and more appreciative than what I'd managed so far. My eyes fell upon the daisy. "Thank you for the flower. It's really pretty." I winced internally. I sounded like an eighth-grader reciting lines for the school play. I dropped my voice and glanced over my shoulder. "I am so hung over today. What was in those drinks?"

Ben laughed, walked around the counter, and kissed my forehead. "I hope you aren't suffering too badly. I have to run. I just wanted to say again that I had a great time last night." He looked down at me. I remembered the kiss by the bike rack. I felt heat rising to my cheeks. I felt like the worst sort of liar. Ben and I had kissed good-night plenty of times, but never before had I imagined he was Clint.

I managed to say, "I did too."

He kissed my forehead again and stooped lower to give my mouth a quick peck. Then he was gone, striding across the gallery and out the door before I could even entirely process that he'd been there.

"So, how was your week?" My mom handed me a glass of wine and sat down on the bench across from me. It was Friday night. We were on the back patio of my parents' house, watching the sunset throw color onto the mountains. Before I could answer, she raised her voice and said, "Boswell, Norman. No!"

Boswell and Norman were my mother's two Bull Terriers. They were currently showing a little too much interest in the cheese plate my mother had placed on the low table between us. Although they were experienced show-dogs, my mother's canines did not possess quite the level of training as the three wire-haired animals I'd seen on the ranch earlier that week. Their skills were apparently reserved for inside the show-ring.

When at leisure around the house and yard, Boswell, Norman and my mother all seemed to share a tacit understanding that my mother did not reign supreme. When she told them not to do something, they tended to look at her for a minute or two with their dark, triangular eyes. I always imagined they were weighing a complex set of variables when they did this, calculating a) how much she meant what she'd said, b) how far away she was, c) how likely she was to try to enforce her command, and d) the possible benefits of defying her. After a delay, they seemed to usually decide to ignore her, and went on doing whatever they were doing.

In this case, however, my mother a) sounded like she meant it, b) was quite close to them, c) was likely to enforce her command, and d) could probably intercede before they could actually make off with any cheese. So Boswell and Norman gave in, turning to wander off the patio exuding an air of disinterest, as if they'd never wanted any cheese in the first place.

Mom watched until their white haunches had disappeared around the low retaining wall that separated the patio from the surrounding desert. She leaned forward and put a slice of cheddar on a sesame seed cracker. She gave me an expectant look. I realized I hadn't answered her question. "Oh," I said. "Fine. Good. I went out with Ben. Twice."

"Twice in one week?" Mom's enthusiasm came through even around the cracker. She'd never met Ben, but she was generally in favor of all activities I could participate in that might lead more rapidly to my marriage. Not that she ever explicitly said this. But it was obvious. And all the more painful because she tried so hard to pretend she didn't care if or when I settled down. Reporting back to her on my relationship with Ben up to this point had been painful for both of us. It had been crawling along at such a slow rate even she couldn't find a way to put a positive spin on it. She took a sip of wine. "That sounds like progress."

I remembered that kiss again, thinking of Clint by the bike rack. I again felt that strange guilt. "I...." I stopped. I couldn't tell my mother I'd kissed Ben while fantasizing about a cowboy I'd developed a sudden but intense obsession with and that now Ben was treating me as if I was an entirely different species of girl than the one he'd been dating up until now.

As if on cue, my phone dinged. I fished it out of my pocket, looked at it, and held it up for Mom to see. "Ben. He says to say hi." I'd told Ben we were having a special family dinner and so I could not go out with him again tonight. It was a total lie. My mom hadn't even known I'd been coming over until I'd shown up with two bottles of wine.

"Oh. How nice of him. Tell him hi back," my mom said. She added, "What's he doing tonight? He could join us."

I resisted the urge to be annoyed. "I'm not going to text him back just now." I set my phone down and took a rather large sip of wine.

It wasn't that I didn't get along with my mother. Eighty percent of the time, she was great. There were just a few points we didn't see eye-to eye-on. My love life was one of them. She felt anyone I went out with more than once should automatically receive an invitation to the next family gathering. I tended to feel that shouldn't happen until someone had given someone else a ring, at the earliest.

"It couldn't hurt to mention it to him," Mom pressed. "He can't be that busy if he's texting you."

"Mom."

She sniffed and sat back, leaning against the bench and assuming a wounded air. She could be relentless on certain subjects. I was afraid she wasn't done.

Fortunately, my father chose that moment to arrive, pulling his battered Ford Explorer into the driveway and stepping through the front gate to meet the onslaught that was what Boswell and Norman considered a friendly greeting.

My father was not a dog person. Boswell and Norman were my mother's, just as the salt-water fish tanks dotted throughout the house were my father's. My parents believed leading rich, separate lives was the key to a happy marriage. They supported each other's interests, but didn't share in them.

This didn't stop my dad from stooping to give Boswell and Norman a few hearty rubs on their firm, broad heads. He saw us, waved, and walked around the side of the house. He set his briefcase down on the bench next to my mother and bent to kiss me on the cheek.

"TGIF," he said, accepting the glass of wine my mother offered him. He sat next to his briefcase, bumped the two inquisitive dog noses away from the cheese plate with his shoe, and looked across the table at me. "How was your week?"

"She went on two dates with Ben." My mother supplied this information in such a bright, happy tone, I had to suppress a cringe.

"Two!" My dad, too, was all enthusiasm now, sitting forward with an intent expression that suggested I'd won the lottery.

For three months during our sophomore year in high school, Trace had become convinced my father was gay. I never did figure out what put her onto the notion, and there were terrible holes in the theory (his long, happy relationship with my mother, to name one). But she went on and on about it for weeks, collecting evidence, reading into his every word and deed. Trace's parents had been going through a divorce at the time. She'd been depressed, so I'd been willing to forgive a lot. I could even take her point, just a little. My dad dressed well, he watched chick flicks with my mom, he genuinely cared about things like who I went to winter formal with, and was in many other ways not a typical dad. Still, her having some grounds for her views made me less happy to hear her go on about it, not more.

Fortunately, Trace got what she deserved in the end. One weekend my parents had left town for an overnight trip to visit my grandmother, who had been having some health issues, leaving me alone overnight for the first time. They'd agreed to let Trace stay over with me. Trace had convinced me to raid my father's dresser, certain we'd find gay porn. Instead, we'd found several sets of nude photos of my mother, a bottle of lube, and a book called, *Sex After Kids: Keeping the Bedroom Steamy While Raising a Family.*

She'd never brought it up again.

"Yeah, two," I said, suddenly wishing I hadn't come over.

Unconsciously echoing my mom, Dad said, "That sounds like progress."

I looked from one shining face to the other and felt a sudden, crushing sense of defeat. I went out with a guy twice in one week and it got my parents this excited? Probably the kind thing would be for me to join the clergy and take vows of celibacy, and thus put us all out of our misery.

"Heels down," Nora yelled. Her voice was at full volume, but it was good-natured. Which was somewhat surprising considering she'd said that same thing to me about four times already.

I was in the middle of my first lesson, which meant I was astride a giant horse named Duke. According to Nora, he was an oversized Teddy Bear of a horse, easy-going about everything, and as beginner-friendly a mount as the ranch could provide. He was gray-going-white, had a blaze and socks you could barely see anymore, and had stood still while I'd fumbled around trying to get my foot into the stirrup.

I'd been nervous driving over to the Tipped Z in the first light of day. It was early, and the light on the mountains was all peach and violet and baby blue. I'd spent the whole drive with a knot in my stomach. It had knotted up further as I drove past all the hostile signs. I'd punched in the gate code, hoping Nora hadn't forgotten our agreement.

Seeing her truck in the driveway had filled me with a sense of relief and only the teeniest little hint of regret. After all, if Nora hadn't been there I would have had to go in the barn and wait. And while I was waiting I might have ended up running into Clint.

But Nora had Duke ready by the time I poked my head around the inside of the barn door. She'd given me a huge smile and said, "We'd better get you mounted up before that sun hits us."

So we'd left the barn and walked through a gate into an outdoor arena, Nora leading Duke and me trailing behind. I'd excavated my closet the night before until I'd found a pair of cowboy boots that were more suitable for a night on the town than riding a horse. But they had a heel and a smooth sole. That was the important part. I'd promised myself that if this first lesson went well, I'd get a more appropriate pair.

In the arena, Nora had stopped, turned, and handed me the reins. She'd said, "If I was my brother I'd talk for like an hour now about respecting the horse, pressure and release, and a million other things. But my personal teaching philosophy is that that stuff doesn't sink in until you have a chance to feel it. You know how to mount one?"

Mercifully, I did know how to mount. So ten minutes after driving past the 'Tours by appointment only' sign, I was sitting on a horse trying to remember what I knew about riding.

The first fifteen minutes were torture for all three of us. The reins were different from the ones I'd used as a kid. Nora showed me how to hold them, but I was awkward. I kept dropping my coil. The first few times I did that, I couldn't figure out how to pick it up again. Nora had to show me three times before I got it, at which point I wanted to sink into the ground with shame.

Shortly after that, things started to improve. I remembered what my childhood instructor had called my 'following seat' and how to move with the horse instead of bouncing around in the saddle. My lower leg relaxed. Nora stopped having to tell me to put my heels down. I started to feel a lot more natural.

Duke sighed and gave his head a shake, his ears flopping around.

"See," Nora said. "You're looking a lot better now. Let's see a trot."

In spite of the early start, it was hot by the time I stepped off Duke and we walked back to the barn together. I was covered in sweat, as was Duke. But I was happy. I felt I'd done a good job. Based on Nora's smiles and commentary, I thought she thought so too. The lesson had been so absorbing, I'd even forgotten to think about Clint for a while.

We were nearing the barn when Nora said, "So this week was about me watching how you already ride. Next week I'm going to start making you change. So be prepared." She gave me a wolfish grin. I grinned back. We stepped through the large side door of the barn, which was pushed all the way open.

The space we walked into was large and dim, with sunbeams falling down from high windows. There was a riding mower parked in one corner and hay stacked in another. A flatbed trailer that hadn't been there when we went out was pulled inside, large enough that it nearly filled the space.

"Hay delivery," Nora said, leading the way around the obstacle. I glanced at Duke. He was unbothered as we edged through the narrow space left to get into the barn.

We walked around the trailer, and that's when I saw Clint.

He was standing up on the stack of hay, heaving bales into place. His shirt was notably absent and his torso was slick and gleaming with sweat. In the early morning light from the high windows, he was quite the sight. I stopped walking, Duke coming to a good-natured halt next to me.

I was staring. I knew I was staring, and that staring was rude. But I couldn't seem to take my eyes off the scene before me. The air was filled with hay-dust. Clint had a lean, useful look to his muscles. His abs stood out in low relief as he bent, picked up a bale, and tossed it up to the next tier on the stack. I was transfixed.

"Erin?" Nora had noticed my absence. She was now peeking back around the nose of the truck that was attached to the hay wagon. I felt my face flush and I hurried forward.

"What are those leggings your brother wears?" I said it more to cover my embarrassment than out of any real curiosity. "I've never seen anything quite like them."

"They're called chinks. Like chaps but with no back. They offer the same protection while you're riding, but they don't get you near so hot."

If she had noticed my gawking, she was kind enough not to mention it. I led Duke around into the aisle between the stalls, where we took his tack off and brushed him down.

We were nearly finished when Nora's phone gave a chime. She fished it out of her pocket and flipped it open, squinting at the small screen. She looked up at me and said, "Shoot, I guess we went a little over. I have to run. Will you put the tack up? Tack room's there." She pointed at a closed door, grabbed Duke's rope, and was gone before I could thank or pay her. I called to her retreating back, "Next Tuesday at the same time?"

"Sure." She waved a hand and glanced back to give me one final grin. Then she disappeared around the nose of the truck.

I stood alone for a moment, looking down at the saddle, which sat on a collapsible rack set on the front of one of the stalls, the bridle, which hung on a hook, and the pad, which lay over the back of the saddle. I listened to the sound of Duke's footfalls fade. The only other sound was the dull heave and thunk of hay bales. Clint was still out there, stacking hay.

I picked up the bridle, which was surprisingly heavy, and opened the door Nora had indicated. Inside was a short, dark hallway. I fumbled along the wall but couldn't find a light switch. I pushed the door open as wide as it would go and ventured in, my eyes adjusting to the dimness.

The hallway stayed narrow for a few feet, then opened into a large room filled with tack of all kinds. Racks of bridles hung along one wall, saddles along another. I strained to see an empty hook where the bridle in my hand might belong. But it was all a dim jumble of ropes and leather.

I stood, feeling lost, until a light flipped on behind me.

I spun around.

Clint stood in the doorway, holding the saddle and pad and looking at me with an expression I couldn't read. He'd pulled his shirt on but hadn't buttoned it. I could see an inch or two of shining skin in the gap.

"Hi." I blurted this out in an inelegant tone that seemed too loud in the quiet room.

"You're Nora's student?" Clint's voice was smooth and calm, just deep enough to resonate.

"My name's Erin."

His hands were full. He thrust his chin towards the bridle hanging in my hand. "That's a snaffle." I glanced from him to bridle. I had no idea what he meant. I knew a snaffle was a kind of bit. Was he trying to give me a lesson on tack? I gave a tiny nod of my head—just enough to indicate I'd heard him.

He waited, as if expecting some greater response. Then he thrust his chin again, indicating a wall other than the one I'd been staring at when he'd come in. "Snaffles go on that wall."

I turned and saw another wall of bridles behind me, where one hook was clearly missing what usually hung there. I hung the bridle up in a spasm of embarrassment as Clint walked by me and placed the saddle on an empty rack along the saddle wall, flipping the pad upside down to sit on top. When he turned around, I was staring at him.

"Thank you." This came out sounding too sincere. I cringed internally as he looked at me. I knew my face was red, my hair was messed up and sweaty. I certainly looked like a total wreck while he was standing there being the most gorgeous person I'd ever seen in the flesh. I tried to think of something more to say, anything to keep him here, to talk to him. "Do you need help with the hay?"

He blinked a couple of times. His mouth cracked into a teeny little smile. It changed his face entirely. He went from seeming aloof and intimidating to sweet and friendly. "That's awfully kind, but I guess you'll be sore enough tomorrow as it is."

He took a step forward. For one wild moment I was convinced he was going to sweep me into his arm and kiss me.

Instead, he extended a hand. "I'm Clint," he said as we shook. "Nice to meet you, Erin."

My beer and Ben arrived at the same time. I saw him walk through the front door as I thanked the server, saw him scan the room, saw his face light up when he saw me. He wove his way through the round, high tables, stopping at one point to let a slim server with a tray through a narrow spot.

I'd arrived early on purpose. I did this partly so I could establish that I would be drinking beer, not pink froofroo monstrosities. I didn't want any more embarrassing drunken episodes with Ben. I'd also done it because my contact with Clint that morning had left me so riled up and restless I'd been pacing my apartment all day like a caged tiger. A caged tiger intent on accomplishing as many household chores as possible, that is. I'd come home intending to write. But every time I sat down to imagine my scenes and characters, I instead spiraled into extended fantasies involving the tack room and Clint's already unbuttoned shirt. I'd resorted to washing towels, cleaning the baseboards, dusting the fans, and finally reorganizing my medicine cabinet. I'd been staring at the expiration date on an old prescription bottle and wondering how I'd managed to hold onto it for six years when Ben had texted asking if I wanted to grab a drink. I'd fled the apartment like it had been on fire.

Ben reached my table, still smiling. "Hey," he said, and leaned in to kiss me. This was new. We'd only started doing the kiss hello thing since the night by the bike rack. He slipped into the seat across from me. "How was your lesson? That was today, right?"

I thought about Clint again: the way his muscles had bunched in his shoulders and forearms as he'd lifted the bale, the sweat glistening on his chiseled abs. I said, "I rode a horse named Duke."

Ben maintained excellent eye contact. "And what did you learn?"

That Clint is even sexier when he smiles. That he can carry a saddle in one hand and a pad in the other. "To keep my heels down."

Ben blinked, the smile fading a little But then the server came to take his drink order. By the time she left I was ready with a question of my own. "How was work?"

Ben waved a hand and told me about some big deal that kept stalling because of something to do with photography. He was wearing an Abercrombie & Fitch t-shirt. It was bright yellow, said A & F on the front, and had a soft, distressed look to it. Not many guys could pull off a shirt that color. But Ben managed it. I wondered what was wrong with me. Why was I mooning around all doe-eyed for some cowboy I had seen a grand total of three times when this very attractive, very nice guy was perhaps starting to like me in a way that might amount to something?

He finished his story. I made a sympathetic noise. His drink came. It was yellow, like his shirt. I was wondering if he'd done that on purpose when he reached across the table and took one of my hands. This surprised me, but I let him. He drew my hand closer, so it was in the middle of the table, and wrapped it in both of his. "Look, Erin," he said. For one horrible moment I thought he was going to break up with me. I had just enough time to wonder what kind of idiot breaks up with someone when she still has almost a full beer, when he said, "I want to apologize."

"For what?" I scrambled around in my memory to come up with something he might have done to offend me. He was looking at me with his perfect eyebrows pinched a little, creating a crease between them.

"For before."

I waited, not sure what to say. I had no idea what he was talking about.

He let out a little sigh. "For the last few months, I've been ... I was." He seemed to be having trouble getting the words out. "I was in a relationship for a long time. That ended before I met you. I was looking for something fun. Something relaxing. I didn't want to get serious. So I kind of kept my distance with you."

This was news. So far we had avoided the topic of prior relationships like the plague.

"But I wish I hadn't. The more I get to know you," he gave me his best, dimpled smile, "the more I like you."

I felt gooseflesh rise on my arms. Was this happening? This gorgeous guy saying this to me, in a public place, no less.

It seemed like it was my turn to say something. "I like you too." My voice came out sounding wan.

He didn't seem to notice. He let go of my hand long enough to take a sip of his yellow drink. I could smell pineapple. When his hand touched my skin again, it was cold.

"I want to ask if we can sort of start over and go forward with a clean slate."

He must have been able to tell I'd been avoiding him all weekend. Apparently, being unavailable immediately after kissing a guy like he was a sexy cowboy did a lot to stimulate his interest in you. I tucked this away in my brain. It seemed like the sort of knowledge that might come in handy later. I said, "Sure. Sounds great." Ugh. Could I have come up with anything more fake-sounding if I'd tried?

His earnest look darkened. He looked down at the table top, gripping my hand a little harder. "Also ...." he started.

"Erin?" a voice said. I looked up and saw Nora walking in with two other girls flanking her. She wore a cute little top and tight jeans. I realized when Ben released my hand and turned in his seat that her brother was not the only one in her family who'd been blessed with good looks.

"Hi Nora." Ben and Nora looked at each other, wearing nearly identical polite smiles until I said, "Ben, this is Nora, my riding instructor. Nora, this is Ben, my ...."

Ben got out of his chair to shake hands with her. "Boyfriend," he said, smoothly finishing my sentence for me.

I thought of the way I'd stopped next to the truck to stare at Clint that morning. Nora had seen me staring. And now Nora knew I had a boyfriend. Although up until that moment I hadn't even been sure that was what I should call him.

Chapter 3

"Has Larson-Juhl called?"

I looked up from the mat I was about to cut. Anne stood in the doorway of the workroom, wearing black pants and a black t-shirt and black heeled boots. Anne was one of those people who can wear all black and look normal instead of like she was trying to make a massive statement.

I hadn't even heard Anne come in, which was unusual. I'd been in this odd, keyed up mood ever since my lesson and what had followed. I kept bouncing back and forth between improbable daydreams of Clint, guilt about Ben, annoyance that Nora knew about Ben, and fear that Nora would tell her brother I wasn't single.

I stared at Anne for a moment, processing. It was 11:00. I'd opened the gallery that morning at 9:00, like usual. I'd checked the messages and answered the phone all morning. Larson-Juhl was the frame supply company from which we bought most of our materials. And they had not called that day. "No."

Anne swore under her breath and stalked off. A moment later I heard her dialing the phone in her office.

I looked back down at the mat cutter. I lined up the blade and pressed, getting the angle right so it wouldn't make a wobble in the corner. I leaned forward, slid the blade to the end of my cut zone, and eased off.

I liked cutting mats. If you were going to be a perfectionist about it (which you had to be if you worked for Anne) it was difficult enough that it required most of your mental attention as well as a fair bit of physical coordination. This meant it did a good job of keeping your mind off things like the guy you were on the fence about telling the sister of the guy you were fantasizing about on an hourly basis that he was your boyfriend.

I opened the mat cutter and rotated the mat, positioning it for the next cut. In the other room, I could hear Anne on the phone. Her voice had the over-amped besty tone she used when she was asking for a favor. I kept cutting.

A few minutes later, I heard the phone go back into the cradle. Anne reappeared in the doorway. "All sorted out," she said. "They're going to overnight it at no charge." I remembered that our Larson-Juhl delivery the day before had been missing a frame for a piece that belonged to a high-end, high-stress client who would not leave his artwork in the gallery overnight. He would bring it in so we could measure it and choose materials while he hovered outside the workroom door. We'd order the frame and he'd take the artwork home. He was scheduled to bring a piece back on Monday morning and pick it up Monday afternoon. So we needed to have that frame ready to go by the time he did the drop-off.

"Good." I made another cut.

Anne leaned against the doorframe and gave me a little smile. One thing I liked about Anne was she didn't carry stress. She'd come in worried about that frame, but now that it was sorted out it was like it never happened. "So, what's up with you the last few days? You're acting like a girl with a crush."

"Am I?" I tried to keep my tone casual. I finished cutting the window in the mat and set it aside, walking to the rack where we kept the glass and scanning the pieces for one close to the size I needed.

"You jump every time I come into the room, it takes you 25 seconds longer than usual to answer simple questions, and you're blushing. Right now, I mean. Blushing."

I could feel the heat in my cheeks and ears as I turned away from the rack. I set my chosen piece of glass on the work table and looked up at

Anne. Her face was friendly, amused, and open. I felt a sudden frantic urge to tell her everything. I'd called Trace twice this week, but both times all I got was five minutes of her partial attention and a lot of banging and cooing in the background. Most of the time I didn't mind. I got that it was difficult to connect with your friends when you'd just had a kid. But I needed to talk to someone and Trace wasn't there for me these days.

"I have this huge problem," I said.

Anne's face went serious and she came into the room, seating herself in a wooden chair that stood near the bins for small pieces of mat board. "Spill," she said.

Now that I had an audience, I had no idea how to sum up my problem. "So, I'm dating Ben." This seemed like a logical place to start. "A couple days ago he introduced himself to someone as my boyfriend."

Anne's eyes narrowed as she took this in. "You don't sound happy?"

"The person he introduced himself to was my riding instructor."

Anne gave a small nod, lips pursed.

I heaved a sigh and plunged in. "Her brother," I stopped. After wanting to talk to someone about this for days, again I felt this hesitation. It was as if telling someone about Clint would make him real, and making him real would steal whatever magic had caused those sunbeams to fall on the hay bales just so and crack that sweet little smile when I'd offered to help him with his work.

Anne waited. Crazily, I wished someone would come into the store at that moment and save me from myself.

The seconds ticked by. The room was quiet except for the distant drone of the radio playing in the other room. I had no choice.

"I met her brother a few days ago. And he's ... well ... he's gorgeous. I mean, amazing." I stopped talking. I'd been right not to want to talk about Clint. Trying to put what I felt about him in everyday terms was like trying to explain an orgasm to a virgin. Not that Anne was a virgin. I didn't know a lot about Anne's personal life. But I did know she lived a bit of an alternative lifestyle.

Anne considered, sitting with her legs crossed, one foot wiggling. Anne never held entirely still. "It sounds like you have a mild case of grass is greener syndrome?" She phrased it more like a question than a judgment. "I only met Ben the once, but he wasn't exactly lacking in the gorgeous department."

I sighed and picked up a glass cutter. "I know," I said. "That's the problem. It's ridiculous. After all these months wishing Ben would pay more attention to me. Now he is, and all I can think about is," I hesitated, before saying, "this other guy."

The bell on the front door jingled—my wish coming true too late to save me. Anne stood, speaking in a low, quick tone to make sure her voice didn't carry to the person outside the frame room. "There's nothing wrong with thinking about someone other than who you're with," she said. "Monogamy is about the body, not the mind. Everyone gets a nutty crush from time to time. Sometimes the best way to get over an infatuation is to go with it. Close your eyes and let your imagination run wild. You get great sex for a while, without cheating on the person you're with." She winked at me, and walked out the door.

I pulled the spinach pastry hors d'oeuvres from the oven and scooped them onto a little hand-thrown ceramic dish my mother had given me when I'd moved into my current apartment. I glanced at the clock, stashed the dirty pan and spatula in the dishwasher, and glanced around the kitchen. I'd decanted a bottle of wine twenty minutes before. It stood on the counter, breathing. A thin line of fragrant steam rose from the pastries. I'd decided against the candles. It had seemed over-the-top. But the kitchen was bright with the late sun. The walls were white, the counter-tops blue tile. Everything looked tidy and inviting. I'd just decided to do one final sweep through the bedroom and bathroom when the doorbell rang. My heart gave a massive lurch and started to hammer.

Trying to compose myself, I smoothed my hair, glanced down at my shirt to make sure I didn't have spinach goo smeared on my stomach, and went to let Ben in.

I'd spent all of Friday night writing middle-school worthy diary entries and soul-searching. Sure, Clint was gorgeous and mysterious. I'd seen him sitting on horseback in a cloud of dust at sunrise, holding a flag and waiting as a herd of horses streamed by. It was the sort of thing you don't see in the real world. It was a glimpse of a different kind of man, a different kind of life.

But I had to be realistic. I didn't even know if Clint was single. I knew he was Nora's older brother and Nora was a couple years younger than me. There was a good chance he was either married or in a serious relationship. There was an even greater chance he wasn't interested in me at all.

Ben was interested. Ben was attractive, gainfully employed, nice, and fun to hang out with. And *interested*. He was interested in me, and I had been interested in him before this whole Clint thing. It was time to stop being an idiot. This morning, I'd texted Ben and invited him over for dinner.

I opened my front door. Ben stood on the little patio outside, holding a colorful bouquet and looking extra handsome in a bright white shirt tucked into a pair of gray chinos. When he saw me, he extended a hand, palm up. Not sure what to do, I put my hand in his. He bowed over it, raising it to his lips to kiss the back. He straightened up with a little smile, and handed me the flowers. "Bonsoir, mademoiselle."

I took the flowers. We'd established early in our relationship that we'd both taken French in college and had attempted one or two fractured conversations since then. "Merci, monsieur." His accent was better than mine. I wanted to say something about how the flowers were beautiful, but couldn't come up with anything that didn't sound trite. I settled for, "Come on in." In English.

Ben stepped inside, closing the door behind him. "It smells great in here."

My mom was a good cook. All through my childhood, she'd been the one who put the food on the table throughout the week. But she did it because eating was a necessary part of staying alive. My dad, on the other hand, was *into* cooking. Weekend meals were his jurisdiction. We'd taken many a long drive around town together, looking for some elusive ingredient. I'd been his apt pupil from the ages of 7 to 13, at which point I'd turned sullen and refused to come out of my bedroom most nights. I'd learned a lot from him, though, and now that I was over being a teenager, I often went over on the weekends to help him put together nice meals. "Thanks," I said, and gestured to the plate of spinach puffs. "Help yourself. Would you like a glass of wine?"

I went to the decanter, pouring two glasses with the awareness that Ben was watching me. This made me jumpy, and I paid extra attention to the glass, the red liquid, the counter. The last thing I wanted to do was knock something over.

Glasses in hand, I returned to the table. I'd spent the whole day preparing for this. But now that Ben was actually here, in my apartment, I had no idea what to say or do.

Ben took a sip of wine, then set his glass down. He walked around the table and slipped his arm around my waist. He kissed me once, gently, and leaned back to look at me. "Thank you for having me over."

I resisted the urge to crack a joke and slip out of his grasp. Instead I looked him in the eye. "Clean slate, right?" Then I closed my eyes, and kissed him.

This time, I did it deliberately.

I thought of Clint. I thought of Clint coming into the tack room. In my fantasy, he didn't turn the light on, and he didn't have a saddle in one hand and a pad in the other. He also wasn't wearing a shirt. He walked up behind me as I stared at the wall of tack and took the bridle from my hand, our fingers brushing. Then he kissed me. He kissed me with a firmness that took my breath away, walking me backwards until I bumped up against the wall and he could hang the bridle on its empty hook.

In real life, in my kitchen, I was now pressed up against the kitchen counter. I could feel Ben's kiss shift from polite to something a lot more interesting. He took the glass from my hand and set it on the counter.

In my head, Clint's lips strayed from my mouth, creeping down my neck to my collarbone while his hands slipped up under my shirt in the back, his rough palms leaving little tingling lines on my skin.

In real life, Ben's hands did the same thing. Except his were smooth and warm. His kiss grew deeper and more serious, slowing down and jerking me back to reality for a moment. Ben was actually a really good kisser. For a few minutes my brain emptied, going devoid of all thought, either of Ben or Clint. I felt my body lighting up, pulses racing from my lips outwards, snaking up and down my spine. My heart was pounding. So was Ben's. I could feel it under my hands, which had untucked his shirt and wormed their way onto his chest.

Ben leaned down so his mouth was close to my ear. "Erin," he said. "I don't want to rush you." I could feel how excited he was, the heat rising off his skin as he leaned against me and the counter. I could feel how excited I was. I hadn't felt this alive since, well, since a time I preferred not to think about just then.

I kissed Ben's jaw. "You're not," I said, and led him to my bedroom.

○

"I slept with Ben." It was Monday evening. Trace and I were in our usual booth in Julio's. I said it because she'd been 20 minutes late and had scarcely looked at me in the half hour she'd been here because she was so busy exchanging texts with her new babysitter. I'd wanted to say something dramatic to get her attention. She only gave me a vague smile without taking her eyes off her phone. That rocked me well past annoyance into real anger.

I looked at Trace a moment longer, giving her one more minute to snap out of it and respond. She continued to stare at the phone, the screen casting a pale glow on her chin.

"Trace," I snapped, keeping my voice down but injecting the word with as much force as I could muster. "I'm trying to talk to you here. But if micromanaging your kid's life is more important than major things happening to your best friend, maybe you should go home and I'll find someone else to talk to."

I hadn't meant to say so much. But as soon I'd started to speak, a little pocket of intense anger I hadn't known I'd been carrying around with me had uncurled and flowed through my whole body. I'd spent the last few days vacillating between an elation that bordered on ecstasy and the dull, anxious feeling of having lied about something important.

When I said her name, Trace looked up as if seeing me for the first time all evening. As I continued my little diatribe, her face went pale. Now her eyes were wide and startled, as if I'd slapped her.

Now that I'd started, I couldn't seem to stop. "Andrew is *home*, for crying out loud. *And* there's a babysitter. Seriously, Trace, you need to let go a little. I don't think the sitter's choice of a bedtime story is going to impact Olivia's chances of getting into Harvard."

Trace glanced down at the text she'd been in the middle of composing. She swallowed. She held her finger on the power key until her phone played the little tone that meant it was shutting down. Her eyes, I was horrified to see, had gone all misty and red-rimmed. She took a deep breath, put the phone in her purse and said, "Erin. I'm so sorry."

Now that I had both her attention and her apology, I wasn't sure I wanted either. I almost wished she'd said something awful, like, "Hold on a sec. Let me send this." That would have entitled me to storm out the door in a white rage.

Instead, she blinked and dabbed at the corner of her eye with her napkin. "You're right. I've been the most wretched friend. It's just that...." She stopped, catching herself on the verge of spiraling back into Olivia world. She looked up and gave me a trembly smile. "See? I can't even stop with the 'me me me' while I'm apologizing to you."

I felt my anger drain away as quickly as it had blossomed. I looked down, fiddling with my napkin. "I didn't mean for that to come out so harsh."

Trace took a sip of her water. She seemed to be regaining her equilibrium. I'd already finished one beer. She was only halfway through her glass of wine. But after the water she took several big gulps and almost caught up to me. "Anything less harsh might not have gotten my attention."

That's when I realized she literally hadn't heard what I'd said about Ben. She knew I'd said something, and it was something she should have heard, but she'd missed it.

Julio's was crowded. All the booths were full. Most of the tables in the center were occupied as well. Mexican music played over the sound system and the buzz of conversation and laughter was loud enough to more than cover anything we might say here. Still, I felt reluctant to repeat myself.

Trace waited, and when I didn't say anything, she bit her lip, took another sip of wine and said, "That last thing you said. Did you say you slept with Ben?"

I nodded, looking down at my beer and thinking about that night. It had been a great night. We'd tumbled into bed, where we'd stayed long enough to burn dinner. Ben had proven to be a considerate but enthusiastic lover—a good combination, as far as I was concerned.

"Was this your first time since...." I nodded as Trace ran out of gas.

"Since Jake," I said, finishing the sentence for her. "Yes, it was." Jake had been my college boyfriend. Trace and I had discussed him enough to last a lifetime.

Trace gave me a sly smile. "Good for you. How was it?"

"It was great," I said, knowing it was true even though it felt like a lie. It had been great, because every time I'd started to cool down or have second thoughts, I'd conjured up a mental image of Clint and gotten myself fired up again. "It was really good for a first time." I said this as if we didn't both know I'd only had a first time twice before, so didn't exactly have a huge selection of partners to compare Ben to. Between the two of us, Trace had always been the wild one. It figured she'd also be the one to settle down first.

"So do you think this could turn into a long-term thing? I thought you weren't sure about him?"

I could tell Trace was trying to ask the right questions, to slip back into the role of best friend she'd occupied in my life for so long. But the longer the spotlight of our conversation stayed focused on me, the more uncomfortable I felt. I almost wished she hadn't turned her phone off so an Olivia-centric message could diffuse the focus a bit.

"I *wasn't* sure about him"

"But you are now?"

I looked out the window. Julio's was in a strip mall. The view was indifferent. I watched a young couple walk past the front of a parked Ford Taurus, a toddler clinging to the woman's hand. I imagined myself as the woman, the man as Ben, and the toddler as our child. The thought made a little surge of panic dart through my body. "I'm sure he's fun for now."

Trace frowned at me, finishing her wine and leaning back in her seat. "That doesn't sound like you, Erin."

This was the problem with best friends. When they're paying attention, they can see right through you.

The server hadn't given us coasters. My beer had left a large puddle of sweat on the table. I looked down and poked at the puddle with my finger, dragging the water out in little lines to make a star pattern.

"Erin," Trace said. Her voice had that stern 'I will root this secret out of you if my life depends on it' quality that always filled me with a mix of annoyance and the warm fuzzies. "There's something you're not telling me."

I'd thought sleeping with Ben would solidify things, bring him into focus, and relegate Clint to some silly dreamscape I had no business dwelling in. Instead, I thought of Clint more than ever.

The server came then, bringing us new drinks and taking our entrée order, giving me a brief reprieve. When he was gone, Trace gave me a nudge under the table with the toe of her sandal. I sighed. "The thing is, I should be head over heels in love with Ben. I thought sleeping with him would move things forward. Instead I just feel," I stopped. *Instead I just feel like I want to set up camp in Nora's tack room and lie in wait for her brother.* "I just feel unsure."

Trace gave me a sympathetic smile. "There's nothing wrong with a casual relationship. It's the 21st century. Sex doesn't have to lead to marriage. You've been single for a long time. I think you should enjoy yourself."

"Thanks, Trace." Somehow her affirmation only made me feel worse. I looked down at the table, and I realized I'd written CLINT in water from the puddle my beer glass had left. I smeared it out before she could notice.

"First off," Nora said, "you ride with too short a rein. I want to see those slobber straps pointing down, not up."

We were sitting in the outdoor arena at the Tipped Z. The sun was just peeking up behind the mountains. Slobber straps, I'd learned earlier, were the leather attachments that connected the reins to the snaffle bit. The particular ones on my horse were a light brown leather with some tooling along the edges and a small Tipped Z brand stamped in one corner. They were quite nicely made. Every time Nora referenced them I couldn't help but think there had to be some more attractive word we could use to talk about them.

I was astride Duke, who had a hip cocked and his ears tipped lazily to the sides. Nora was on a chestnut mare named Sally. Sally was an interesting brownish red. She had no white on her anywhere. Nora was wearing a pair of chinks similar to the one's I'd seen on Clint. As she sat on her horse, she had one hand resting casually on the horn, her reins so long I wondered how she'd have any control if her mare decided to get uppity on her.

I never had told Trace about Clint. We'd had a great talk. After I'd spilled the beans about Ben, I'd asked why she was so worried about Olivia. She'd confessed Andrew so far had been about the worst parenting partner she could have imagined. The night had ended in her shedding a few tears and giving me a long, fierce hug good-bye while promising to be a better friend.

I'd gone home, gone to bed, and had a dream involving Clint and the tack room.

I hadn't seen Clint this morning. There was a huge stack of hay in the barn where the truck had been last week But other than Nora and two wire-haired dogs, I hadn't seen a soul.

"What do you do if your horse runs off?" I said this in response to her comment about my reins.

Nora gave me a blank look. "Duke won't run off. But if one did, you'd just pick up one rein and bend him to a stop. Now, I want you to go to the top of the arena and walk a circle."

After the first lesson, I'd been sore. Clint had been right about that. A week later, I was feeling good again. I was also pleased to feel myself moving with the horse a lot more easily from the start. I could feel myself relaxing into a position that had once been natural for me. I pointed Duke up the rail and we walked to the top.

Nora reoriented her red mare so they still faced us, saying, "I want a quality circle, and not on the rail. Walk around the barrel there and keep an even distance from it at all times. Keep a nice bend in Duke's body, and, no, you're collapsing in. He's going to want to hurry on that side because he'd rather be down here with me and Sally. That's okay. Try again. Remember to use your legs to bend him and support him and keep him in that turn."

An hour later, I was exhausted. I'd had no idea when I'd asked Nora to give me lessons that I was hiring the most precision-obsessed taskmaster on the planet.

We had spent thirty minutes on the circle. It had taken that long before I could keep Duke from cutting in on one side or dishing out the other. Nora kept stopping me to demonstrate how she and Sally could walk a perfect circle without hands, even though Sally was 3 years old and had only been started that spring, and Duke was a seasoned ranch horse.

After the circle, Nora had taken pity on me and let me trot and canter along the rail for the last fifteen minutes. That had felt great. I'd been smiling in spite of myself by the time we stepped off. It was hot by then, and Duke's neck was sweaty when I petted him to thank him for the ride.

Nora and I walked side by side back towards the barn, the breeze cooling the sweat on our skin. I could smell horse and leather and sand. I felt relaxed and happy.

"I don't want to pressure you or anything," Nora said as we led our horses back into the barn. I glanced at the stack of hay. No Clint. "But it's hard to make much progress if you only ride once a week. You have a good seat, and you're confident and natural on a horse. I think you could get somewhere if you put the time in."

STEFANI WILDER

I thought about the meagre paycheck I brought in from the gallery and the half-finished novel I was not writing at that very moment. Nora's lesson price was reasonable, but it wasn't nothing. I was about to say something neutral along the lines of, "I'll think about," when Clint walked in.

He stepped through the small door near the parking area as I fell back to let Nora go first down the aisle between the empty stalls, one of the wire-haired dogs at his heels. As usual, the mere sight of him sent a series of sparks down my spine. He looked at me and saw I was looking at him. For a moment, our eyes locked. It was a shock to have him appear so suddenly: the real Clint, flesh and blood, standing right in front of me again.

He was wearing his hat. He tipped the brim in my direction, like a cowboy in a movie. I expected him to say, "Ma'am." Instead he said, "Erin, right? How was your ride?"

"Oh." I felt as startled as if I'd been addressed by Duke. "Well, I spent half an hour trying to walk a circle." I regretted my own honesty the moment the words left my mouth. I should have tried to come up with something more impressive to say, something that would have made him conjure up an image of me loping freely through the sunshine with my hair flowing behind me on the wind.

But Clint didn't seem surprised. Instead of turning dismissive or superior, he cracked his adorable smile. "Most won't stick with it so long." As he said this, he walked towards me. I felt dizzy with the certainty that this was it: something was finally about to happen. He was going to reward my perseverance with something extra special. He stopped right next to me and extended a hand. My heart did a backflip and started beating triple-time.

His hand reached past me and smoothed Duke's forelock, then ran down the gray gelding's neck. "Did he give you a good one?"

My heart was still hammering. I was so close to Clint, I could smell the light scent of the soap he must have shaved with that morning. I'd heard his words. Although my mind was scrambled, I believed my command of the English language had not deserted me entirely. But I had no idea what he was talking about.

Clint glanced away from Duke and must have registered my blank expression. "Duke," he said. "Did Duke give you a good circle?"

A ridiculous, trembling laugh escaped me. "Yes. Yes, he did."

Clint gave Duke a pat on the shoulder and walked off as Nora poked her head back out of the stall barn to see what had happened to me.

I stood up from my chair as my desktop faded to the blue screen that informed me my computer was shutting down. Raising my arms above my head, I felt several small pops in my spine.

I glanced out the window. The sun was starting to fall. My stomach gave a little rumble. I padded barefoot into my kitchen, enjoying the feel of the cool tile floor under my toes. I looked in my refrigerator. Condiments rattled in the door, but the shelves showed a depressing lack of options. A wedge of cheese stood next to a carton of milk and a hank of withering beet tops I'd been intending to use in a salad but hadn't. I threw the beat tops out, closed the refrigerator, and stared indecisively out the window.

I'd spent the entire day producing words for my novel. I'd been so giddy and high over my (admittedly brief) interaction with Clint, I'd let Nora talk me into committing to riding on Sundays as well, and either getting a lesson, if nothing was going on, or helping with ranch work if there was some sort of activity going down that I could be guaranteed not to screw up. Nora had cheerfully said that they were sometimes a bit shorthanded, and the days I worked for them would count as credit towards the days she gave me lessons. She said it might end up breaking about even.

That had been all the additional persuasion my addled brain had needed. I'd agreed. But on my drive home I had given myself a stern talking-to. I had laid down the law. I'd agreed with myself that if I wanted to keep taking riding lessons, I needed to make sure I did not let them take over my Tuesdays and Sundays. Tuesdays and Sundays were for writing, and writing was the key to the entire Grand Plan of my life. Without writing, I was a late-twenty-something making a laughable wage at an art gallery. With writing, I was a struggling artist.

So I'd marched into my apartment with a purpose, put my phone on silent, taken a quick, cool shower, and gotten down to work. I'd closed all programs on my computer except Word. And I'd written. All day. I'd written quite a lot and was feeling proud of myself for exhibiting such maturity.

But now I was hungry, and I had no food. My choices were either to go out, go shopping, or go hang out with my mom.

I wandered into the bedroom and picked up my phone, which I'd left to charge during its silent day. I unplugged it and woke it up, and my heart gave a clench. Not the good kind of clench when you see someone you had been hoping to hear from called. No. Sitting in my notification bar were the words: "15 missed calls." They were all from my mother.

My mouth went dry as I frantically unlocked the screen. The first call had come about twenty minutes after I'd gotten home from my lesson. I hit the screen to call her back. As the phone rang on the other end, I began to pace. My father was supposed to be on his way to Iraq. He was a chemical engineer and consulted for the military. They regularly flew him overseas for reasons he could not discuss with us. I knew my mom had been scheduled to drive him down to Davis-Monthan Air Force Base that morning.

It seemed to take an eternity for her to pick up, during which time I imagined every sort of lurid accident that might have left my father injured, maimed, or even dead. I was in a cold sweat by the time she interrupted the ringing. Her voice was tense and unhappy. Instead of her usual greeting she said, "Where have you *been* all day?"

"Mom," I said, a sudden lump in my throat. "What's wrong?"

"They've been kidnapped. There's no doubt of it. The police were here, and they found tire tracks."

"Kidnapped?" I felt my panic solidify and quicken, my mind filling with the unpleasant image of my father with a sack over his head and a gun pressed to the small of his back, stooping to get into a van. Then the second part of her sentence sank in. I adjusted the backdrop of my mental image to Sonoran desert instead of busy street in Baghdad. I felt a chill run up my spine. This was very, very bad. I moved away from the window and spoke a little more quietly. "Oh my god. They came to the house? Where were you?"

Mom's tone became more impatient. "Taking your father to the base. When I came back, they were gone."

I blinked several times, my mind doing a looping scramble. I felt my panic cool a notch. "Wait, Mom. Who was gone?"

She released an exasperated sigh. "Did you listen to my voicemails?"

My fear was starting to fade, morphing into annoyance born of being so badly scared. "Mom," I said, trying to keep my voice even. "Is this about the dogs?"

"They've been stolen," my mother said.

It wasn't only that the loss of Boswell and Norman was a hard thing to take seriously after the narrow escape from maiming and/or death my father had just experienced in my mind. It was something that went a little deeper for me. As I jammed my phone into my purse, fished out my car keys, and hurried down the steps on my way to go over and do what I could to comfort my mother, I admitted something I had previously kept under petty good wraps.

I'd long been harboring mild jealousy issues regarding Boswell and Norman.

I had my reasons. The year I'd left for college had been a big one in my family. My father had been offered his contract with the military. Two years in Iraq would mean great professional opportunities for him, not to mention putting my parents in a different tax bracket. After the first two years, he would come home, after which he would only need to make the trek overseas once or twice a year.

And so I'd left for college and my father had left for Iraq within months of each other, leaving my mother alone without even my father's fish. (He'd given them to a friend because she didn't know how to keep them alive.)

That's how Boswell and Norman came about. My first trip home from school, they'd been there: two wriggling white puppies who had stolen my mother's heart. I had tapped down on any feelings of jealousy because, really, who could blame her?

But the puppies had been only the beginning. They weren't just any puppies. They were show-quality Bull Terrier stock, my mother had informed me proudly as they'd bounced across the yard chasing a blue ball as large as they were. And she was going to show them.

It had been the start of a new era. Soon, Mom needed a new house because our old yard wasn't big enough for Bull Terrier energy levels. That's when she'd single-handedly demolished all my childhood memories by moving from our little house at the edge of town out onto a small acreage with a large, secure yard. And as if that hadn't been bad enough, she didn't just show the dogs. She *showed*. It seemed like every weekend she'd be loading up and taking to the road in her new Subaru Outback—its back fitted with a grille and custom carpeting to make a comfortable traveling room for the dogs. She drove all around the country to compete in breed shows. Boswell and Norman did well, even winning sometimes.

They became my mother's new family.

I resented them. It annoyed me that I would call to tell my mother I was coming home for the weekend and she'd say that was fine but she wouldn't be around. Most of my friends had clingy parents who were hounding them for more visits, more time on Skype, more news of their lives. When I called home (it was usually me calling), I got a play by play dissection of the last show.

Things had evened out when Dad came home. Mom had slowed down a little. Boswell and Norman entered a golden stage of pseudo-retirement. Mom still showed them sometimes, and she also had them at stud. Which meant she had a website about them with pictures and fees and a contact form you could use in case you wanted your female dog to produce the newest heirs to the Boswell or Norman line of Bull Terriers.

To say my feelings were ambivalent as I drove to my parents' house that afternoon wouldn't be entirely accurate. I was glad nothing had happened to my father, and of course, I didn't want anything to happen to Boswell and Norman either. I was just having a little trouble taking the whole kidnapping thing seriously.

But when I pulled into our driveway, I could see a small section of the parking area was cordoned off with yellow police tape. The light was failing. But after I parked my car and walked around the tape, I could see two skid marks there, deep in back, shallower in front, like someone had floored the accelerator on their way out. I recalled how my mother always drove when the dogs were in the car, careful not to slam on the brakes or accelerate too fast so they wouldn't get knocked around. I thought of the two dogs tumbling in a heap and hitting the back of the van (it had to be a van that had taken them, right?) with little yips of surprise and pain.

That was when I felt the first beginnings of outrage. It sank in that someone had come to my parents' house and taken my mother's dogs. It was the sort of thing that happened in Disney movies. And yet it left me feeling angry and violated and helpless all at once.

I found my mother on the back patio, an open bottle of wine on the low table where normally there would also be a cheese plate that would need to be defended from two inquiring white muzzles. Today there was no cheese, and no Boswell and Norman. I felt my heart sink further.

My mother had never been one to cry. As I sat down across from her and poured myself a glass of wine, she looked at me, dry-eyed, and said, "They say there's little hope. Stolen dogs are almost never recovered, particularly with breeds that have so few characteristics that distinguish individuals." She trailed off, shaking her head.

I could see the problem. Boswell and Norman were both pure white. Even some of my parents' good friends couldn't tell them apart.

My mom drew in a deep, ragged breath. "And your father doesn't even know. He's still in the air."

Chapter 4

"I'm so sorry." Ben gathered me in his arms the moment I opened my door. I didn't even have the energy to pretend he was Clint. I just leaned my head on his shoulder.

It was Wednesday evening. I'd stayed Tuesday night with my mom. I'd gotten up early to have time to shower and change before work, but Mom had been awake already, sitting at the kitchen counter sipping coffee and staring out the window with a dull expression. I hadn't wanted to leave, but when I'd asked her if she wanted me to come back after work she'd said no, she wanted some time and space.

So when Ben texted asking if I wanted to go out, I'd written back saying I didn't feel up to it, at which point he'd called and asked what was wrong. His initial reaction had been like mine, but as I'd explained I could feel him realizing why it was a big deal. When I was done, he'd offered to bring over Chinese food.

Since I'd gotten home from work, I'd done nothing but text and email every single person I could think of, sending them photos of Boswell and Norman and asking them to send them on to everyone they knew, promising a reward. The police had said this kind of strategy usually didn't work, but sometimes if the kidnappers thought there was more to be gained by giving the dogs back than keeping them, they'd respond. So I'd emailed and texted friends, posted on every Craigslist within 100 miles, and then I'd run out of things to do.

When Ben had offered to come over, I'd thought it was nice of him. But now that he was here, stepping back from our hug to look at me with an earnest, concerned expression, I felt a sudden odd sense of claustrophobia.

"How's your mom holding up?" His eyes searched my face. I uncharitably wondered how he would possibly be able to up the ante if real tragedy ever struck my family.

"She's devastated," I said, taking a small step backwards.

Ben nodded, face solemn under his perfectly mussed shock of blond hair. "Is there anything I can do to help?"

I took the plastic bag of Chinese food from his hand. "Feeding me is a good start."

We adjourned to the table. As I unpacked the food, Ben walked into the kitchen and opened cupboards and drawers, poking around until he found plates and forks. It struck me as a tad over-familiar for where we were in our relationship. He smiled when he saw me watching him, carrying the plates over to the table. At a loss for any other response, I smiled back.

We scooped piles of food onto our plates and ate in silence for a minute or two. Around a mouthful of General Tsao's Chicken, Ben said, "So where have you hung posters?"

I stared at him, a forkful of Mongolian Beef poised halfway between my plate and my mouth. "Posters?" I repeated.

Ben looked up, wiping his mouth on one of the napkins that had come in the plastic bag. "Yeah. Isn't that what you do when a dog gets lost?"

I had to bite down the urge to remind him that Boswell and Norman had been *stolen* not *lost*. It was highly unlikely anyone was going to see them running around on the side of the road and bring them home. I reminded myself he was trying to help. "I sent their picture to every contact I have in my email and phone."

Ben nodded. "I saw that, and the reward. But wouldn't posters, you know, build on that?"

I wanted to tell him that my mom had friends all across the country, breeders and other showers and advocates for the Bull Terrier breed. I wanted to say hanging posters would be about as much help to her finding her dogs as a kid with a lemonade stand is to his family's bottom line. But then I realized that if I shot this down, I'd be stuck with Ben in my apartment with nothing to do except what we'd done the last time he'd come over. And I wasn't in the mood. So I said, "After we eat, maybe we can make some. And then you can drive me around and help me hang them up."

You never notice how many people you know until all of them are concerned about you at once. Or, rather, all of them are concerned about your mother. The fact that my dad was out of the country lent the dognapping a whole extra layer of tragic heft, and mere hours after my emails went out, legions of women banded together, organized themselves, and worked out a way to bombard my mother with a steady supply of casseroles for the foreseeable future. I could hardly blame her when she started to pretend she wasn't home. Without Boswell and Norman around to wreak havoc on the dishes left like offerings at a shrine for the hungry, it didn't even matter if the covered dishes sat outside for an hour or two before my mother retrieved them.

But even the most attentive of friend networks cannot stay infinitely concerned about lost dogs. By Saturday evening, the sheer volume of delivered food was dropping off. I noticed as I pulled into my parents' driveway the police tape was gone. When I let myself through the front gate, there was only one covered dish with a note on it set next to the front door. I picked it up with a sigh and let myself into the house.

The police had turned up nothing. While my mother seemed to think they weren't trying very hard I, for one, was astonished they'd bothered to even call back with updates, particularly when the updates amounted to a total lack of leads. Likewise, the emails and texts and three dozen posters Ben and I had hung around our respective neighborhoods had produced no results of any kind. We were all losing hope.

My mother had made her way rapidly through the stages of grief, and had settled into a sort of detached acceptance that worried me. In spite of the lukewarm reception I got every time I came by, I kept dropping in each day. Each day it seemed a little sadder that there was no hurricane of compact, muscular dog-flesh there to slobber on my pant-legs and cover everything I owned in a dusting of short white hairs.

I carried the dish to the kitchen, attempted to find a place for it in the refrigerator, gave up, and left it on the counter. The house was quiet, but I knew my mother was home. I poked my head out the back door to find the porch empty, and headed for her workroom.

Professionally, my mother was an illustrator. She drew illustrations for medical texts, and her work was somewhat sought-after. When I'd been a kid, she'd taken as much work as she could, and I had many memories of sitting on the floor playing with my Breyer horses while my mom perched at her drafting table with photographs of organs pinned up along the wall behind her.

A similar scene greeted me today, except instead of an array of hearts or lungs, the wall behind my mother's desk was populated with photos of her two missing dogs. Boswell and Norman's young lives and careers had been documented far more extensively than my own had. Not long ago, this fact had irked me a little. But when I walked around the corner and saw my mother's head stooped over her drafting table, the wall of dogs beyond her, I had to step back into the other room for a moment to get hold of myself so I didn't walk in crying.

The next time I stepped around the door, I knocked on the frame. Mom swiveled in her chair, her glasses perched low on her nose. On the table before her was a half-finished illustration—the two dogs looking out of the paper with bright eyes and pricked ears. She made a vague gesture towards the page. "It's therapeutic, I guess."

We looked at each other. She set her pen down and stood up with a sigh.

There was a long silence, and I said the only thing that came to mind. "I brought you some food."

Her eyes narrowed, then she gave a small laugh. "For a minute I thought you were serious. Have you seen the refrigerator?"

I tossed back the last of my coffee and set my travel mug in my cup holder. I was almost starting to get used to this getting up at the crack of dawn thing, and I was gaining confidence. I'd hardly even noticed the terrifying signs as I'd typed in the gate code and driven onto the Tipped Z.

I stepped out of my car. The three wire-haired dogs were standing near the barn, sniffing politely in my general direction. They had never barked at me since that first time.

Nora's truck was not in evidence, and this made me hesitate in a way the ominous signs had not. This was my first Sunday out at the Tipped Z, and I had no idea what to expect. I walked slowly towards the barn, half hoping Nora's old truck would rumble around the bend, and half hoping it wouldn't.

As I neared the barn, I heard voices. I paused outside the small door that led into the area where the hay was stacked. I listened for a moment. When I recognized Clint's voice, a small surge of adrenaline shot through me. I could hear his end of the conversation, and I realized he was talking on the phone.

"... another bad one yesterday. No, no. Nothing like that. Just a lot of tension."

A pause while someone on the other end spoke. Clint gave a short laugh.

"She's got her daddy's looks, that's for sure." His tone was appreciative.

The comment sent a little chill through me. I wondered who he was talking about. Not me, certainly. For one thing, Clint had never seen my father.

One of the wire-haired dogs came and sat at my feet. I squatted down to rub its ears, giving myself an excuse to continue to eavesdrop.

"I don't know what her deal is, though. We spend all this time working on our communication, then at the first sign of trouble it all goes out the window."

He stopped again and said, "uh huh" a couple of times. He sighed. "There's no doubt when she's relaxed and loose she's something to feel. I just don't know if she has long-term potential, you know?"

There was another pause as Clint listened. The dog gave a small sigh.

"Yeah. Good point. There's no real rush. There's not necessarily a downside to keeping her around for a while."

I realized what he must mean as I felt my cheeks go red with some strange blend of embarrassment and shock. I don't know why I was surprised. Ranchers weren't renowned for their progressive views on women.

Clint's tone changed as the conversation shifted towards wrapping up. "Sure, sounds good. Thanks Wyatt."

There was a beep as he turned off his phone. I realized I was squatting in the doorway in a position to have overheard a rather intimate conversation. I also felt like someone had placed a thirty pound boulder in my stomach. To learn Clint was both not single and sort of a chauvinist in one fell swoop was a lot to take.

I scrambled to my feet and stepped through the door, trying to make it look like I had walked straight up from my car.

The inside of the barn was dim. The large doors on the other side were open, letting in the morning light. Clint was leaning against the stack of hay, one booted foot propped up behind him, a dog sprawled at his feet. With the light of the door in the background, he was mostly silhouette. I felt that fire run through my veins even as I berated myself for being such an idiot. I don't know if he favored his mommy or his daddy, but one of them had sure passed on the right stuff.

He'd been staring down at the dirt floor when I entered, but now he looked up. He heaved himself off the hay. "Erin," he said by way of greeting.

Every time he said my name, I was impressed he remembered it, although the more I was around the Tipped Z the more obvious it became that Nora didn't exactly have a crush of students. From what I could gather, I was her only one.

I said hi in a squeaky voice that sounded like it belonged in a cartoon character.

STEFANI WILDER

Clint looked at me. There was no trace of embarrassment or concern that I might have caught what he'd been saying a moment before. His tone was even and relaxed. "My sister should be here any minute."

I could see he was on the verge of walking off, and even after what I'd just heard, I wanted to talk to him. Maybe if I could talk to him more, he would come tumbling off his pedestal and I could see him as a normal person instead of some enticing, half-shadowed specimen of manhood. At the same time, that phrase, "When she's relaxed and loose," stuck in my mind like a burr, conjuring up truly pornographic thoughts of how relaxed and loose I would prove to be for him, if I was ever given the chance.

I felt my opportunity slipping away as my mind remained resolutely empty of anything remotely conversation-worthy.

Clint took a step towards the door, then turned back as if remembering something. "It was your dogs that were stolen, right?"

I grasped at this conversation topic like a life preserver. "Yeah, my mom's. My parents live across the road from you, you know, if you go through the new subdivision and across the wash. There's an older neighborhood back there."

Clint nodded. "We had some taken once." He thrust his chin at the wire-haired dogs by his boot. "Must have been ten, fifteen years ago now. These dogs don't look like much, but they've been bred for ranching for generations. They come from this one little area where my dad grew up, and in some circles they're pretty sought after." Clint shook his head. "We had a litter posted for sale and someone came in at night and took them all. Makes your skin crawl, thinking of someone sneaking onto your land that way. My only consolation is those pups probably ended up in pretty much the same lives they'd have had anyway. People don't want these dogs for their looks." As he spoke, Clint stooped and ran a gentle hand down the dog's back.

I tried to reconcile the Clint who talked about stolen puppies with genuine concern with the one who had just been saying he was only with his girlfriend for the sex and wasn't sure she was long-haul material. "These were my mom's show-dogs. Bull Terriers. She got them when I left for college. She couldn't have been more attached to them. I guess someone took them because of their bloodlines."

Clint gave a little grimace and kicked at a stray pile of hay with his boot. "Some days the world makes you sick."

Behind us, I heard the sound of a rumbling engine and the crunch of tires on sand. Clint straightened. "That'll be Nora. I best bring the horses in."

○

"You take this," Nora said, offering me the rubber handle of a metal rod with a flag on the end. It was like the flag I'd seen Clint using that first day I'd seen him as he sat in the middle of the road at dawn.

I was sitting on Duke, feeling like I may have made a mistake. In theory, I accepted that some horses were okay with things like flags flapping around their heads. My personal experience with horses, however, told me quite another thing. I'd once been unceremoniously dumped by the horse I was supposed to be learning to run barrels on because I'd unzipped my sweatshirt.

Nora must have recognized the expression on my face. She gave a little laugh. "Don't worry," she said. "Duke is as broke as they come." She raised the flag and pumped her arm. The flag snapped and crackled in the air, inches above Duke's ears. I tensed, trying to organize my reins enough to contain the flare-up I was certain was coming. But Duke just sighed and cocked a hip.

Nora jigged the flag a little more. In a quick series of movements, she whacked Duke all over his body with the fabric. She wasn't hitting him hard, but the flag was noisy. I'd never seen a horse in my life who would tolerate that kind of chaos. Still, Duke stood like a statue.

Nora reached up and placed the flag in my hand, closing my fingers around the handle like a mother handing out lunch-money. "These are working ranch horses," she said. "They know the drill." That was all well and good for Nora to say, but I knew enough about horses to also know their behavior could change dramatically depending on who is on their back.

She turned away from me and swung onto her horse. She wasn't riding Sally today. Instead she was on a gleaming bay gelding named Paul who she rode with a thick woven rawhide band around his nose instead of a bit. Once she was on board, she looked over at me. I was aware I was holding the flag like a grenade with the pin pulled. "Flap it around a little," she said. "Get used to it."

I flexed my wrist so the flag dipped approximately one inch, then brought it back up. Nora's laugh was so loud Duke's head came up a little and his ears swiveled in her direction. "Erin, I promise. He won't dump you. Now shake that flag or I'm going to leave you behind."

I shook the flag. Duke stood still.

There was the jingle of tack behind us. I turned in my saddle to see two men approaching. One was Clint, and he was leading the most gorgeous horse I'd ever seen. It was a few inches shorter than Duke, and beautifully proportioned, with square conformation and striking coloring. The unbroken black of its legs faded into the creamy tan of the coat. A buckskin.

The other man was a slightly taller, rangier version of Clint with perhaps an extra 25 years under his belt. He was leading a red horse with four tall white socks. Two of the wire-haired dogs walked beside him. Nora looked over as the two men swung into their saddles. "Dad, this is Erin. Erin, my dad, Hank."

Hank tipped his hat, but said nothing. Both his horse and his son's horse stood quietly. I had always imagined the sort of horses that had the spunk to work cattle would be fidgety and restive, but these four were the picture of relaxation. Both Hank's horse and Clint's horse, however, were wearing heavy ornate bits, and it looked like Clint had two sets of reins, one attached to the bridle and the other to a little band of rawhide that went around the horse's nose, like Paul's, but skinnier. Maybe they got uppity when they got around the cattle.

Then I noticed something else. "Hey," I said. "Why am I the only one with a flag?"

Twenty minutes later, I was sitting alone near an open gate. Just behind me was a large, bushy mesquite tree. To my right was an unbroken expanse of dried grass and sagebrush. To my left was the fence line and the new pasture the cattle were supposed to go into.

I reviewed Nora's instructions in my mind. The cattle were going to be coming from my right. Most of them knew the drill and would go through the gate without trouble. Every now and then, however, one of the young ones would get a bit agitated and would dive for the cover of the mesquite tree. It was my job to sit on Duke, far enough away from the gate that I wouldn't interfere with the cattle going through, but close enough I could turn one back if it got on the wrong trajectory.

I practiced shaking my flag, glaring into the eyes of an imaginary cow who was thinking about trying to squirt past me. Nora had told me to be confident and firm, and everything would be fine.

I was not confident. Sitting on Duke's back in the gathering heat, I could feel the ill-advised third cup of coffee I'd had adding extra pressure to my bladder. I tried to ignore it, vowing to myself that however this day turned out it would not include a scene involving a herd of cattle charging over the ridge to see me squatting in the bushes.

"Relax," I said, reaching down to pat the mottled gray of Duke's neck as if he was the one who needed reassurance.

We waited. The sun rose higher. I started to wonder if this was some sort of sick hazing ritual: a joke the ranch folk played on the greenhorns to see how long they'd sit alone in the sun before realizing what was what.

I had myself half convinced I'd been cruelly tricked, when a change came over Duke. He'd been half-dozing in the shade of the mesquite, but now his head popped up and the energy in his body changed so dramatically, I grasped at the horn with the same hand that held the flag. But he didn't move. He pointed his ears at the horizon, and stared.

I stared too. I couldn't see or hear a thing.

Then I saw the dust, and a moment later, the cattle. For a second I thought it was going to pan out like a scene in the movies—panicky animals stampeding among dust and boulders, riders galloping and calling as they cut off the lead heifer again and again, steering the spooked herd away from cliff-faces and canyons and bandits and whatever other terrors a screenwriter could come up with.

In fact, the cattle came over the top of a nearby ridge at a slow shamble. One dark red cow was in the lead, walking with purpose but not anxiety. More reddish bodies clustered up behind her. One horse and rider paced her on the left, keeping her from swinging into the open country. I couldn't see the others.

I sat up straighter in my saddle, and took a deep breath. I practiced shaking my flag one more time.

In no time at all, they were there. The lead cow spared me only the briefest of glances before walking confidently through the open gate. The rest of the herd followed on her heels, most of them appearing not to see me at all.

It was not a huge herd, maybe 20 or 30 animals, total. Half of them were through the gate in no time.

I was beginning to think I'd been spared, when a group of three young cattle that had lagged came sprinting up from behind, pursued by Clint on his trotting buckskin and one of the dogs. Clint brought his horse down to a walk as the three youngsters plunged in among the rest of the herd. He spoke a word to the dog. It dropped to the ground, eyes intent on the cattle. Two of the three young animals slotted right in with the others, but the third seemed to have too much forward momentum. It continued straight, missing the gate and coming at me.

Duke saw the calf at the same time I did. I could feel his body coil beneath me like a spring. "Oh shit," I muttered.

The calf trotted closer, hesitant now that it had taken a few steps away from the herd. I could see its wide-set brown eyes assessing us, trying to determine if it could dodge around on one side or another. I felt frozen, paralyzed by the stony gaze of an adolescent bovine.

"Erin, the flag," Nora called. She, Clint, Hank and the dogs were all watching me now. The potential for embarrassment was huge.

Her words and the fear of making a fool out of myself snapped me from my trance. I shook the flag, giving Duke a little squeeze with my legs and tipping him one step forward.

The calf stopped walking, eyes growing even wider.

I shook the flag some more and asked Duke for one more step.

The calf turned tail and ran, its red haunches disappearing behind one of the fully grown females as the last of the herd ambled through the fence.

I felt a sudden flush of pride as Hank stepped his horse up to the open gate and executed a perfect 180 degree side-pass maneuver, first swinging the gate out from where it rested against the fence, pushing it halfway to closed, then spinning his horse on the haunches and continuing to side-pass until the gate was closed. He flipped the latch down, and patted his horse's neck.

My sense of accomplishment faded a little at that, but then I heard Clint say, "Nice work."

He was behind me and to my right. I had to turn my head to look at him. I was certain he was talking to his dad. Instead, he was looking at me with his little quirk of a grin.

I felt myself beaming at him.

Nora said, "All right. Let's get out of this bloody heat already." She led us all down to the valley at an extended trot I knew I would pay for the next day.

"You sound like a real natural." Ben's tone was ironic, and he was grinning as he regarded me from a few cushions away. I'd just finished recounting my adventure with the stray calf and the flag, complete with the part where Nora had to remind me what to do.

We were on my couch, and my feet were in Ben's lap. He'd been giving me a foot rub while I told him about my day. It was only the fact that his strong hands were still squeezing the ball of my left foot that kept me from kicking him.

"Even some of the most gifted actors suffer terrible stage fright before the curtain call." I tried to make my tone lofty, and I stuck my nose in the air to drive my point home.

"What would you call this then? Cow fright?"

I decided it was worth the risk. I kicked him, gently, in the arm. Then I placed my foot back into position for rubbing.

"Hey," he protested. "I'm trying to develop a complete understanding of your morning." But he continued the massage.

It was Sunday evening. Outside, the light was failing. Inside, we'd consumed most of a bottle of wine. I had returned to my apartment that morning and, as I'd promised myself, devoted the rest of my day to writing. But after last Tuesday's disaster, I hadn't silenced my phone. Which meant when Ben had texted at five asking what I was up to, I'd invited him over even though I hadn't met my target word count.

The problem was, even though I'd ostensibly been writing all day, I hadn't produced more than a few hundred words. I hadn't produced more words because of Clint. I had been distracted enough by the rest of the morning's events that I hadn't had time to dwell on the conversation I'd overheard while I was still at the Tipped Z. But as soon as I'd gotten home, my mind had seemed intent on setting that single scene on repeat in my head, dissecting each word and phrase, trying to parse the underlying meaning of his half of the conversation.

Part of my writing had even amounted to transcribing the chat I'd overheard in as close to verbatim as I could manage. I'd read somewhere a few months before that the more times you remember something, the more inaccurate that memory becomes. Since then I'd suffered from this low-level paranoia that some of my most cherished childhood events hadn't happened, or hadn't happened as I recalled them. I knew I was going to be remembering this scene a lot, and didn't want it to lose accuracy.

Not that this memory was one to cherish. It was one to agonize over. It seemed I had struck out about as hard as I could on the Clint front. First, Nora is the first person to ever hear Ben refer to himself as my boyfriend. Second, I learn Clint is both not available and not desirable.

But the part of the conversation I kept coming back to all day, kept reading and rereading on my computer screen, was the part where he talked about long-term potential. Reading those words gave me this ridiculous little thread of hope to cling to. I found myself trying to explain away the rotten things he'd said with the rationale that there was nothing wrong with casual sex if both parties were consenting. Who's to say Clint wouldn't settle right down once he did find someone with the qualities he was looking for in a life-partner? So what if his tone discussing his love-life had sounded about as passionate as someone recapping the day's activity in the stock market? Maybe he just hadn't found the right person yet.

By happy hour, I was sick of myself—sick of mooning over a transcription of a conversation I hadn't been supposed to hear, sick of daydreaming about Clint instead of Ben, sick of remembering Clint's lean form leaning against the haystack. I needed to focus on Ben. Ben was real. Ben was attractive and interesting. Ben had good taste in wine.

Except one glass in I'd somehow devolved into telling Ben all about my morning with the horses, skirting as close as I could to the subject of Clint without actually raising it.

"I'm trying to impress upon you that I was slightly impressive this morning." I made a grand gesture with my wine glass as I spoke.

It was a lie, of course. I didn't think I'd even managed to impress the calf.

Ben grabbed my ankles and pulled, dragging me down the couch until I was flat on my back, then swinging himself out from under me so he was lying on top. "I'm already impressed with you." His tone was serious. He'd set his wine glass down. He now took mine from my fingers, placing it on the coffee table next to his. He was always so careful not to spill the wine.

He kissed me.

I thought of that morning. I thought of walking into the barn the same way I really had, seeing Clint leaning against the bales. Instead of hesitating in the entryway, I strode up to him, wrapped my arms around his neck, and pulled him down to kiss me. He was a taller man than Ben, and he wore tall heeled boots, but he bent to meet my lips as soon as he got over his surprise. His kiss was fierce and passionate. The thrill of it raced through my veins like fire. A moment later, he heaved me onto a stack of bales with as little effort as he moved hay, swinging himself up and on top of me. I could feel his belt buckle pressing into my stomach.

On the couch, Ben slipped his hands under my shirt. In my head, Clint did the same. I arched my back as a small moan escaped me. I could feel the heat building between our bodies, the pulse of our kiss quickened.

In my apartment, my phone rang. The fantasy shattered, and I turned my head. Ben's lips trailed onto my neck. "Let's pretend we can't hear it." His words were mumbly against my skin.

"It's my mom." I was one of those nerds who customized my ringtones so I knew who was calling without having to go look. I squirmed until Ben rolled aside, removing his weight from my chest. "She never calls me unless something's wrong."

I reached for my phone, ignoring his quizzical look. I answered just in time to prevent the call from going to voicemail.

"Erin," my mom said when I answered. I didn't like her clipped tone.

"What's up Mom?" I sat, trying not to look at Ben and attempting to straighten my twisted shirt.

"I got a call from the police. They arrested some dog thieves."

"And?" This seemed like good news, but Mom sounded anything but happy.

"They caught the thieves after tracing back from a suspicious sale. They found a warehouse where there were almost a hundred show-quality dogs in kennels, all probably stolen."

I waited, sitting forward on the couch and resisting the urge to pepper her with more questions.

"But the thieves had somehow gotten wind the police were coming. They started letting dogs loose."

I realized my heart was pounding, probably from a combination of what I'd been doing with Ben/Clint and the suspense of this unnecessarily drawn out tale.

"They think about 20 dogs ran off the property before the police arrived, but they have four Bull Terriers. One is a female but they think there is a chance one or two of the other three are Boswell or Norman."

"That's great news!" My voice was too loud in the quiet of the apartment.

"But they're not," my mom said. "They sent me a photo. None of those four dogs are familiar to me. They're bringing them down, though, and want me to come by the station to be sure."

"Bringing them down from where?" I said, my heart beginning to sink.

"Florence," my mom said. "That's where the warehouse was."

There was a silence on the line. I looked up at Ben, who was watching me with a curious expression. I asked the looming question. "What happened to the dogs the police didn't recover?"

My mom was silent for a long moment before answering. "They ran off into the desert."

Chapter 5

"Would you like me to wrap this up for you?" I lifted the small oil painting off of the counter and gave its new owner a questioning look.

The woman standing in front of the register treated me with a suspicious squint, as if I was teasing her somehow. "It's not a gift," she said, slotting her credit card back into her overflowing wallet and dropping it into a leather purse that likely cost as much as a month's rent at my apartment complex.

"We use protective foam and brown paper, so the frame doesn't get dinged before you can get it home."

The woman waved a weary hand and turned away from the counter, as if I had suggested something outrageous and she didn't have the energy to argue with me. I carried the painting to the back room.

Midway through my wrapping job, I heard Anne arrive. A moment later, the sounds of animated conversation drifted back to me. By the time I returned with the wrapped painting, the unfriendly woman was smiling. I handed her the painting, which she took without acknowledging my existence. I beat my retreat to the back room as Anne walked the woman to the door.

It was Monday, and I was exhausted. I'd gone with my mother to the kennel where the Bull Terriers were being held. They had turned out not to be Boswell and Norman. It was obvious even to me, although the police had seemed skeptical, insisting we hang out with the dogs for a few minutes, "Just to be sure." This had made my mother furious.

After leaving the kennel, my mother had informed me that she was going to drive to Florence and search the area. She'd offered to drop me at my apartment on her way out of town, but I'd insisted on going with her.

So we'd arrived in the desolate town of Florence, Arizona close to 10:00 PM. The wine and the drive had combined in my empty stomach into something that was no longer sitting well. We'd spent hours combing the outskirts of the town, windows rolled down, yelling "Boswell, Norman. Come!"

Needless to say, they hadn't come. On the way home, I'd had to have Mom pull over so I could be sick on the side of the road.

I heard the jingle of the bells on the front door as I ran the ATG dispenser along the back of the frame I'd been in the process of closing when the unfriendly woman had arrived. A moment later, Anne appeared in the doorway, dressed in white capris, platform sandals, and a breezy black tank-top. "Nice work," she said. "That's a good way to start the week."

The little oil had been by a well-known local artist, and its sale alone was enough to mean the gallery would have a decent week. "Don't thank me," I said. "She marched right in and asked to see Gary's stuff. When I started to tell her about his process, she told me she'd prefer to look alone."

Anne's eyes narrowed as she looked at me. Her mouth curved into a mischievous line. "I hope the reason you look like you could use eight more hours of sleep is because you've been taking my advice about your cowboy crush?"

I thought of the steamy but interrupted interlude on the couch the night before. "Unfortunately," I said, cutting a piece of backing paper and setting it onto the frame, "I am exhausted because my mother got a lead on her dogs and dragged me to the booming metropolis of Florence in the middle of the night, where we spent hours driving around disrupting the sleep of the locals."

Anne's expression turned serious. "Oh, I'm sorry Erin. If you need to go home...."

I thought of the way I'd spent my Sunday afternoon (staring at my transcription of Clint talking about his girlfriend). The last thing I needed was more unsupervised time in my apartment.

Before I could answer, my phone beeped. It was sitting on the work table. Anne didn't care if I sent and received texts while I was on the clock. Still, it made me feel a bit awkward to hear one come in with her standing there. She seemed to sense my discomfort. "Anything good?" She gave the phone a meaningful look.

I reached for the phone. The text was from Nora. "So sorry busy tomorrow. Clint will fill in same time."

I stared at my phone, my tired mind somehow unable to process this turn of events. Clint would fill in? As my riding instructor? I felt suddenly unsteady on my feet.

"Erin?" Anne said, her voice filled with concern. "Are you okay?"

I couldn't speak. I handed her the phone. She read the text and lost the worried look. She set the phone back on the work table and gave me a wicked smile. "That sounds like a promising development."

"Or a horribly embarrassing one." I regained my voice and motor skills, picking up a razor to trim down the edges of the backing. "This is a disaster. I've only had three lessons with Nora, and only during one of those was she actually trying to teach me anything. He's going to see I don't know what I'm doing."

Anne had not lost the satisfied smirk. She leaned against the doorframe. "Most men like nothing more than the opportunity to show off their expertise."

I thought of Clint's wordless chin thrust in the tack room, followed by the unhelpful comment, "It's a snaffle." This memory did nothing to ease my doubts. "I'm not sure he's the teaching type."

The gallery phone rang and Anne straightened. As she turned to leave, she said, "I can't wait to hear how it goes."

I walked into my apartment and tossed my purse onto the couch, hanging my keys on the hook by the door and sinking into my favorite armchair. I'd texted Trace a few hours before to cancel our standing Julio's date. I didn't feel up to the crowds and the Olivia photos and the drinks. My stomach was still unsettled. As I popped the footrest on the chair, my phone buzzed. I gazed at my purse on the other side of the living room and considered ignoring it. But a moment later I heaved myself out of my chair.

The text was from Ben. "Have a fun girl's night!"

I scowled at his sweet message and threw myself back into my seat, not bothering to text him back to let him know I wasn't out. I stared out the window for a moment, then called my mom. The house phone rang and rang until the answering machine picked up. I tried her cell.

She answered around the sound of wind. "Erin?" she said. She always seemed surprised when I called her cell phone, as if it was something normal people did not do.

"Hi Mom." I could hear road noise in the background. "Where are you?"

"Florence." A car horn blared in the background. "People here aren't the friendliest." The connection was crackly and her words cut in and out.

I pictured my mom creeping along the shoulder of the highway with the window down, calling for dogs that were certainly nowhere nearby. I felt my heart sink. "Don't you think it's about time to head home?" But before she could answer, the call dropped. I resisted the urge to hurl my phone at the wall.

On the one hand, I couldn't blame her. More details about the dog thieves had been disclosed. It looked like the warehouse in Florence had been the hub of a well-orchestrated operation that had been running in Tucson and Phoenix. All the dogs the police had recovered had been valuable, many with wins and recognition in their breed registries. The police thought there was a good chance these were the people who had taken Boswell and Norman.

Which meant my mom's two Bull Terriers were loose in the desert, lost and alone. It was not a heart-warming thought. I could hardly blame my mother for terrorizing the town in an effort to find them before they died of heat exhaustion.

Suddenly, I couldn't sit in my apartment all night. I walked to my computer and turned it on, pulling up the poster Ben and I had made and loading a fresh stack of paper into my printer.

Half an hour later, I carried a stack of posters and a roll of masking tape to my car. In the car, I sat indecisively for a moment, then fished my phone out of my purse. I sent Ben a text. "Up for an impromptu trip to Florence?"

I turned on my engine and cranked up the AC. The interior of my car was stifling, even though my parents had overruled my desire for a green car and purchased me a white one instead, saying it would be a lot cooler in the summer.

I stared at my phone, feeling sweat bead on my upper lip. Ben wrote back. "Italy? I'm game."

"Arizona. More poster hanging."

"Sure. Be right over."

"I'm in my car. What's your address? I'll pick u up."

There was a long pause. I wondered if Ben had to look up his own contact information. Another text came in a few minutes. "Not at home. At your place in 10."

I waited, trying to ignore the jealous little part of my mind that started to wonder what he was doing not at home at 6:00 on a Monday evening. I diverted myself by turning on the radio.

Nine minutes later, Ben's truck rolled into my apartment complex. He parked, leapt out of the driver's seat, and jogged to my car. He grinned as he settled in beside me, leaning over to kiss me on the cheek. "What happened to girl's night?"

"I canceled it." I put my car in reverse and maneuvered out of the parking lot. "I hope I didn't pull you away from anything interesting?"

Ben turned to look out the window, and I remembered how getting details about his life when he wasn't with me was about as easy as walking a perfect circle on horseback. I never seemed to be able to get any concrete information out of him. I waited as I pulled onto the road, thinking he would offer up some answer. Instead he said, "I'm always up for more Erin time."

I considered pressing the issue, but decided it would make me seem clingy. Instead, I filled him in on the Boswell and Norman situation while we drove. "So," I said, stopping at a stoplight. "I realized there's a decent chance someone around Florence will see them and pick them up. Mom's been up there two days in a row, driving around and calling for them, but it's a lost cause."

Ben was silent. I turned my head to look at him. He was wearing a charcoal gray t-shirt that made his hair look particularly blonde. He was giving me this funny look. "What?"

"You're a good person," he said. "A good daughter."

I didn't know what to say to that. Fortunately the light turned and I could look back at the road.

○

"I gather you used to run barrels." It wasn't phrased as a question.
I ran a quick mental check of what I knew Clint knew about me.
It wasn't much.

I hadn't told Nora many details about my previous experience with horses, and Clint nothing at all. But here he was, tossing this at me as if I was wearing a label on my shirt.

I was once again astride the stolid Duke, sitting in the slanted morning sunlight in the outdoor arena at the Tipped Z ranch. Clint was across from me, sitting on his buckskin horse, who I had learned this morning was a mare named Penny. That was all I had learned this morning, because so far Clint had said exactly nothing to me other than to answer when I asked his horse's name. I had arrived to find Duke and Penny saddled in the barn aisle. Clint had handed me the reins without a word, and walked off.

I had followed him, walking through the gate he held for me feeling more self-conscious than I had on my first date. I had mounted when he'd mounted, and now here he was, throwing this out at me with no preamble whatsoever.

I tried to make light of it. "How can you tell?"

Clint squinted. His hat was pulled low, and his eyes were bright in the tan of his face. I wondered why he didn't invest in a pair of sunglasses. I didn't say this, though. I was finding Clint considerably more intimidating without his sister present. "Your legs."

I leaned to the side and looked at my legs. My heels were down, and the horse hadn't taken so much as a step yet. Also I was still wearing my ridiculous fake cowgirl boots, which I had not yet had a chance to replace.

I tried to think of some witty rejoinder, but could come up with nothing.

"I could throw a loop around your ankle," Clint added, unhelpfully, as my silence stretched. I looked from the toe of my boot back to Clint. He patted the rope tied to one side of his saddle. "Pull you right off your horse."

I gave a weak little laugh, failing utterly to see his point. I didn't doubt he could rope my ankle, but didn't that have more to do with his roping skills than my riding? And what on earth did it have to do with me running barrels as a twelve-year-old?

Clint didn't appear to move, but his horse stepped forward, walking at a steady pace until she had covered half the distance between us. Then she stopped. I had no doubt Clint had asked the horse to do both things, but I hadn't seen his hands or legs so much as twitch.

A breeze kicked up and stirred the hair at the nape of my neck. The Tipped Z ranch was preternaturally silent. I racked my brain for something to do with my legs other than what I was currently doing.

Clint waited for so long I was afraid he wasn't going to say anything else, ever. Finally, he added, "Look at my legs."

I thought wistfully of Nora. Nora did not *stop* talking during a lesson. There were no pregnant pauses, no painful stretches of silence while she waited for me to fumble towards what was clearly an obvious concept.

I looked at Clint's legs. He was wearing his chinks, and the toes of his boots were dusty and well-worn where they poked through the stirrup. "Could you rope my ankle?" he said.

For a second, I thought he was raising the issue of my non-existent rope-handling skills. But then it came in a flash. Clint's legs were draped around his horse in a soft bend. There was no space between his calves and the horse's sides.

I glanced back down at my own feet, and saw what he meant. My legs were braced in my stirrups. My heels were down, but there was a good three inch gap between my ankle and Duke's dappled side. I relaxed my legs, surprised when I realized how much tension I'd had in those muscles.

"Good." Clint said. "Now he knows where you are."

I couldn't help but think Duke had likely known I was on his back even before I was touching him with my calves, but somehow got the idea Clint was not in the mood for flippant commentary. I kept my mouth shut. Clint added, "Keep them like that the whole ride. Seat, legs, hands, every time you ask him to move. Now, walk."

I gave Duke a little squeeze with my calves and he amiably began to walk. I drew in a deep breath and tried to get myself to relax. Clearly, Nora and her brother had a different teaching style. That was all. This was going to be fine.

We hadn't taken more than two steps before Clint said, "Stop." I pulled back on the reins and Duke stopped. I looked over to see a pained expression on Clint's face. He looked as if he'd witnessed someone run over a cottontail rabbit with a truck. Deliberately. I took another deep breath.

He walked his horse a few steps forward so he was once more facing me. Again, I didn't see him move. "What did I say right before I asked you to walk?" His tone, at least, was patient.

I scrambled to remember. "Keep my legs down?"

"Seat, legs, hands," Clint said. "Look at Penny. I'm going to ask her to walk, then stop." With a slow, deliberate movement, Clint set his reins down, looping them around his saddle horn and crossing his arms over his chest. Penny started walking. She walked a compete circle around me and Duke and stopped when she and Clint were back where they had started.

"What did I move?" Clint said.

I had been a good student in school, with history being the one exception. It wasn't that I didn't care about history as a whole, it was that I didn't see the point of memorizing specific dates. This was usually only a problem on tests, but during my sophomore year I'd had one particular teacher who had loved to ask impromptu questions of the class during lectures. I had lived in fear of his calling on me, because every time he asked me what year the Berlin wall came down, or what year Martin Luther King was shot, I could only gape at him and fumble around in my textbook until he called on someone else.

That was how I felt with Clint. I had seen him move nothing. I had watched his feet, and they had not budged. His hands were clearly out of the picture. I felt that old panicky sensation of not knowing the answer to what was obviously not a difficult question.

"I'll go again," Clint said. I stared at his calf, convinced I'd see some little wiggle or tap. But Penny started walking, passed around my one side, then the other, and stopped again in front of me. I wanted to cry with frustration.

Clint read my blank look, and gave up. "My hips. My hips are what moves. My seat changes, so she knows to go. It's only if she doesn't go that I use my legs. Watch again."

I raised my eyes to Clint's slim, Wrangler-clad hips and thought about other ways in which their movement might be interesting. I tamped the thought down as Penny started walking again. They looped around in front of me. I watched, and I saw it: a little tilt in the pelvis, a shift in his seat position. Penny stopped. "I exaggerated that time so you could see."

Doubtful, I looked down at Duke. He had his ears cocked to the sides and appeared to be dozing.

Clint spoke as if reading my mind. "That horse is as sensitive as this one, and even if he wasn't, you should ride him as if he was. For stopping, your pelvis should be like you are sitting now, rotated back. For forward movement, you should sit straight up in the saddle and open your hips. Now try again."

I prepared myself, thinking about my legs in contact with Duke's sides, and my pelvis.

I tilted my pelvis so I was sitting up straight in the saddle, thinking *walk* with all my might.

Duke's ears came up, and he started walking.

"The man is insane," I said to my mother. "He seems to think I have control over every single muscle in my body."

It was Wednesday evening, and I was at home, talking half to vent my feelings on my disastrous lesson with Clint and half to fill the silence. My mother had been driving to Florence every day. Boswell and Norman were as lost as ever, and it was still two more days until my father came home.

"You do have control over every muscle in your body." My mom said this without smiling. Her face had a tired look. Her eyes were distant. I knew she'd be all right if the dogs were never found. My mother wasn't the sort to let tragedy derail her. Still, this was taking its toll. I bitterly thought it would have been kinder if the cops hadn't told her about the warehouse. Boswell and Norman stolen because they were valuable was one thing. Boswell and Norman wandering through the desert, dying by degrees, was quite another.

I gave her a look and leaned forward to load a slice of cheese onto a cracker. I had made the cheese platter, trying for some sense of normalcy. Mom had yet to join me in eating anything. "Well of course I do. But I mean, like, really precise control."

Mom didn't respond. She was doing the thing where she was staring blankly into the desert. I stopped talking, my mind wandering back to my time on horseback with Clint. I appeared to be a glutton for punishment. Even though the lesson had been a disaster, even though a sane person probably would have been well over the Clint thing by now, I was more obsessed than ever.

The lesson had seemed to go on forever. I'd realized once I got back to my car it had felt long because it had gone on for an hour and a half. An *hour and a half* of "wiggle your left toe," "block his forward movement, no, be gentle," and "release release release." Clint had made me feel like I'd never even seen a horse before.

But he'd also made me feel something else. There were these little glimmers throughout the ride, moments where I forgot about how hot Clint was, how much I wanted to haul him off his horse and see what was underneath the chinks, moments I forgot to overthink everything he was telling me. In those moments, I felt something with Duke. I'd ask him to disengage his hindquarters and he just would. It would happen with a sort of smooth grace, as if Duke had been waiting all along for me to ask the right way.

And every time that happened, Clint would say, "There." He'd say it in this soft, satisfied tone that made gooseflesh rise on my arms.

After the lesson, he'd said almost as little as he had before. But he'd helped me untack and let me lead Duke back to the pasture. Then he'd walked me to my car and tipped his hat and I'd shoved one of the leftover Boswell and Norman posters into his hands because I'd been unable to think of anything else to say or do. And I'd driven home and had a feverish day of thinking about Clint on horseback and Clint not on horseback.

"How's Ben?" My mother turned away from the view of the mountains, making an obvious effort to rally. "When do I get to meet him?"

"He's fine." I brushed cracker crumbs off the bench next to me. "He helped me with the posters in Florence."

"That was nice of him." My mom leaned forward and put some cheese on a cracker. She went still again, turning her head once more towards the open desert. She sat in stiff silence for a moment, then sighed. She turned back to me. "You know what I can't get out of my head? That stupid book about the two dogs and a cat that travel all across Canada to get home."

"The Incredible Journey?"

"Yeah. One of the dogs was a Bull Terrier. I keep thinking they'll pull it off, somehow. I'll look up and see them bounding out of the wash. But I know it's impossible. Between the heat, the lack of water, the cactus...." She shook her head, setting the cracker down so she could pick up a napkin to dab at her eye.

"Oh, Mom." I left my chair to sit on the bench next to her, putting my arm around her shoulders. "We need a distraction." I pulled my phone out of my pocket, and texted Ben.

"The flowers are for your mother." Ben said this half an hour later, stepping through the gate where he would have usually been accosted by an enthusiastic canine greeting party, and stooping to kiss me on the cheek. He moved his lips close to my ear, adding, "You have a monopoly on kisses though. And there's more where that came from."

I felt a shiver race up my arms and had a sudden flashback to that morning. When we'd been untacking Duke, there had been a moment when Clint had reached up to take the saddle off. I'd been standing by Duke's shoulder, adjusting the knot on his halter, and Clint's shoulder had been so close to mine I could feel the heat in his shirt. All he'd have had to do was rotate his highly communicative hips, and his lips would have brushed my forehead.

I shoved Clint out of my mind and took Ben's hand, leading him around the back of the house to where my mother was looking expectantly over her shoulder. She rose to greet Ben, the flowers were handed over, and introductions were made. I could see by Mom's smile and the fact that she brought out her favorite vase that she already liked him.

And what wasn't to like? Ben looked good in the soft evening light, his forearms showing to advantage below the rolled up sleeves of his pale checked button-down shirt.

We settled back into our seats and my mother and Ben began to rattle through the basic questions. Where do you work? Where did you go to school? Do you like your job? Oh that's interesting, I didn't realize people did that. It was a relief for me, at least, to sit back and listen. I already knew most of the answers on both sides, so didn't have to pay much attention.

Then I heard Mom say, "And do you ride?"

I looked up, a twinge of nerves activating in my stomach. I didn't like it when Ben and Clint overlapped, even when it was only conversationally.

Ben looked surprised. "Horses? No." He gave a little laugh that suggested only people with a strange disregard for their own health ride horses. Then he added, "But I think it's great Erin is getting back to it. So many people are always waiting until tomorrow." He put his hand on my hand, which was resting on my leg.

My mother beamed at him. "Erin's had 'seize the day' down since the moment of her birth."

They both laughed. Ben's hand gave a little squeeze.

I thought of another moment from my lesson. I'd been having trouble getting Duke to step his hind underneath him, and Clint had been telling me to reach back further, to get my leg behind his balance point. When I'd gotten it wrong a few times in a row, he'd swung off Penny, walked up next to Duke and wrapped his large, warm hand around my calf.

I'd turned to putty in the saddle.

He'd adjusted my leg and cupped my boot-heel in his other hand, raising it towards Duke's side. Duke had stepped over before the heel even touched him.

Clint had been back on Penny before the blood in my veins had stopped surging. He'd said, "Leather soled boots with a good heel are ideal for riding. Smooth leather, no rubber at all except on the heel."

I thought of his strong, calloused hand on my ridiculous blinged out cowgirl boots and vowed to go shopping before I set boot on the Tipped Z again.

"Which reminds me," I said, hoping to contribute to the conversation in a way that would suggest I was, in fact, existing in the present with the rest of the world, "I need some new boots. The ones I've been wearing aren't cutting it."

Most mothers love to take their daughters shopping. This was not the case with mine. My father had been the one to go with me to pick out my prom dress. Mom gave me a mild look and said, "Maybe Trace can get a babysitter."

"I could go with you." This came from Ben, and I realized my tactical error too late. In trying to make conversation, I had made it seem like I wanted company on my boot buying excursion.

○

"Do they *all* have rubber soles?"

It was Friday afternoon. Ben and I were in Western Warehouse, systematically going down the rows of boots and finding them lacking. Clint had said two things: leather sole, good heel. So far we had yet to find a single boot that met even the first requirement.

Most of the boots on the wall, in fact, made the dance-style boots I'd been wearing to my lessons look positively understated. There were some that were a little more utilitarian looking, but they all had rubber soles. Every single one of them.

"Here's one." I looked over at Ben. He held a boot in his hand. The toe was black, and looked demure enough, but when he tipped it in my direction I could see the top was an elaborate montage of lacy inlays and paisley shapes. But it did have a leather sole, and a good heel.

Ben handed it over. I slipped it on my foot. The fit was okay. I walked around in it for a moment, made awkward by the fact that my one leg was now 2 ¼ inches taller than my other.

Ben picked the other boot off the shelf and examined the tag. "How much are they?" I said.

"$529."

I stopped walking. "What?"

He checked the price tag again, as if it might have changed in the last three seconds. "Yeah," he said. "$529."

"As in, five hundred and twenty-nine dollars?"

"Plus tax," Ben put in helpfully.

I had the boot off my foot and back on the shelf before you could say Cotton Eyed Joe. I gazed at the row of footwear in despair. Computing complex sums in my head had never been my gift, but it didn't take a genius to know the price tag on those boots was out of the question if I wanted to eat for the next two months.

Ben was still holding the other boot, gazing into the dark tunnel of its upper as if there was a fascinating world of dancing pixies in its depths. When he spoke again, his voice was low and strangely hesitant. "Erin," he said. "I could get them for you."

If I had been uncomfortable a moment before, it was nothing to what I'd felt now. I sat down on the wooden stool with a built-in mirror that was placed in the aisle to facilitate removal and reinstallation of footwear. I pulled my socks off. "Ben," I said, feeling panicked all of a sudden. It would be the most horrible form of irony for Ben to spend over $500 on a pair of boots I intended to wear while swooning over a hot cowboy. "No, you can't do that."

"I've been meaning to get you something," Ben said. "Really, it would be fine."

I shoved my socks back into my purse and slipped my sandals on. I knew that Ben had a good job, and $500 to him was not at all the same as $500 to me. But still. I turned to him. "No, Ben. Just no." It came out a whole lot more harshly than I meant.

Ben looked startled, then downcast. He set the boot back on the shelf.

I looked around. We were surrounded by racks of boots. George Strait was on the radio, and chose that moment to say, "I ain't rich, but, Lord, I'm free."

I stood for another moment, feeling an intense need to escape. "I think we should go," I said.

It was an awkward drive home. I made a few half-hearted attempts at conversation, but Ben was subdued. He wasn't not responding, but his normal cheerful manner had vanished. As he navigated his truck into the parking lot of my apartment complex, it occurred to me I still didn't know where he lived.

He didn't pull into a parking spot, even though there was an empty guest space next to my Hyundai.

I opened the truck's door, then looked over at him. He was staring out the front windshield, his expression closed and distant. I said, "Ben, I'm sorry. I didn't mean to be a jerk. Thank you for shopping with me."

He turned. His smile was forced, but he leaned over to kiss me on the cheek. "It's okay, Erin. It's not your fault."

I didn't know what to say to that. Clearly, it was my fault. Things had been going fine up until the point I'd bitten his head off for offering to do something nice for me.

I stepped out of the truck and dragged my purse out from where I'd stashed it behind the front seat. Ben said, "I'll call you soon." I nodded and closed the door. He drove off, brake lights winking as he went over the speed hump near the swimming pool. Then the truck engine revved higher and his black tailgate disappeared around the edge of the front office.

I stood in the sunlight, blinking, until I realized my eyes had tears in them. I squinted down at the ground, telling myself it was nothing. Ben and I had had our first fight, was all, and first fights were bound to happen, sooner or later. Weren't they?

That's when I saw the envelope. It lay at my feet, a plain piece of mail, the kind everyone gets every day. It had a little plastic mailer window in the front, and the logo of a law firm where the return address belonged. Someone must have dropped it getting out of their car.

Glad for something to do, I picked it up and took a step towards the office, then realized if it was a neighbor I knew I could slip it under their door.

I read the address, and my heart seemed to stop beating.

BENJAMIN AND KIM KELLER
3429 Painted Trail Blvd
Tucson, AZ 85748

I stared at the envelope. Keller was Ben's last name. I knew that. I'd seen it on his emails plenty of times.

But who was Kim?

Chapter 6

"He's married," I said. "That's the catch. That's the problem with this great guy who has been going around seeming perfect in every way imaginable. *Married*. He married four years ago. I looked up the court records."

I was at Trace's house. I had driven over straight after the internet had confirmed my worst fears, surprised to find myself teary-eyed and shaken. I hadn't dropped in on Trace randomly since some time partway through her pregnancy, when she'd made it clear unexpected visits were no longer all that welcome. I'd texted her on the way, to warn her, not giving her a chance to back out. Sometimes you just need to talk to your best friend.

She'd met me at the door with a concerned expression and a hug, and led me to the living room, where Olivia was holding court in a playpen full of stuffed animals. "Forgive the mess," she said with self-conscious laugh.

I could see an open diaper bag sitting near the front door, and a pale green towel of the kind new parents must always have within reach draped over the arm of the couch. Otherwise, the house was spotless.

Trace and Andrew lived in one of the new subdivisions that had sprung up all over the edges of Tucson like sandspur after a rain. It was a bit cookie-cutter for my taste, but the ceilings were high, the windows were large, and the interior was a welcome cool after the crush of heat outside. It was more than one step up from my apartment, so who was I to judge?

We'd settled onto chairs in the living room, Trace perching on the edge of hers, her eyes on Olivia, as if the extra second it would take for her to get out of a reclined position might make the crucial difference in a case of choking or suffocation by stuffed animal.

I hadn't waited for her to ask what was wrong. I'd blurted it out. Now it hung there in the air between us, the horrible truth, all the more three-dimensional now that I'd said it out loud.

"Married?" Trace said. "Are you sure he's not been divorced? You know how long it takes the mail to adjust to that sort of thing. I still get things addressed to Trace Cox, even after all this time."

She had a point, but I'd already thought of that. "I searched the records, under his name and hers. No divorce. Nothing." I paused, staring out the living room window, which overlooked an empty street lined with a row of identical entryways and closed garage doors. "And it explains a lot. Why we've never gone to his house, for instance. He always comes to me."

Trace was frowning. Olivia laughed and flung a toy at the mesh side of the playpen. It bounced back towards her, something inside its stuffed body rattling.

We sat like that for a while. Trace was clearly trying to come up with some other way to explain the incriminating piece of mail. But there wasn't any way. Ben was married. Every time I'd kissed him, every time we'd gone on a date, and that day we'd tumbled into my bed while dinner got crispy, he'd been cheating on his wife.

The thought made me sick to my stomach.

Finally, Trace sighed. It was a sigh of defeat. "I'm so sorry, Erin."

Somehow, that made it even worse. I found myself blinking back angry tears. "The stupid thing is I don't even like him. I mean, I do like him, but I haven't been sure how much. All I seem to do is fantasize about this...."

Olivia let out a sudden wail. Trace leapt out of her seat, stooping over the playpen to see what the problem was. To me it had sounded like a happy wail, but then, I wasn't the mom here.

Trace adjusted the blanket Olivia was sitting on, and set the rattling toy back within reach. She sat down again. "I'm sorry," she said, looking over at me. "You were saying?"

I was almost relieved. I'd been on the verge of telling Trace about Clint. Which I didn't want to do. Trace's over-mothering had also shifted my emotional state from weepy to annoyed. It was a welcome change.

I waved a weary hand. "I should have seen it coming, is all." I sighed, looking back at the blank scene out the window. "And now I have to tell my mom." It figures I would put two and two together mere days after inviting Ben to the house.

"You should talk to Ben first," Trace said. "You at least owe him the chance to explain."

"I don't *owe* him anything." I said this in as fierce a tone as I could muster.

Trace was looking at me with the cool, steady gaze that always made me squirm.

I sighed. "But of course, I'll talk to him."

"If it is true, you're better off without him."

The comment made me smile bitterly. *Thanks for that one, besty. Really useful insight there.* I couldn't decide which was more upsetting: Ben's betrayal, or Trace's utter lack of interest in it.

I left Trace's a half an hour later. Olivia had gotten fussy, and I had found myself growing less comforted by the minute. As I walked down the sidewalk that ran from her front door to the street, I was surprised to note I was growing less sad and more angry. When I got into my car, I turned the key in the ignition and sat for a moment, sweating as the AC started to do battle with the heat. I sat, staring at the empty streets of the subdivision. As I sat, I grew more angry. As I grew more angry, a strange sense of resolve built up in my mind.

I reached for my purse, and pulled out the envelope. I stared at it for a moment, then punched the address into my phone.

"Do a U-turn," the chirpy robotic voice instructed as I set the phone on my passenger's seat.

I did a U-turn.

Six minutes later, I was in a different subdivision, though if I hadn't just made the drive from one to the other I might not have known that fact. Like Trace's, this one was full of uniform houses with well-groomed fronts and flat roofs.

"Your destination is on the right," my phone informed me.

Heart pounding, I let my car drift up to the curb.

Ben's house was a lot like all the other houses on the street. It had a little covered entryway at the front with some faux stone around the door.

My heart was hammering and my hands were sweating, even though the interior of the car had cooled off.

I killed the engine. I didn't give my righteous anger time to be dissipated by rational thought. I picked up the envelope, left my car, and marched up to the door of the house.

As I walked through the heat, I tried to anticipate all possible outcomes. Perhaps Ben wasn't home. He might have called some buddies and gone out drinking. He might, at this moment, be sitting in a bar complaining about me. He might be home but drunk, sloppy with the sting of my refusal to let him buy me boots.

But somehow it never occurred to me his wife might answer the door.

I rang the doorbell and waited in the still, hot, evening and was completely unprepared when a blonde woman cracked the door and said, "We don't accept solicitations."

I was so startled, I almost missed my moment. The door was swinging closed again, nearly there, when I said, "Wait. I'm not selling anything."

The door paused in its closing, but didn't reopen.

"I think I have some of your mail." I held up the envelope like an all access pass to the true secrets of Ben Keller.

The door swung back open, and I could see the woman in full now. She was tan and slender, with a large, high chest strapped into a bursting tank-top. She said, "Oh, okay." She didn't smile or apologize for trying to close the door in my face. She extended a hand. Her nails were painted an electric blue. I handed her the envelope, and she looked at it.

I was starting to think I'd gotten the wrong house, that maybe there was some crazy explanation for all of this after all, some way out for Ben that I hadn't seen. Any moment this woman's forehead would crease and she'd hand the envelope back, saying something about this being the wrong house, the wrong Ben, revealing how I'd leapt to the wrong conclusion.

But then I heard his voice drifting in from the other room. Ben, unmistakably. "Kim," he said. "Who is it?"

Kim began to close the door again. "Nothing," she said. "Just someone returning a piece of our mail."

She wasn't going to ask my name or extend the transaction with any sort of small talk or chit chat. The door was closing, blocking out the tile-floored entryway it had briefly revealed.

Perhaps it was better this way. Clearly, Ben had a wife, and he lived with her. There was nothing else to say. I should leave: walk from his front door to my car and never answer a phone call or a text or email from him again.

The door was almost closed. I was about to turn to go. And then I saw him walking out of a doorway into the hall, his face showing nothing more than mild curiosity. He was looking at Kim's back saying, "Did you even say thank—"

As he spoke, his eyes shifted to me. I saw his face register a mix of surprise and horror.

The door closed, and there was the sound of the dead bolt turning.

○

I pulled into my parents' driveway and parked, flipping off my headlights and sitting in the dim interior of my car. I resisted the urge to check my phone. I had put it on silent the night before, as soon as I'd left Ben's subdivision, and was now avoiding looking at it because I was equally afraid he had contacted me and he had not contacted me.

It was only 4:30 in the morning, and I hadn't slept a wink.

After Kim had closed the door in my face, I'd walked back to my car, expecting to hear the door open behind me, expecting to hear Ben call my name, expecting him to run after me and beg forgiveness.

He hadn't. I'd driven home through the fading evening, nursing my wounds.

When I'd gotten home, my apartment had never seemed so empty and quiet, my life never so devoid of people I could talk to. In spite of her promises, Trace had let me down again. I'd left her house feeling worse, not better.

I'd consoled myself with the knowledge that I'd found out, that I'd stopped the sordid situation before it had progressed any further. But it was cold comfort. I'd poured myself a glass of wine and watched *Pride and Prejudice* which, unsurprisingly, did little to lift my spirits. I'd gotten into bed and tossed and turned until I'd realized my room was incrementally brighter than it had been an hour before.

And now, here I was, sitting in my parents' driveway even though I knew they'd be asleep.

If Boswell and Norman had still been at large, approaching the house this early without waking my parents would have been a tricky business. As it was, I let myself in through the gate without difficulty, and walked around to the back patio. I settled onto one of the benches and sipped the coffee I'd bought on the way over. I watched the sky grow pale along its rim, my mind mercifully still for the first time since walking out of Western Warehouse the day before.

That's how my dad found me half an hour later. He came shuffling out the side door looking unshaven and rumpled, the skin beneath his eyes a little puffy. "You're up early," I said, rising to give him a hug.

He hugged me back, put his hands on my shoulders, and held me at arm's length, no doubt reading the tear tracks on my face like a fortune teller reads lines in a palm. "Jet lag," he said. "What's your excuse?"

"I think it's time for me to retire," my dad said. We'd made more coffee but were still in the yard. I'd just finished telling him about Ben. Unlike Trace, he'd listened attentively. When I was done, he didn't try to make me feel better about it. "One quick trip overseas and I come home to two lost dogs and a broken-hearted daughter."

His tone was light. He meant it as a joke. I forced a wan smile. "We do miss you when you're gone."

The side door opened and Mom walked out. Unlike Dad, she always ran a brush through her hair and put on jeans and a t-shirt before leaving the bedroom. She looked better than the last time I'd seen her. She gave me a long, measuring look, poured herself a cup of coffee, sat down next to my dad, and asked if everything was all right.

Dad told her, which was nice. I'd had enough of explaining about Ben for a lifetime. Though they were trying to hide it, I could see they were disappointed. My chances of finding a spouse before I turned fifty had just plummeted from decent to nil. Still, Mom had the good form to call Ben a cad and to say the flowers he'd brought had made her sneeze. Then my father offered to challenge Ben to a duel, which actually made me laugh.

And that's when we heard the hoof-beats.

I picked up on it before anyone else. As soon as I finished laughing over the duel comment, it drew my attention: the clip-clop of a horse trotting out, moving at good pace and covering country. It was a sound that reminded me of the day I'd "helped" Clint and Nora move cattle.

I was certain my sleepless night had me hallucinating, but I turned towards the sound anyway. I stared down past our dog-secure fence and the sandy wash that ran behind.

Dad heard it next. "What's that?" He also turned to look.

The hoof-beats were closer now, and I could hear the jingle of spurs.

Then there was a bark. My mom stood up so fast she almost knocked the coffee over. A white streak blasted out of the wash, running for the back gate, tail a furious blur in the morning light. Mom was running down the slope of the back yard, unlatching the gate, and Norman was collapsing against her legs, pink tongue lolling, black triangular eyes nearly squinted shut with the force of his canine grin.

Dad and I were hot on Mom's heels. But as fantastic as it was to see Norman, I was looking towards the sound of the approaching horse.

I had reached the fence line when I saw a blur behind some mesquite trees. A black leg appeared, then three more. Penny trotted through the wash, dark-rimmed ears pricked as she took us all in.

Clint was on her back.

He looked like he had the first day I'd seen him. He was wearing his flat brimmed hat. His face was in shadow in the weak morning light. He was riding Penny's big trot without rising, and as he came through the wash I saw why. A white, dog-shaped form was draped across his lap, held in place by the saddle horn, Clint's hips, and a hand resting on its ribcage.

Penny dropped to a walk. She picked her way up the other side of the wash as everyone but Norman stared at Clint in stunned silence. My mother had stooped down to pet her prodigal terrier, but now she straightened. Everything was quiet except for Norman's happy whining, as if a spell had been cast over the desert.

Clint rode up to the gate and stopped, his hand leaving Boswell's side to tip the brim of his hat. "Erin," he said.

At the sound of his voice, the spell was broken. "Hi," I said, stepping forward to put myself between him and my parents. I didn't want Mom rushing forward and spooking Penny. I couldn't think of anything else to say, though. Later, I would make a list: I could have thanked him for finding my mom's dogs, introduced him to my parents, asked him how he'd done it, offered him water or coffee or my immortal soul. Instead I gaped at him like a simpleton.

My mother's eyes had gone wide, her face pale as she stared at the white shape in Clint's lap. "Is he?" Her voice came out in a thin quaver. She tried to take a step forward but was hampered by Norman's presence at her feet. Her face was stricken. That's when it registered in my addled brain that Boswell wasn't moving.

Nora had told me they trained the Tipped Z's wire-haired dogs to jump up and ride in the front of the saddle. They taught them this because it was useful for the dogs to be able to go horseback when they have to cover long distances to get to the cattle.

This was different, though. Boswell was not a passenger. He was baggage. His front feet hung on one side of the horse, hind legs on the other, and his head lolled in a way that did not suggest good health.

Instead of answering, Clint swung down from the saddle. His movement was fluid, and he somehow continued to support Boswell as he stepped down. Once on the ground, he tied up his get-down and lifted the dog off Penny before any of us could offer to help. Leaving

Penny standing at the gate, he stepped through. I stepped out of his way, wondering if I should go hold his horse so she didn't wander off.

Once inside the fence, Clint lowered Boswell to the sandy ground. The rest of us were still staring, still struck dumb by the surprise of seeing him. He knelt, producing a small knife from a pocket in his chinks. Boswell was tied at the ankles, trussed like a roast pig.

Clint cut the ties in two efficient strokes, and rubbed his hands over the furrowed fur until the grooves were gone. As Boswell gave a low groan, a palpable tension left the air.

Clint stood. My mom rushed to kneel in his place, and Norman began a fierce campaign of face-licking to assist in reviving his partner in crime. Boswell gave another groan and shifted so he was lying on his stomach instead of his side.

The sight of the obviously not dead Boswell seemed to inject new life into all of us. My father stepped forward and offered Clint his hand. "We can't thank you enough," he said. "I'm Carter."

"Clint," Clint said. They shook. Clint looked back down at Boswell. "The one's snake bit," he said. "I gave him the antivenin. Had to dope him to get him on the horse. I'd have brought them in the truck but that one," he nodded towards Norman and gave a small shake of his head. "Couldn't even get near enough to toss a rope. Didn't want to save one just to lose track of the other."

"What's your last name?" my Dad said. "I'll run inside and get the checkbook so we can get you the reward."

Clint looked at my father, then at me. I realized I had so far failed so say anything beyond a single syllable greeting. Now Clint seemed to expect me to explain something—clear up a misunderstanding I didn't know was taking place. Or say his last name?

But the sleepless night coupled with the dream-like experience of having Clint materialize out of the desert at sunrise with my mom's lost dogs proved too much for me. My brain was on overload. I couldn't speak.

Clint waited a second or two before looking back at my dad. "No reward," he said. His tone was both friendly and firm, leaving no room for argument.

Then he was leaving. He walked back through the gate and swung onto Penny's back. My mind was screaming at me, *Say something say something say something.* But my lips were still.

Clint paused for one more moment as he slipped his get-down back through his belt and collected his reins. He looked down at the two white dogs. "Shouldn't wonder if they're both a fair bit dehydrated."

He turned Penny on her haunches and trotted back the way he'd come.

"Hey there sweetie," Nora said, looking up from snugging Duke's cinch down when I walked into the barn. Her tone was expansive, as if she hadn't seen me for a year rather than a week. I did a quick scan of the barn. No Clint.

I carried a warm, lumpy package containing a thank you card from my mother and a batch of my father's chocolate chip pistachio cookies. My father had also insisted I bring a blank check with me, in case Clint changed his mind about the reward thing.

It was Sunday morning, and I was reporting in for my second day of "helping" at the Tipped Z.

"Hi," I said, trying to match her bright tone but failing. I held up the package. "My parents sent these for your brother."

Nora straightened and turned to look at me, her expression curious. "He told me, under no circumstances am I to accept a reward." She was smiling.

"It's a card and some cookies. He's my parents' new hero."

"Dots found them," Nora said, nodding down at one of the little wire-haired dogs that was sprawled in the barn aisle. "We were out repairing a fence and when we were done we couldn't see her. That's unusual, you know. These dogs have a work ethic. We were looking around, puzzled, and the wind died a bit. We could hear this faint barking in the distance. Our other dogs started whining so we mounted up and went to look for her. We found her standing on top of a big rock. One of your mom's dogs was standing a few feet away, growling. The other one was lying in the sand beneath a saguaro. The one lying there looked dead. The other one ran off when we tried to get close, but it followed us when we rode off with the other one. So I guess it's Dots who deserves the cookies. Not us."

Hearing her name, Dots got up and walked over. She was a strange white and gray brindle shade, with three brown splotches on her otherwise gray face. I guessed those markings were her namesake.

I knelt down and rubbed the dog's ears. She endured the contact with a patient air, not moving away, but not exactly loving it like Boswell and Norman would have. "Thank you, Dots," I said. I looked up at Nora. "Should I really give her a cookie?"

My parents and I had spent the bulk of the day before spinning stories, trying to figure out what had happened to Boswell and Norman between the morning they were released from their Florence prison and the moment Clint brought them home. We had a lot of time to sit around talking that day. We took the dogs to a clinic that saw animals without appointments. They'd required quite a bit of attention.

Both the dogs were appallingly thin and, as Clint had suggested, dehydrated. After the initial excitement at seeing my mother had worn off, Norman had turned out to be limping badly on two legs. He'd had cactus spines embedded in every paw, a large, thin scrape along his ribs that required stitches, foxtails in his ears, and the pads of his feet were tender—abraded and burned.

Boswell was in even worse shape. The snake bite was just below where his front right leg connected to his chest. The area was large and swollen, the punctures standing out like angry quotation marks. Even when coaxed into walking, he would not bear weight on one of his hind legs.

The vet, much to everyone's relief, had returned the verdict they would both be fine given a month or two to recover. She'd said it had been a near thing with Boswell, and guessed he wouldn't have made it through the day without antivenin.

Now I knew how they'd been found. But the space between Dots staking them out and their captors releasing them into the desert outside of Florence would remain forever a mystery.

"Don't you dare," Nora said, her tone appalled but still friendly. "My dad would never forgive you. Those are working dogs," she added in a deep, husky voice that suggested she was impersonating someone.

I smiled. "Is there something else I could do for you guys? Some other way of saying thank you? Those dogs mean the world to my mom. She's really grateful." I stood up, still holding the awkward package of cookies.

"Actually, Clint did ask me to see to something. Come on."

Mystified, I followed Nora into the tack room. She flipped on the light. At the sight of the hanging bridles, my favorite Clint fantasy filled my head—the one where he came in after me and swept me up in a kiss, taking the bridle from my hand, pushing me up against the wall, and returning the bridle to its proper hook. I felt my heart begin to beat harder.

Nora took the cookies, setting the package on a small countertop near the fridge. I relinquished them with mixed relief and reluctance. I wanted to be sure Clint got them, but I was glad not to have to hand them over myself.

"Clint said you need some better boots," she said. "Seemed to think you'd do a lot better keeping your toes pointed the right way if you had a leather sole." She smiled at me. Just as my heart started to fall at the thought of how horrible my riding must have been for Clint to ask his sister to upgrade my footwear, she added, "Said you're a fast learner, too, and you, 'Showed an interest in riding with quality.' Just in case you can't tell, that's about the highest compliment my brother is capable of dishing out to someone who's not actually Ray Hunt or Richard Caldwell."

My heart did something in my chest that felt like a pre-death spasm. I thought back to our lesson: the long, painful silences, the distressed winces. Was Nora making this up?

If she was, she wasn't done. She leaned her head a bit closer to mine and said, "If you want the truth, I think my brother might have a bit of a thing for you." She leaned back and winked broadly.

I felt dizzy. Were we talking about the same person? How could Clint have a thing for me? He didn't even speak to me, other than to note the many millions of ways in which I could not operate my body properly while on horseback. And besides, didn't he have a girlfriend? The poor woman who wasn't long-term material but he was keeping around just because?

It struck me that this was a perfect opportunity to dig a little, to ask Nora some questions about what Clint liked in a woman, how long he'd been with his girlfriend, or if perhaps they had broken up.

But my mouth betrayed me again. All I managed was a strangled, "He sure doesn't seem like he likes me."

This set Nora laughing. She turned away from me and directed my attention to a row of boots set along the far wall. "No, I don't guess you're wrong about that. Anywho, I dug around in my closet and Mom's and Grandma's, and I've got five pairs for you to try. Hopefully one of them will do the trick."

I stared at the boots. They ranged in size and style, but they all shared the same basic characteristics: solid construction, good heal, leather sole. "Nora," I protested. "I couldn't possibly take a pair of boots from you. I went shopping on Friday. I couldn't find anything, but I haven't given up."

Nora was eyeing my feet with a calculating expression. "Oh don't worry," she said, picking up a pair of tall boots with a worn teal upper and brown toe. "These will be on loan for when you're here. Part two of Clint's request is I'm to take you shopping. We all know you won't find anything worth spending money on at these western stores." She waved a dismissive hand in the general direction of Western Warehouse. "Now come on," she says. "It's heating up out there. Best try these on."

I parked my Hyundai in my spot, got out, fished the boot box out of my back seat, and locked the car. Stepping onto the sidewalk, the sun was a riot of orange and pink in the sky behind the complex. I smiled to myself.

I should be feeling guilty that I'd wasted an entire Sunday—hadn't written a word. As it was, it was hard to regret the day.

Nora had given me a lesson. I'd tried to keep everything Clint had said the week before in mind. That, combined with Nora's constant stream of feedback, had resulted in the best ride yet. There were times I had actually wished Clint would walk by so he could see me.

We'd been untacking our horses when Nora had said in a deceptively casual tone of voice, "So what are you doing with the rest of your day?"

I'd been preoccupied with wondering if Clint was going to put in an appearance before I had to leave. So I'd said, "Oh, nothing. I have Sundays off." Of course, this wasn't true. I intended to go home and write three thousand words of quality fiction, but I didn't generally say that to people.

Nora had said, "Good. You can come down south with me. There's a boot shop between here and Benson. They're the real deal. I have to pick up some repairs. They keep a small number of quality pairs in stock. I'm sure they'll have something that will work for you."

And so, I'd spent the day with Nora. It had been a fun day. So fun, in fact, I'd forgotten to think about Ben. That lasted until I rounded the corner of my building to see him sitting on my stoop.

My heart gave a heavy thud, as if it had dropped dead out of sheer horror. I stopped in my tracks.

Ben was one second behind me. He looked up as I saw him, and I saw his posture shift from the pose of someone who has been waiting a long time to someone who is very nervous. He stood, standing between me and my front door.

I considered turning on my heel and walking away. But I was tired. As much as it had been a fun day, it had also been a hot and dusty day. I wanted a shower and some reheated leftovers. I wanted to crawl into bed knowing my new boots were waiting for me to slip on again on Tuesday.

Seeing Ben, and having him standing between me and what I wanted, filled me with a remarkable jolt of anger. I took a step forward.

"You," I said. "Why are you here?" My voice was filled with venom to an extent that surprised even me.

"Erin," Ben said. He quivered in place, as if he wanted to take a step forward but knew better. "You haven't answered my messages. But please, let me explain."

It was true I had been studiously avoiding him, deleting any message he sent me. I was done being a cheatee.

I took another step forward, and spoke again. I was aware my volume was too loud for the quiet evening, but I didn't care. "Explain? *Explain?* You can *explain* the fact that you are married to a woman named Kim? That you live with her? There's an explanation for that?"

He started to speak, but I didn't let him. I was riding a wave of anger and indignation and self-righteousness. "No," I said. "No, Ben. I don't think there is anything you can say that will make it any less sordid than it is. I am done. I'm done with you. I don't want to see you again. Ever. Please go, now, or I will call security."

I stepped off the sidewalk and made a point of gesturing, directing him past me like a crosswalk guard.

He was silent, staring at me. His blonde hair was tinted orange in the sunset. His face looked nothing but sad. He waited like that for a moment, his lips still but his eyes asking me a question. I thought about all the times I'd lied to him, by kissing him as if he were Clint. That made me feel worse.

I knew this was the moment I was supposed to relent, to give him a chance to clear his name. But I didn't. After a few seconds had ticked past, I repeated my 'it's safe to cross' gesture, encouraging him to go.

His head and shoulders drooped. He began to walk. Which was when I noticed the box sitting on my steps. I didn't want to stop him, to tell him he'd forgotten something, but he seemed to read the expression in my eyes. "Those are for you," he said. The words were no more than a whisper as he walked by.

I poured the last of the wine from the bottle into my glass and flopped back onto my couch. I had intended to be in bed by now, immersed in blameless dreams. It had been such a *good* day. Ben had ruined it. Utterly.

The boot shop outside of Benson had turned out to be the front room of an old stucco-covered adobe house, and the couple that ran it had turned out to be sweet and eccentric. The man had crouched over my foot like a fortune teller, commenting on the relative proportions of my heel and toe-box, the state of my arches. He'd thumbed the callous that always seems to build up on the outside of my right foot and nodded sagely, as if its presence there confirmed a deep secret he'd always suspected the truth of but had never been able to confirm until now. He'd gotten up, pulled a pair of boots down from the overcrowded shelving that lined the walls, slipped them on my feet, and told me to walk.

They'd been tight going on. But after I'd clomped around the store for a few minutes, I could tell the fit was good. Really good. But he'd shaken his head, asked me to remove the left one, disappeared into the back of the shop with it for a moment, and returned. "It was a little tight over the outside here," he'd said, handing it back to me and running a thumb over where my pinkie toe would reside when the boot was on. "Try it now."

When I'd put the boot back on, it had fit like a glove.

The boots had cost considerably less than the Western Warehouse ones had, and the kindly couple had given me a discount. Nora had picked up her repairs, and we'd left.

We'd driven through a monsoon on the ride home. After the rain had stopped, we'd rolled the windows down, enjoying the cool air and singing along to twangy country songs. I'd been feeling full to bursting with some happy emotion I couldn't quite put my finger on when we'd pulled up next to my car in the Tipped Z parking area. As she'd killed the rumbling truck engine, Nora had said, "We'd better get some dust on those boots before you go home."

She'd taken me riding again. Really riding. She'd put me on the bay horse named Paul she'd ridden the day we rode out to move the cattle, and we'd headed out in the late afternoon. The ground had been damp after the rainfall, the harsh edge taken off the desert for a short while. We'd clattered up a trail that wound up the side of a ridge, moving between the trot and the lope. Nora had whooped and laughed and I'd done the same, remembering what it was like to be a girl on a horse, listening to the sand flinging up from under hooves and pinging off the mesquite trees next to the trail.

I hadn't wanted to come home to find Ben on my stoop. I'd wanted to ride that high. And I certainly hadn't wanted to spend the evening staring at four cowboy boots lined up in a row on my coffee table, wondering if Trace was right, if I did owe Ben a chance to explain himself.

There couldn't be a bigger contrast between the boots I'd purchased with Nora and the ones Ben had gone back to Western Warehouse to buy. My boots, the ones I picked out with Nora, were a soft brown leather with a darker brown top. There was an extra strip of leather across the arch which I'd learned was called a saddle vamp, and the leather of the sole protruded past the leather of the heel, creating a deep notch for a spur to rest on.

The boots from Western Warehouse were nice boots, I was sure, but the leather was finished in some kind of varnish. They were all shine and paisley/lace decoration. They were stiff and straight and hard. They were the product of a factory. Mine had been made by hand.

But that didn't change the fact that Ben had gone back and gotten them for me, then sat on my stoop for who knows how long, waiting to deliver them.

I took another sip of wine. My head was spinning. I thought back to Nora's comment in the barn that morning, her little quip about Clint liking me. Had she been joking? Was there any possible way it could be true? In spite of spending all day with Nora, I hadn't seen Clint. He'd never appeared. It was as if he'd vanished after finding my mother's dogs and bringing them home.

I groaned and slumped on the couch so I was lying on my stomach, adjusting one of the end pillows so it was underneath my chin. I'd wanted to fall asleep thinking of chasing the red haunches of Nora's horse up the edge of a ridge, laughing. Instead I kept seeing the sadness in Ben's eyes as he'd walked away, leaving a boot box on my doorstep.

"I tried to come in yesterday," the woman on the other side of the counter said, her tone accusing, glaring down at her work order with a sour expression.

"We're closed on Sunday," I said. My mouth had a cottony quality, and my eyes were sensitive to the light. It wasn't quite as bad as the morning after the night I'd had the grapefruit drinks with Ben. Not quite.

"I'm saying, I tried," the woman said. She was short and round, with a pinched mouth that was especially pinched right now. "I don't think I should have to pay a storage fee for late pickup." She pointed at a line on the work order.

I took the slip of paper back from her. The date at the top read May 8. It was currently well into August. It might even be September. I wasn't honestly sure at that moment. I handed the paper back to her, pointing at the date as she'd pointed at the line. "The storage fee is added after you haven't picked your framing up after three weeks. If you'd come in yesterday, even if we'd been open, you still would have been late by at least two months."

I was aware I could have been more polite about this, but this was a huge problem Anne struggled with. People dropped off their artwork, ordering expensive moldings and archival materials which Anne had to buy, then disappeared for half a year sometimes, leaving her having to keep their art stored safely and also out the money and labor of the frame job. And I had headache. And Ben had given me a pair of $500 boots I didn't need anymore.

The woman's mouth got even tighter. "I didn't know about that policy. You can't charge me for something I didn't know about."

I tapped the bottom of the work order, which was a carbon copy of one that had been handed to her when she'd left her artwork. "It's outlined right here at the bottom, right above your signature agreeing to our policies."

Her mouth could apparently not tighten any more, but her nostrils flared. She handed me her credit card and stared at me with an accusing expression the whole time I rang up the transaction. I found myself growing angrier the longer she glared. It was a $15 storage fee on a frame job that had cost $438. She'd left her art here for three months. I was of the opinion the fee should go up each week a piece was left, but Anne disagreed, and she was the boss.

I handed the woman her receipt and card. She grabbed her neatly wrapped package and stormed out. I sighed as the bell on the front door jingled, my anger souring into remorse. If Anne had been there, she'd have mollified the woman without waiving the fee. I'd let a customer leave angry, which was the number one thing you were not supposed to do.

I wandered back into the frame room and resumed work on the four little canvases I'd been framing before the woman with the pinched mouth had walked in. Which meant I also resumed my brooding over Ben and Clint and the four boots that were still on my coffee table at home.

The boots from Ben had at first seemed like such a tender gesture. But the more I thought about it, the less I was sure. I was aware that many men had illicit relationships with women they weren't married to, and most of these operated around the man providing a certain amount of monetary assistance to the woman, apparently to compensate for the fact that he could not acknowledge her in public.

Thinking of the boots that way made me want to rush home and shred them to pieces with a utility knife.

But the thing was, Ben *had* been seen with me in public. A lot. He'd gone out with me all the time, hitting places near his house. He'd wanted to meet my parents. How does that jive with 'adulterer?'

My head ached and the sour taste in my mouth clung despite me downing an entire glass of water. I decided I needed something stronger.

I was in the kitchenette, making a cup of coffee, when Anne arrived. She swept in as usual, energetic and perky, dressed well, her shoulders square, her air confident.

Anne was one of those women who seemed to have no interest in marriage. It wasn't that she couldn't get guys. It was quite the opposite. She had a robust social life. I'd seen her out on dates with more than one eligible bachelor. I'd also had enough frank discussions with her to know she was not shy in bed. She knew what she liked and how to make it happen.

She stopped in the doorway of the kitchenette when she saw me at the coffee maker, taking in my haggard expression at a glance. Her eyes flicked over me from head to toe, registering my soft-toed clogs, nearly worn out jeans, and soft, distressed t-shirt. Anne had never once talked to me about what to wear to work, but I guessed this outfit was pushing it. Still, it had been the kind of morning where I'd wanted to wear all my old, favorite, nearly worn out clothes.

"Bad night?" Her tone was sympathetic, underpinned with a hint of amusement. But before I could respond, the bell on the door jingled. She hurried out to see to her customer.

My phone buzzed. It was on the table next to me because Trace was 20 minutes late, as usual. I was sipping my beer and trying to contain my rage. Trace *knew* what had happened with Ben. She knew it. And still, she wasn't here.

I was in our normal booth at Julio's, gazing out past the young tree between me and the parking lot. I put off looking at my phone for a moment because I knew what it would be. Outside, a little boy helped his toddling sister step down the curb while their mother watched with a smile. The boy, to my eye, didn't look like he'd be much assistance if the sister made a misstep. But the mom didn't intervene. She let him help. Although the girl rocked back drunkenly on one heel when she stepped down, she didn't fall. When she regained her balance, she clapped her hands and ran to her mother, who picked her up and put her in a car seat.

That was how parenting was supposed to work. You're supposed to mostly watch, letting your kid explore, experiment, and develop confidence. You're supposed to make sure they don't stick their fingers in an electrical socket or fall into a pool. You're not supposed to monitor every breath from the moment of their birth until they move out.

I looked down at the text Trace had sent. "So sry. New sitter. Didn't like her sent her home. Sry sry! CU next week."

For some reason, the fact she hadn't even bothered to type out the word "sorry" is what put me over the edge. I stared at the text, seeing sparks at the edges of my visions. I swallowed and tapped out my reply. "Next week is off. You can get in touch with me in 18 years or so, when you're ready to be a friend again."

My finger hovered over the send button. I was aware that part of the anger I felt pulsing in my skull should rightfully be directed at Ben, not Trace. But in some ways, Trace's betrayal seemed worse. The whole point of having a best friend was so she could scrape you off the floor when a guy smeared you. Guys usually ended up smearing you. That was life.

"Hey girl!" an enthusiastic voice said. Startled, I punched send and looked up.

Nora was beaming down at me.

"Hey," I said. Then it sank in what I'd done. I turned back to my phone, the consternation written all over my face.

Nora said, "Uh oh. Bad news?"

I released a sound that was midway between a moan and a death-rattle. "I just sent my best friend a really, really mean text. I was just going to type it, then erase it, you know? It's kind of the way I vent sometimes. But then...." Unable to go on, I handed her my phone.

Nora took it. She was wearing low-rise jeans and a button-down shirt tied in a little twist at her waist. On anyone else it would have looked contrived or ridiculous. On her it looked good. Her eyes widened as she read what I'd sent Trace. "Oh, yeah. Ouch."

My phone buzzed again. I jumped like someone had kicked me under the table. "Was that her?"

Nora tapped my phone. "Nope," she said. "Someone named Ben. He says, 'I hope you read this. I'm going to give you some time and space, but I will still be thinking of you every day. And please, when you're ready, let me explain.'"

I looked back out the window. Traffic was whizzing by in the street. I had the mad urge to walk out to the sidewalk, stick my thumb out, get in the car with the first person who stopped, and tell them to take me anywhere that wasn't here.

Nora watched me a minute, then set my phone on the table with a slow, careful movement, like I was a rattled horse who might be startled at the slightest thing. I put my head in my hands.

I was aware that I was making this awkward for Nora, that I should rally and say something light-hearted and stoic, give her leave to laugh and walk off to meet her friends. Instead, I stayed silent.

She watched for a moment. Her air was more curious than put off. Finally, she slid into the booth opposite me and set down her purse.

I was in some sort of Ben/Trace induced daze of self-pity. I said nothing as Nora pulled out her own phone and sent a message. Then the server came over and she ordered a Modelo Especial, like I was drinking. She saw my bottle was low and added before the server had left, "She'll have another one, too."

My phone was still sitting on the table, dark and silent. No response from Trace. Nora saw me looking. With one deft swipe, she scooped it up with her own and shoved them both into her purse. "Okay," she said. "Tell me everything."

"I love beer," Nora said. "But this is going to have to be my last one. I've got to give a riding lesson in the morning. A student who shows some real promise, too."

I laughed. We were nursing our third beers, and my mood was a good deal improved. Nora had stopped into Julio's to grab a taco-bowl to go, on her way to meet a group of friends elsewhere. The text she'd sent was to let them know she wouldn't be coming. When she'd told me this later, she'd read the look of horror on my face and waved a hand. "Oh don't worry. It's nothing like your besty standing you up. It's a big old troop from high school. They go out all the time and it's real casual, you know? They go to Maloney's. No one cares who shows and who doesn't. To be honest, I'm pretty over that scene. I was only going tonight because I hadn't in so long. I'm relieved to have an excuse to miss it." She'd grinned, sipping her beer.

I *had* told her everything—the hopeful start of my relationship with Ben, my foundering friendship with Trace, my independent parents, my empty apartment, my budding collection of cowboy boots. The only thing I'd left out was my massive infatuation with her brother. Even three beers in, I couldn't seem to bring myself to direct the conversation to Clint.

She'd listened, taking it all in, her eyes keen and interested. It had all poured out of me, a flash flood forming out of nothing but one quick rainfall.

When I'd gotten it all out, she'd been quiet a moment. She'd said, "You know what I think?"

"What?" I'd said, suddenly nervous for some unknown reason.

"I think you need a fresh start, a clean slate. Forget about Ben and Trace. You can take the boots back to Western Warehouse, you know. They'd give you in-store credit. Or, if you know Ben's last name and he paid with a card, they might be able to credit them back. That would be a pretty sweet punch in the guts, wouldn't it?"

Our food had arrived then. Over the course of the next hour, I'd loosened up considerably. It wasn't that Nora made light of my struggles, or tried to diminish them or solve them. She acknowledged them and we talked about them a while, then there was a logical point at which the conversation moved on.

We'd eaten and chatted about horses and ranch stuff, boots and saddles, leg position while asking for the canter, dog training, and all sorts of other things. By the time we were sipping our third beers, I was almost glad Trace hadn't come.

"Well, hopefully your student isn't too hung over to ride," I said, squeezing my lime so it fit down the neck of my bottle. "She's shown some poor decision-making skills these last two nights."

Nora grinned and picked at the gold foil on the neck of her bottle. "There's nothing wrong with a little liquid self-medicating," she said. "As long as it doesn't go too far."

We were quiet for a minute. I felt a sudden warmth towards Nora. She was so relaxed and self-assured, and so generous. She could have spent the night out dancing. Instead, she'd stayed here with me. "Thanks for hanging out."

She waved the comment by as if it were a persistent fly. "You're better company than the crowd at Maloney's, anyway."

There was a buzzing sound in her purse. We both looked at it like it might contain a snake. Nora reached over, fished both phones out, and looked at their screens. "It's mine," she said. "I think you might be ready to regain possession rights to your own device, don't you?"

She slid my phone across the table as she checked hers. I unlocked the screen to see nothing. No response from Trace, nothing more from Ben. I put it in my purse.

Nora was reading her text. "It's from my brother."

Startled, I tried to imagine where Clint might be right now. "He's up late," she added. "He's usually down for the count by 8:30." Before I could say anything, Nora's eyes went wide and she looked up at me with an expression I couldn't read. Gleeful? But sly? Some cross between amazed and utterly smug?

"Nora," I said, my curiosity rising from 'dying to know' to 'on the verge of rupturing.'

She texted back before she answered me. Then she gave a theatrical sigh. "This is the problem with brothers," she said. "They're always asking for favors."

I waited. I could feel my heart pounding in my palms where I had them clasped around my cool beer.

She seemed to enjoy drawing out the tension. She picked her own beer up and tipped it back, taking a long swallow. "But at least I don't have to worry about getting out of bed tomorrow anymore."

My head was about to explode. I was sure. Any second now, there would be a massive detonation, Julio's would go silent, and everyone would stare at the mess I'd left in the booth. "Nora." My voice came out in a desperate whine.

She fixed me with a smug, direct gaze. Her face could barely contain her smile. "Clint asked if he could teach your lesson tomorrow."

Chapter 7

When I'd had lessons as a kid, all my teachers had told me horses could sense your emotions. You can't be scared of a horse because they'll pick up on your fear and get nervous. You can't get angry at a horse because they'll get defensive. Not expressing your fear or anger is not enough. You can't even *feel* it.

Knowing this left me in an impossible situation. Clint had asked to teach my lesson. Clint had *asked*. He'd texted Nora and asked. He'd done this at 9:00 PM—later than he was usually up. Had he been lying in bed thinking about me? Was that even possible?

Nora had been singularly unenlightening as to the question of why. Why did Clint want to teach me? When I'd asked her, she had put her phone away, still looking smug, and said she didn't know. He hadn't said.

So I was left to ride my bike home, tumble into bed, and wake up to the chiming of my alarm to realize I needed to get out the door and over to the Tipped Z and that Clint would be the one there to greet me.

Too nervous to eat anything and disinclined to drink coffee due to the impact this would have on my bladder, I downed a glass of water and pulled on my boots. Ben's boots I had put away at Nora's suggestion. I'd placed them back in their box and shoved the box to the back of my closet. They could wait there until I was ready to deal with them.

I arrived at the Tipped Z early. So early, in fact, I considered driving around the block a few times. But I didn't. I parked my car in front of the barn structure, glancing around at the empty yard. Nora's truck wasn't there, of course, and the dogs didn't greet me when I stepped my new boots into the dust of the parking area.

I walked into the large room with the hay where I'd seen Clint hoisting bales and overheard him talking about his girl dilemma. Today the space was quiet and empty, the large bay door across the way standing open, sunbeams illuminating dancing dust motes on the cool morning air. The nerves that had been churning in my stomach since Nora had gotten the text last night began to settle.

I took a few steps in, tentative in my solitude. The aisle of empty stalls was deserted. No horses. No dogs. No Clint. The tack room door was closed.

I walked to the open bay door and looked out over the landscape. The Tipped Z was an old ranch. Many of the fences had the look of having been there quite a long time. Against the back wall of the barn stood a long, worn hitching post made of smoothed tree trunks bigger around than my thigh.

A movement in my peripheral vision caught my eye. I turned my head. There was Clint. He was still a good distance away, leading Duke and Penny, his hat brim tilted to block the rising sun. Three wire-haired dogs were with him, flanking the horses like an honor guard.

I didn't have long to stand and watch him unobserved. Any moment one of the dogs would run forward, announcing my presence. But I had a small space of time where I could watch Clint thinking he was alone.

He reached a gate and flipped it open. He pointed a hand and Duke went through first, walking in a little arc around the gate and stepping under to face the way he'd come. He waited quietly while Clint sent Penny after. For some reason, as Penny passed between the upright post and the gate, she got a little agitated. She tried to bolt ahead, her body stiff, head high.

Clint didn't even look at her. He gave the rope a calculated pull which somehow stole all her momentum, bringing her head around, disengaging her hind and parking her right next to Duke as if nothing at all had happened. Clint came through the gate, latched it, and set a brief hand on Penny's neck. Then he started walking again. The two horses followed.

One of the dogs saw me. It snapped to attention, and all three ran across the yard. I was almost used to the stiff way they greeted people, but it still alarmed me a little when they all came up at once, hair along their backs bristling, ears held high. I knew these were cattle dogs, but it didn't take a great leap of imagination to believe they were trained to attack the unwanted visitor on cue.

There was a low whistle from Clint. The dogs dispersed, disappearing into the interior of the barn. I looked back to Clint, watching as he strode easily through the dust, the fringe on his chinks swinging.

When he was within earshot, I expected him to say something. Some greeting or explanation, some preamble about why he'd asked to give my lesson. Instead he gave me a brief nod, led the horses up to the hitching post and tied them, then disappeared into the barn without uttering so much as a syllable.

I was determined not to be bothered. Clint was a man of few words. I could be okay with that. I could get used to it. I wasn't a huge talker myself. I could appreciate both silence and solitude.

Clint came back with a wooden box with a handle, filled with grooming supplies. He set it on the ground between the two horses. It appeared he was not going to be the first one to speak. I said, "I guess I'm a little early. Can I help tack up?"

He looked at me. His eyes were bright shards in the tan of his face. I met his gaze, trying to appear relaxed and confident, trying not to let on that it felt like he was looking past my eyes at something deeper.

There was a long silence. It began to feel like I had asked to ride Penny in the Fourth of July parade. I had to resist the urge to stammer a retraction, to say something like, "Or I can stand here and watch you. That'd be fine too."

Finally, Clint looked away from me, reached into the box, and picked out a soft curry. It was pink, with glitter embedded in the semi-transparent rubbery plastic. It looked totally out of place in his hand.

He handed it to me. As I took it he said, "Tacking the horse sets the tone for the ride that follows."

I remembered the way he'd handled Penny's scare at the gate—the one quick pull on the rope to keep her from crashing off, the one gentle stroke down her neck.

I accepted the curry and walked up to Duke, giving him a pat on the shoulder, acutely aware that Clint's eyes were on me. I began to rub the curry in gentle circles, fluffing the coat enough to work the dust out but not applying enough pressure to irritate. Clint watched for a moment, then returned to the box. He picked out a similar curry, this one green but still sparkly, and began to work it over Penny's creamy coat.

Silence fell. While it was less awkward now that we had something to do, I felt the need to fill it in spite of myself. I progressed from Duke's shoulder up his neck and said, "What happened at the gate there?"

Clint was rubbing Penny under the neck. She lifted her head and tipped it to one side, eyes half closed, helping him reach the right spot. "She's green. She can still get troubled in confined spaces."

I waited, but it appeared this was all the answer I was going to get. I tried to think of another question, a way to prompt him to go on.

Clint glanced over at me. His hand stopped rubbing Penny's neck. His face took on the pained expression I'd first seen when I'd asked Duke to stop by pulling on the bit out of nowhere. "Now, see," he said. "You got to keep your mind on the horse."

At first I didn't know what he meant. Then I realized he was looking at Duke. I had not been looking at Duke. I had been looking at Clint. When I did look at Duke, I realized I'd worked the curry up his neck and had probably been rubbing the same place for a while, bumping the base of his ear in clumsy manner. Duke was a horse with impeccable manners. He wasn't pulling away or pinning his ears, but he had gone stiff. His body was leaning a little away from me.

My hand went still. I felt like I'd failed some kind of important test. I took a step back, like a kid who's knocked over a small, fragile trinket after being told not to touch anything. I felt my heart sink down to reside in one of my new leather-soled boots.

"So," Clint said, and I jumped because I hadn't heard him walk around Penny. He was right next to me. I could smell the scent of dust and leather. How could someone in spurs walk without jingling? "Can you see where he's tense?"

I looked at Duke. Three weeks ago, I'd have seen an utterly relaxed horse. He stood with a hind end cocked, his head down. But his ears were tipped a teeny bit back instead of drooping out to the sides, and the long muscle that ran down his neck seemed stiff.

Not giving myself time to second-guess anything, I took a step forward, shoving the curry in my back pocket. "Here?" I said. I set my hand on the muscle in the horse's neck and gave it a gentle rub, working my hand like I'd massage my leg if I had a cramp.

Duke stood in the same pose for a moment longer. Then he sighed. His head dropped an inch. His ears relaxed. He licked his lips.

Clint walked around to Duke's face and ran a hand down the horse's head, smoothing his forelock and watching me work on his neck. "That's right," he said. "But too much of a good thing can grow stale."

My hands flew away from Duke's neck as if I'd received an electric shock. Silence fell again, punctuated by the cries of the morning birds. I looked at Clint to see he was looking at me. His eyes had settled on my face. His expression was speculative. "Most people," he said, and stopped. The silence stretched for so long I had to resist the urge to shift my weight or look away. "Most people wouldn't see that little bit of stress, even if you pointed it out to them."

With that, he walked back to Penny, leaving me feeling some mix of exhilaration and relief.

○

"So how did it go?" Nora said as soon as I answered my phone, not bothering with customary conversation-starters and jumping straight to the subject I most wanted to talk about while simultaneously most wanted to not talk about.

"Okay, I think." I was in my apartment, showered, seated at my desk. I had been staring at a blank computer screen for about 45 minutes before Nora called. "He let me groom and tack this time."

There was a long silence—so long I thought the call had dropped. I held my phone away from my ear to look, but the screen still showed the photo of Nora I had snapped in Julio's the night before, holding her bottle of Modelo Especial and grinning.

She said, "This is my brother we're talking about? The one who never goes out without his chinks and is conversationally impaired?"

"Yes," I said. "And I only got in trouble once."

Nora laughed then, a long, full peal that had me smiling too. "He really must like you."

The comment hung there, buzzing on the line between us. I bit back my reservations, forcing my tongue into action before I could miss another perfect opportunity to ask the critical question. "Nora," I said. "Does Clint..."

My voice failed as I spoke his name. I had to stop and regroup. Nora waited. I managed to go on, to ask the question that had been burning my mind for weeks. "Does he have a girlfriend?"

I didn't know what to expect. I tried to prepare myself for anything from, "Yes, but he doesn't like her," to "Um, he's gay." Instead, Nora said, "No. Not that I'm aware of. But he's not the biggest sharer on the planet."

I gathered my courage and pressed ahead. "It's just I overheard him one day. He was on the phone talking to a friend, and he was talking about a girl. It sounded like he was thinking about breaking up with her because he couldn't see the relationship turning into a life-long commitment."

I left my desk chair and walked to my office window. It looked out on an indifferent view of the sidewalk that ran between my building and the next. A skinny, pale guy in baggy sweatpants was walking his black pug, squinting into the light as if it hurt him.

"What?" Nora said. She sounded incredulous. "When was this?"

I told her, recounting the way I'd been coming in for the lesson and he'd been leaning on the hay.

There was a silence. I could almost feel her thinking. "Wait," she said. "Tell me what he said. Verbatim, if you can."

As it so happened, I had a transcript of the conversation. I still had the file saved on my computer. Feeling ridiculous, I walked over to my desk and pulled it up. I read it to Nora, trying to make it sound like I was struggling to remember rather than reading off a screen.

When I got to the part where Clint said something about long-term potential, I thought I heard her stifle a laugh.

I finished reading. There was a pause. "That's all." I said. "That's what I heard."

Nora did burst into laughter then. She'd clearly been holding it in. Released, it went on for a while. She was gasping by the end. I was trying not to be annoyed. I left my screen and returned to my window. The guy and the pug had disappeared.

Finally, Nora got herself under control. "I'm sorry, Erin. It's just, it's just so funny. Clint would never talk about a woman that way. Mom would gut him."

"What was he talking about then?" I tried to keep the irritation out of my voice, but didn't entirely succeed.

"Penny, for God's sake. He was talking about Penny. His *horse*. Clint starts a few young ones each year, but he's real picky. He only finishes out the ones he clicks with, that take to their job and love it. Penny's defensive about some things. She'll fly apart over next to nothing, But then when you want her to put some effort in, she's kind of lazy. Not a winning combo."

Beyond the first part, I was having trouble following what Nora meant. But the overall message was clear. Clint was single. Clint was not a chauvinist. Clint did not keep enthralled women waiting at his beck and call so he could have casual sex with them.

Nora was still talking. "To make one into a bridle horse takes about six years, you know. So it's a big deal. Clint likes to be able to finish what he starts. Wyatt, the guy he was talking to, has a slightly different philosophy. He's a professional colt starter. He's also my brother's only friend and the only thing they ever talk about is horses. "

I was so overwhelmed with relief, I couldn't think of anything to say. I stared at the manicured gravel and gray-green shrubs that lined the sidewalk outside.

Nora piped up again, her tone playful now. "You sure do sound interested in the state of my brother's romantic attachments."

She had me there. I decided to take a page from Clint's book. I didn't answer.

Nora laughed again. "Well, that's fine." She sounded as pleased as if she'd won the lottery. "You don't have to come right out and say it. Tell me about the rest of the lesson."

I told her about most of it. I told her about how Duke and I had managed a serviceable circle from the start. I told her about how Clint had me and Duke face him and Penny, and mirror him as he stepped Penny's front feet one way and then the other. I told her about the trotting to the fence line and softening Duke to a stop, then hurrying him into a canter departure going the opposite direction. I told her all the plain facts.

I didn't tell her about the moment I had looked up from one of my canter departures to see Clint with a tiny smile on his lips, or how that smile had converted my entire bloodstream into something sweet and hot. I hadn't told her how every time I got something right and he said, "There," it sent a shiver down my spine.

And I didn't tell her how at one point I was having trouble getting Duke to step his front over and, frustrated, I'd given him a kick in the shoulder. Clint's mouth had hardened when he'd seen that, and he'd been off Penny and walking towards me in a heartbeat. I'd gone still in the saddle as he'd walked up. Without preamble, Clint had reached up and set two fingertips, lightly, against the bare skin of my lower arm.

I'd been too confused to say anything. He'd been so close I could have poked him in the ribs with my boot toe.

He'd said, "Can you feel that?"

My mouth had gone dry. "Yes."

Clint's hand had left my arm. He'd put the same two fingers, applying the same amount of pressure to Duke's shoulder. "So can he."

On cue, Duke had stepped over.

Clint had turned back and looked up at me, his eyes shaded by his hat brim. "You're weight is on the shoulder you're asking him to move, and you've got too much pressure on his mouth. You're physically inhibiting his ability to do what you're asking. I'm not saying to never kick a horse, because sometimes you have to. But before you kick one, make sure it's him who's making the mistake."

Then he'd been walking away from me and climbing back onto Penny.

I didn't tell Nora about that part.

She listened, asking questions, genuinely interested in the details of my ride. As we spoke, I realized how pleasant it was to have a conversation with someone that wasn't about babies or dogs, or filled entirely with vapid small talk.

Then, abruptly, Nora said, "Oh shoot. Boss is here. Gotta go."

The phone clicked and went silent. I stood a moment longer, still staring out the window, realizing it was only Tuesday and I'd have to wait until Sunday before I could return to the ranch.

"How you doing, kiddo?" my dad said. "Is everything all right in the world of Erin?"

It was Saturday morning. We were in the kitchen at my parents' house. The counters were covered in bags and boxes and bundles, and my dad was up to his forearms in flour. We were busy making the hors d'oeuvres for the party my parents were throwing in honor of Boswell and Norman's safe return to thank everyone who had brought casseroles and forwarded emails.

"Oh, yeah. Everything's good." I was at the sink, scrubbing and rinsing fruits and vegetables and starting the chopping.

My father was a huge fan of all things pastry. Puffs and wraps and flaky treats were his ultimate specialty. Most of his creations were elaborate and original. I swear my parents only entertained at all to give him an excuse to go nuts in the kitchen.

Dad paused in the middle of rolling out a sheet of soft dough. He looked at me, eyes narrowed. I did my best to keep my squirming internal.

The truth was, I was feeling remarkably all right. Sure, Ben had turned out to have a wife. And even after I'd personally spoken with that wife, he'd bought me an expensive pair of boots and brought them to my apartment and waited all day to give them to me. He'd then declared his intention to give me time and space and he *had* given me time and space. At least a million times a day, I found myself wondering what he would say if I did give him the chance. And each time I realized I was wondering this, I forced my mind to consider another subject.

But the other truth was, Clint had asked to teach my lesson. And the lesson had been good. Although Clint's longest speech to date had been reprimanding me for kicking his horse, I still felt there had been a shift between us: a subtle but critical difference in the way he looked at me.

"Come on, now," Dad said. "I know you liked Ben. But we don't have to talk about it if you don't want to."

"I didn't actually like Ben," I said. The words came out in a tumble. Dad cocked an eyebrow at me. He'd turned away from the counter and was standing facing me, flour-covered arms held away from his body so he wouldn't get his clothing dirty. It was a lost cause. He was dusted with white all over. Within the hour my mother would come into the kitchen and ask him why he hadn't worn an apron.

"I mean," I struggled to explain. "I did and I didn't. There was always this feeling he was holding back. Like I didn't really know him. So it was hard to be truly excited about the relationship since there was a wedge between us. I thought he was just reserved, but it turns out the wedge was named Kim."

Dad, satisfied, turned back to rolling out his dough. "Well, I'm glad he didn't break your heart."

Dad (for no earthly reason I could discern) liked to listen to ethnic Greek music while he baked. I listened to the wailing vocals and fast-paced plucking overlaid by the rocking clunks of the rolling pin. I prodded around my heart a bit. The Ben thing had not been pleasant, but I was confident my father was right. My heart was not broken at all. In fact, any time Clint came near it did it's best to make sure it throbbed so hard as to be audible.

A moment later, Dad asked the inevitable question, his voice casual but sly. "Any other interests?"

"Dad," I said. "Give me some time here. It's been a week."

"Your mother can't stop talking about that cowboy who brought Boswell and Norman back. Maybe you should ask him out?"

I felt my body stiffen. I tried to keep scrubbing with the same rhythm as before, trying not to give away the fact my veins seemed to light on fire at the very mention of Clint. I scrambled around, trying to find a response that was both neutral and believable.

Fortunately, my mom's two terriers swept into the room as if summoned by their names. Although a week had done a remarkable amount to restore them to their usual exuberant selves, they were still thin, and they tired easily. But now they cruised into the kitchen like sharks with wagging tails, black noses raised to sample the air.

"Boswell, Norman. Out," my mother said as she came walking in their wake.

The two dogs ignored her. Norman came up next to me. I could hear him whuffing next to my hip. I was glad my mom had her dogs back, but there were a few things I hadn't missed. I raised one bare foot and set it on Norman's broad chest, pushing him slowly but firmly away.

"Erin," my mom said. "Be gentle."

I did not dignify this comment with a response, and Mom was in too good a mood to be perturbed. She perched on one of the stools at the counter and moved a pair of reading glasses from the top of her head, settling them over her eyes and looking down at the notepad she was carrying. A Micron pen was in her other hand. "We've heard back from almost everyone," she said. "Erin, your friends the Crosses replied with a yes for three."

I felt myself freeze up. Norman, undeterred, pressed close again. "Three?"

My mother had insisted on inviting Clint and his family. Insisted. I had tried to stall, to divert, to fudge, to put her off with, "I'll text Nora in a minute." When I had failed to produce their mailing address within twelve hours, she had forced me to give her Nora's cell number. So they'd been invited. I had been certain they wouldn't come, or Nora would come alone.

But the RSVP said three.

Mom tapped the line on her notepad with her capped pen. "Yep, three. You two better make double batches. There are going to be a lot of people here."

Several hours later, I was in a state of near panic. This morning, I had dressed in a pair of old capris and a stained shirt. Without putting much thought into it, I'd thrown my favorite jeans and a top into my bag to wear for the party. At that point in time, I had envisioned helping my dad with the baking for most of the day, staying at the party long enough to say hi to everyone and circulate for a while, then heading home. This morning, I had assumed Nora might put in an appearance. But considering I hadn't heard from her since Tuesday, I had doubted it. I had never dreamed Clint would come.

The prospect of Clint showing up was terrifying. It was one thing to be a scrubby mess when I arrived at his barn for riding lessons. I would be quite another to see him out of that setting—to see him socially. And at my parents' house, no less.

I stared at the mirror in my old bedroom. It was full length, and had a wobble towards the top that made my neck look twice as long as it really was. I was used to this oddity. Normally, I didn't even notice. Today, it was all I could do not to put a foot through the offending glass. Trying to decide how I looked by staring into a funhouse mirror seemed to sum up more things about my life than I cared to admit.

Fortunately, the lower portion of the mirror was normal. My favorite jeans were not my favorite jeans for naught. They were the perfect fit. Snug but not tight. Flattering but not revealing. The top I had grabbed was essentially an embellished tank. It fit me well, and it was blue. Blue, Trace had told me more than once, was my best color. I had my hair done in a loose twist at the nape of my neck, and had left a few shorter strands out to frame my face.

I looked fine. I knew that.

The problem was, I wanted to look more than fine. I wanted to look stunning. I wanted to transform like the main character in the ever-popular makeover movie. I wanted to turn from something unremarkable into something that would make Clint's jaw hit the floor.

I stared at myself in the distorted mirror for another moment, then flipped off my bedroom light with a sigh. There wasn't time to run home for a change. Even if there had been, I had nothing better to wear.

I tried for an air of nonchalance as I walked back into the kitchen. My dad had been chased out by my mother. I could hear the shower running. Mom was arranging the platters of finished flaky treats far enough back from the edges of the counters so Boswell and Norman couldn't reach them. They weren't ill behaved enough to actually jump and grab things, but anything they could get their lips on while their paws were on the floor was a different story.

Mom barely glanced at me as I walked in. "You look nice."

I sat at the counter and picked up a spinach puff. The pastry outside was still warm. "So do you."

Mom was wearing a pair of flowing linen pants and a black sleeveless top, her hair twisted into a disarrayed bun. She did look nice. More than nice. My mom was, in fact, a beauty. Even now that age had crept into her face and softened some of the lines that had once been firm, she was still stunning.

I did not take after my mother. I was like my father: good-looking enough. Normally I was fine with that. Normally I was able to look around and recognize that I should count my blessings.

But some days, I looked at my mom's flawless profile and wondered why I couldn't have favored her a bit more.

My mom waved a hand at my compliment, as if to indicate she knew I was lying for her benefit and wouldn't dignify the comment with a response. She glanced around the house, scanning for last-minute things to adjust or tidy. She fussed with a flower arrangement, gave the counter a final wipe and said, "Those are for the party, you know," as I started in on a second spinach puff. But she was teasing. I made no reply. I was trying not to wonder when Clint would arrive.

"Your friend Nora called," my mom said then, putting away the towel she'd used to wipe the counter and going to the kitchen window to look out towards our driveway.

"What?" Adrenaline shot through my body as if my mother had injected me. "Did she say who the three guests are?"

"Yes, she told me about the special guest she wanted to bring. She wanted to ask my permission first. She's a very polite young woman. Of course, I said it was okay."

The pastry had turned to ash in my mouth. I swallowed. "Said what was okay?"

"Oh," Mom said, turning away from the window. "The Jones' are here. You can always count on them to arrive right on time."

I glanced at the clock on the stove. It said 5:00. I glared at the glowing green numbers as my mother swept from the room to greet her first guests.

The invitation had identified this event as an open house. Normally, I liked open house style parties. They meant people would drift in and out in waves. You had more time to talk to different groups, it was less crowded and noisy at any given moment, and people with kids came early and left early.

In this case, however, it was agony.

By 5:45 I had been certain at least five times I heard Nora's truck rumbling into the driveway. Every time this happened I ended up gawking over my shoulder at the gate, heart going into spasms in my chest. Eventually, the party got loud enough I couldn't hear cars arriving at all. And that helped.

So when I glanced around and saw Clint striding through the front gate, it surprised me so much that I stopped in the middle of my sentence.

I was talking to a woman named Sue, who was a friend of my mother's from art school. Sue was the sort of artist I found unrelentingly tiresome. She liked to talk about her art. A lot. And she liked to talk about public response to her art and the hidden meaning in her art and the reason why her art didn't get into more galleries. I typically dealt with Sue by nodding and smiling a lot, and escaping the conversation at the first viable opportunity. Today, she was proving extra difficult to get rid of. She kept asking for more details about the theft of Boswell and Norman, the conditions the stolen dogs had been kept in, the distance between Florence and Tucson, and all sorts of other things. I had been explaining we didn't know the exact setup of the warehouse because we hadn't seen it.

Sue didn't seem to notice that I trailed off without finishing my thought. She said, "It does inspire a surprising degree of pathos, doesn't it? I have often used the symbolism of cages in my work, but always with regard to the human psyche. I wonder...."

I hardly heard her. In a shocking act of rudeness my mother would have scolded me for if she'd been there to overhear, I cut Sue off. "I'm so sorry, but I need to greet someone." Before she could segue around my leave-taking and back into conversation (Sue was adept at this), I scurried off, making my way around the small clusters of chatting people to where I'd seen Clint.

He'd stopped inside the gate and was now looking back out. Dots appeared then, poking her small gray face around the leg of his jeans. Nora came a moment after, letting the gate swing shut behind them.

Of the three, only Nora looked happy.

"Erin!" Nora said, hurrying towards me with her arms open. She gave me a hug and looked around. "Wow. What a crowd."

Clint and Dots drifted after Nora, as if tethered to her by an invisible elastic cord. Dots was rigid, staring around the yard, her ruff a little raised. She was so close to Clint's leg she sometimes bumped into him while they walked.

"Hi Clint," I said.

Clint, too, had been looking at the crowd. Now he shifted his gaze to me and managed a quick smile. He started to raise his hand, as if to tip his hat, except he wasn't wearing one.

He was dressed in the closest I'd ever seen to normal clothes. His jeans were still Wranglers, but they were one of the more stylish varieties, with a little wear that looked factory installed. He was wearing boots, but they were clean boots, and they were under his jeans so they didn't stand out. His shirt was a plain short-sleeved button-up, and his hair was clean and combed. His face was freshly shaved and free of dust smudges. He was still stunningly handsome, of course, but his outfit screamed 'Nora.' I kind of liked him better in his native state.

"Erin," Clint said to cover his confusion over not having a hat on.

"Your mom wanted us to be guests of honor," Nora said, either unaware of or uninterested in her brother's evident discomfort. "But I said it wasn't us, it was Dots. Dots is the one who deserves the recognition."

"That's a great idea." I tried not to sound as doubtful as I felt. Dots looked about as comfortable as if she'd been thrown into a pen of lions.

"And of course, Dots won't get in a car if Clint isn't in it, and would probably rupture herself if she had to be around this many people without Clint nearby too. So that sealed it. I had to drag them both along."

Nora said this casually, her voice light and quick. But she caught my eye when she said the last sentence. I understood. Nora hadn't done this because she thought Dots deserved special attention. She'd done it to get Clint here, to hang out with me.

The nerves I'd felt earlier seemed suddenly insignificant, like being annoyed by one bee only to discover what a swarm is like. If Dots had been a more normal dog, I'd have squatted down to rub her ears. As it was, she looked like she might take my hand off if I tried that.

There was a silence that was one beat too long. I said, "Thank you for coming." This was meant to be directed at Dots, as a joke, but Nora said, "Oh, we wouldn't have missed it."

Then there was a bark, and Boswell and Norman were there, surging forward to investigate this strange dog in their domain. Bull Terriers are not known for being especially friendly to other dogs. I had a terrible vision of Boswell and Norman, now restored to better health and vitality, descending on Dots and ripping her to pieces. All three dogs were stiff, hackles raised, when my mother's voice rose over the din. "Oh good," she said. "Our guests of honor have arrived."

It turned out Nora was right. Dots would not leave Clint's side. Boswell and Norman determined quickly she was not nearly as interesting as all the people who might be setting plates down within their reach. After a moment of tense sniffing, they wandered off. Dots showed no interest in following them. She stayed as near Clint as she physically could.

My mother did not seem to pick up on the evident discomfort of two out of three of the honored guests. She took Nora by the arm and set out to introduce the three of them to every person at the party.

Before I could follow, I was waylaid by one of my parent's neighbors, Walter, who was at least 500 years old and hard of hearing. He asked me what kind of dog Dots was. I spent the next ten minutes trying to indicate I didn't know, all the while surreptitiously watching the progress of Clint's smooth head. He was taller than most of the people in my parent's yard, so it was easy to keep an eye on him.

"Strange coat," Walter said.

"They're cattle dogs," I supplied. Clint had just been introduced to Sue. He shook her hand but didn't smile.

"They like cats?"

"Cattle. Cattle. Cows." I dragged the 'o' out as I said the last word.

I didn't mind Walter. He was a sweet man, and a good neighbor: the sort of person who would loan you a stick of butter for your cookies, or come barging over with a shotgun when you're house was being robbed. I also had sympathy for his deafness. I knew he'd lost his hearing flying planes in Vietnam, knew it frustrated him to always be one step removed from the conversation.

"They like cows?" He looked, if anything, more confused.

"For herding." I made a gesture with my hands that was meant to indicate grouping something up. Walter's gray eyes followed the movement of my hands. He blinked a few times. I despaired of ever getting the message across. Then his face cleared.

"Oh, she's a cow dog," he said. He rocked back on his heels, face breaking into a smile. "When I was a kid, my neighbors had cattle." And from there he was off, telling me a long, elaborate story while I only half-listened—an arrangement more comfortable for both of us.

The major downside of attending parties at my parents' house was that all their friends had known me all my life. This lead to them feeling they had a vested interest in my success, or lack thereof. By 8:00, I was exhausted. I had escaped from Walter to be waylaid by Kris, a colleague of my father's, who was the sort of brittle, forceful person whose well-meaning questions left you feeling interrogated. The night had gone on from there. I'd had to explain over and over that yes, I was still single. No, the guy I had been dating wasn't here; that hadn't worked out. Yes, I was still working at the gallery. No, I had no intention of going back to school.

I hadn't told anyone I was writing a book. I felt that was best kept to myself until it was done. The upside of this was I didn't have to field inane questions such as, "What is your book about?" or "When do you think it will be published?" The downside was it made it seem like all I was doing was working part time at an art gallery. No one came right out and said it, but almost everyone I spoke to tried their best to encourage me to do something more worthwhile with my life.

Finally, the crowd had started to thin a little. I had long since lost track of Nora and Clint and Dots. I was, in fact, convinced they had slipped out at some point. When the family I had been saying goodbye to walked out the gate, I found my way to a bench that was tucked into a corner made by the house and the patio wall. It was an out-of-the-way nook I favored for escape when parties got later. It wasn't as obvious as going to my room, but it got me out of the thick of things. I collapsed onto the wooden seat, noticing the throb in my feet and the dryness of my lips.

It was a cool night. A breeze stirred my hair as I sat. I closed my eyes and lifted my face. I could smell the sweet tang of fallen mesquite beans and the fading heat of the day.

When I opened my eyes, Clint was there, his appearance as sudden as if he'd materialized out of a puff of dust. Dots was still at his side, but she was more relaxed now. She stood with her head turned towards the open desert, ears up, tracking the sounds made by some small animal in the underbrush.

I found I didn't have the energy to scramble to my feet, to say something clever, or worry if my hair twist had gotten messy. I gave Clint a small smile.

He smiled back. It was that small, sweet smile that made fine wrinkles at the edges of his lips. "Nora said you like beer."

That's when I noticed he was carrying two sweating bottles, limes perched in their necks. I accepted one and, with a sigh, Clint lowered himself onto the bench next to me. Dots followed suit, collapsing into a heap next to his feet and settling her head onto her paws.

And then, suddenly, I was alone with Clint, sitting in the fair desert evening, gazing out into the black night. I didn't say anything at first. I squeezed my lime down into my beer, licking the tangy juice off my fingers and smelling the smooth, sharp scent that drifted over from Clint.

"Thanks for coming," I said. The party was still going on a little distance away. We could hear voices and laughter and the low throb of the music pouring out of the porch speakers. I wondered where Nora was.

At first, Clint's only answer was to reach down and smooth the ruff on Dots' neck. After several minutes, he said, "People think there's no more need for working animals. Working dogs, working horses. They think you can do it all with an SUV and a GPS unit. But with an animal that's trained the right way, you leave them their self, their independent mind. They can fill in for you, pick up on something you might have missed."

I understood he was attempting to explain why he had come, and it hadn't been to socialize. I waited, but he stopped there.

It was enough. He'd come for Dots. Not for me, not for Nora.

I sipped my beer and wondered at the puzzle that was Clint. "Parties probably aren't your thing."

His head turned towards me. He seemed to be examining my profile in the low light spilling out the kitchen windows. "Yours either." It wasn't a question.

"The joys of filial duty." I looked down to pick at the label on my beer bottle, then stopped when I realized I was fidgeting. Fidgeting, my mother had told me often, was not an attractive habit.

Clint leaned back into his seat, extending one hand along the back of the bench so it was reaching in my direction. It was nowhere near me, really, but I could feel it there, like a magnet, sending out a pulse that made the hairs on my arm stand up.

"You're an only child?"

I felt a shiver run up my arm, as if Clint had actually touched me. As far as I could remember, this was the first thing Clint had ever asked me about myself.

"I am," I said. "And I was a mistake. My mom didn't want kids, although she'll happily tell you now that she no longer regrets the decision to keep me."

I realized as soon as I stopped talking that this was not the sort of information one should be volunteering during one's first ever real conversation with the subject of one's wildest fantasies.

Clint didn't seem put off. He had turned back to face the desert, but his gaze was soft, unfocused. "Motherhood," he said. He stopped. I waited for so long, I thought maybe he wouldn't go on. He shifted, sitting up straighter and bringing his arm down off the back of the bench. "I think we don't give it enough weight." He dropped his eyes to the bricks of the patio and gave his head a little shake. "What it does, physically and emotionally. It's a total coup." He reached down to smooth Dots' ruff again.

I didn't know what to say. No one had ever responded to the "my mother didn't want me" anecdote this way before. Most people gasped as if I'd repeated the trashy headline from a tabloid and supplied some response like, "That's horrible," or "I can't believe she told you that," as if it wasn't more of an accomplishment to be loved in spite of not being wanted than to be adored unconditionally from day one.

I thought of Trace. She hadn't responded to the nasty text I'd sent from Julio's. I had suffered nagging regrets all week. Still, it was undeniable. Before Olivia, I'd had a best friend. After Olivia, not so much.

I resisted the urge to say something inane like, "Yeah," or, "Totally." I tried to come up with something weightier, more philosophical.

Then there was the scrambling of toenails on brick. Boswell and Norman churned around the side of the house. They ran up to the bench, shoving their white faces towards our beers. Dots sat up quickly, her expression offended, while Clint gently but firmly took Boswell by the collar and set him back about two feet. Confused, the dog surged forward again. Clint did the same thing. There was no anger in his correction. He used precisely the same amount of force as he had the first time.

By the third time, Boswell hung back instead of barging into Clint's space. Clint ran a gentle hand along his head and back.

Meanwhile, Norman was slobbering all over my favorite jeans. Clint turned to look at me. "They'd respect boundaries if they had any." His voice was quiet, just audible over the breeze rattling the mesquites.

Before I could try to prove myself talented with animals by giving Norman a new way of looking at the world, my mom appeared, strolling with Nora around the patio. "Here you two are," she said, smiling. Clint rose to offer her his seat.

"I may need a favor today, Erin." Anne spoke as she strode into the gallery, heels ringing on the tile. I looked up from my phone, which I'd been staring at while I sat behind the front counter.

It was Monday morning, and I'd still heard nothing from Trace. As much as I hated going to Julio's and waiting 20 minutes for her to show up, as much as it had been so long since our nights out had consisted of anything more than her obsessively checking her phone and rattling on about her kid, I felt dull today, weighed down by the knowledge that I had scuttled over a decade of friendship with one nasty text.

"Oh?" I set my phone down and looked up. Anne was wearing a slim pair of flared black slacks and a deep red top. She looked tall and well-formed, like a fashion designer's sketch of a casual Parisian.

"We got a huge order from Southwest One Bank. They called it in on Friday, and they want it done today. It's all stock frames, but it's 40 pieces, and they won't be able to bring the certificates until this afternoon. I hate to ask because I know it's your night out with your friend, but is there any chance you could stay late and help me finish?"

I glanced again at my dark phone. "I'm not hanging out with Trace tonight," I said, not entirely succeeding in keeping my tone neutral. "So that'll be fine."

Anne stood a moment, her sharp eyes interested. "I have to make a few phone calls, but as soon as we're in the frame room, you're going to have to explain."

She strode off. I resumed my blank staring.

After the party, I had been so high on my Clint experience I'd been unable to sleep for half the night. This had left me foggy the next day when I scrambled into my car to get over to the Tipped Z. Nora had met me in the barn, triumphant and unapologetic, laughingly explaining the lengths she'd had to go to, the arguments she'd made, to get Clint to agree to take Dots to the party. "When I first brought it up you'd have thought I'd asked him to donate her to charity," she'd said, her laugh ringing around the barn.

I'd glanced over my shoulder nervously, and she'd patted my arm. "Sorry, darling. He's not here today. He and my dad headed up to Cave Creek this morning. Somebody's fancy show horse has developed a nasty habit of kicking out during the lope, and they called in the cavalry. So you're stuck with me today."

It had been a fun day anyway. We'd gone out on the trails again. Nora had told me a bit about leaving the reins slack and steering the horse from behind, using the hindquarters like a rudder to keep the horse balanced through the twists and turns of the trail. We'd galloped around the hills like a couple of teenagers until the sun had been so high we could feel the sweat baking off our skin. We'd headed back happy.

But today, my budding friendship with Nora seemed like less of an accomplishment in the face of my massive fallout with Trace. The more

I thought about it, the worse I felt about the whole thing. Sure, she'd been a lousy friend from approximately the moment she got pregnant. But what was a year and a half compared to such a long history? Like Clint had said, motherhood was a coup. Trace was having to reimagine herself, and I wasn't giving her any slack at all.

I picked up my phone, half resolved to text an apology. Then the gallery phone rang. Anne called from her office, "Will you grab that Erin?"

"I'll cut the glass, you do the flats," Anne said. "We won't know how big the windows will need to be until they bring the certificates, so we'll have to do those at the last minute."

It was 3:00. The gallery had been busy for a Monday. This was the first chance we'd had to start on the job for the bank. As we set up our respective tools on opposite sides of the work table, Anne glanced at the clock. "It's going to be a late one," she said with a grim twist of her mouth. "Thank you for agreeing to stay, Erin."

I gave a little nod and positioned a piece of mat board, lining it up for the first cut. Anne thumbed a glass cutter, her expression skeptical, and judiciously pulled a new one out of the supply cabinet against the far wall. "Now," she said, bending over a piece of glass, "what's up with Trace?"

I considered lying. It would be easy enough to say Olivia had a cold. "Oh, nothing. It's just that I'm a lousy friend and I'll probably never speak to her again." I was aware I was dramatizing things, but this had been eating at me all day. I wanted to give it the proper conversational weight.

Anne scored the glass and popped the sheet apart with a deft knock of the heel of her hand. "Why don't you tell me exactly what happened? Start from the beginning." She glanced at the stack of glass next to her and said, "No shortcuts. Goodness knows, we have the time."

So I told her, starting with what had driven me to my annoyed moment in Julio's: Trace's paranoia during pregnancy progressing into the ever-increasing helicopter mothering, and finally her total failure to be there for me through my breakup with Ben. When I got to that part,

Anne looked up in the middle of a cut as if I'd hit the pause button. "Wait, what? You broke up with Ben?"

"I found out he was married." I set another squared off mat in my pile of finished flats.

Anne let out a low whistle. "Okay, we'll get to that next. Let's stick with Trace for now."

So I went on. When we finished with Trace, we segued into the entire Ben story and the thing with the boots, which required me to mention my elevated status as "sort of part time ranch helper" at the Tipped Z, and Clint's appearance at my parents' party.

By the time I finished, it was 3:45. We had most of the cutting done. Anne, while listening, was increasingly distracted by the obvious fact that the certificate delivery had not happened at 3:30 as promised. She straightened, setting her glass cutter down and placing her hands on her lower back to stretch. "That's quite a lot to process, Erin."

I nodded unhappily, flipping my second to last mat onto the finished pile. "At first I felt proud of myself for telling Trace off. But now I feel miserable."

Anne leaned one hip against the work table, regarding me with her direct gaze. "Well," she said, "sometimes things need to be addressed, and cool-headed discussion doesn't do them justice. You tried to talk to Trace, and she didn't step up. Now you've made a more dramatic statement, to which she's responded with exactly nothing?"

I gave a little nod, feeding my last board into the cutter.

"So I think you should consider writing her a letter or email, apologizing for the nasty text but spelling out your feelings, explaining how you've rarely felt so much in need of a friend and how it's a big deal she hasn't been there for you. Then leave it with her. Some people emerge from the daze of early parenthood and turn back into people who can have social lives. Some don't. It's the reality of family dynamics."

I nodded again, feeling like a bobble-head doll but also surprised to find my eyes stinging with the threat of tears. I didn't want to cry in the work room with Anne. I took a few deep breaths and said, "What if they don't bring the certificates today?" just as the bell on the front door jingled.

Several hours later, Anne and I were in a booth at a sushi restaurant, sitting underneath a massive painting of a Japanese character in a frame that was coming apart at the corners. I had seen Anne notice this, but she'd made no comment. She'd ordered edamame and a drink almost before settling into her seat as I'd groped for the beer list and picked from the unfamiliar names at random.

It was quiet in the sushi restaurant. An older couple sat at a table across from the door, and four men in suits were tucked into the opposite corner.

Once we'd gotten going on the framing, Anne and I had functioned like a well-oiled machine, flying through the 40 certificates in less than two hours. After talking about Trace and Ben, our conversation had moved to less charged topics. For the last hour, I'd even forgotten to feel awful about the fact that I wasn't going to Julio's. Then, towards the end of the pile of certificates, the prospect of reheated leftovers in my empty apartment had loomed. Fortunately, Anne had offered to buy me dinner to thank me for late night.

Now, with the server departed, Anne released a small sigh and looked around, rubbing her thumbs. If they were anything like mine, they were raw with shallow glass and paper cuts. We'd framed more in a day than we usually did in a month.

It was strange to be out in public with Anne. I was used to her presence in the gallery, where she was the head honcho, the one in charge. Here, we sat across from each other. People looking at us might think we were friends, or sisters.

When I'd been younger, I'd often wished for an older sister. And now I suppose I did think of Anne in a similar capacity. I admired her. She did everything with an air of relaxed confidence. In her car on the way over, she'd driven with one hand on the steering wheel, the other near the gearshift, as if she was used to driving a stick but found herself unexpectedly in an automatic. But in spite of having known her for years, I knew very little about her interior life. I knew she wasn't married, never had been. I knew she didn't have kids. And given how she went after the things she wanted in life, I doubted she'd wanted either.

"Did you ever want to be a mom?" I said this without thinking. I froze as soon as the question left my mouth, as if some exterior force had taken over my brain and forced the words out without my permission. I was not in the habit of asking people personal questions. It always felt like prying. But, on the other hand, Anne and I had spent the last many hours discussing the state of my relationships and friendships. It seemed only fair I show some interest in her.

Anne's mouth tightened in a strange way I hadn't seen before. She removed her straw from her water, setting it down on the table. "No," she said. "I never did. And because of that, two relationships that would have progressed into marriage," she paused, eyes on the little puddle of water her straw had made, "didn't."

"Oh." This, I reflected, was why I did not ask personal questions. Some people, like Ben and Anne and Nora, knew the right thing to say in any awkward conversational outcome. I tended to end up blinking and staring like an owl woken from sleep at high noon.

Anne's eyes were distant as she stared off over my shoulder. "When you're young, they tell you it's the women who can't live without having kids." Her voice reverted back to her normal tone as she went on. "But you know, in my experience it's usually that men want to be fathers."

I wondered if that had been the case with Andrew and Trace. Trace had never been one to gush over babies before she had her own.

Anne continued, seeming not in the least shy to share the details of her life, now that I had asked. She sipped her water. "But I think it's for the best, anyway. Without kids, marriage is an institution of questionable value, particularly for the woman. I have learned to appreciate my autonomy."

Our drinks came. Anne placed a rapid-fire sushi order I couldn't follow in the slightest. When she finished she added, "That should be enough for both us of, Erin, but order anything else you'd like."

I hadn't even looked at the sushi menu. Neither had Anne, that I had seen. I hoped I didn't look as awkward as I felt as I said, "Oh, no. That all sounds great."

When the sushi came, it *was* great, which surprised me. My prior experience with sushi had been limited to California rolls and other tame selections deemed friendly for beginners. Anne was no sushi beginner. As two large platters were set down before us, I stared at the array of colorful, sauce-covered presentations with surprise. Some were coated in avocado, some were deep fried, some had tiny, crunchy eggs clinging to their outer layer. I wondered if my dad had ever had sushi like this.

We spent most of the dinner in companionable conversation, chatting about work. We made our way through our beers and the elaborate rolls, decimating the artistic tableau but enjoying ourselves enough to make up for the destruction.

We were near the end of our second beer, and we'd both slowed down on eating, when Anne said, "Your friend, Trace. Have you tried to get to know her kid?"

I looked at Anne, confused, I set the beer I'd been sipping back down onto the table. "Get to know her? She's nine months old."

Anne began to consolidate the remaining sushi pieces on a plate so the server could carry away the empty platters. Her tone was matter-of-fact. "Kids are never too young to get to know. They don't have speech yet, and they can't do much by way of physically controlling themselves, but they're people from the moment they're born."

I decided I wanted another sliver of the fried roll. I moved one from the platter onto my own plate before Anne got around to moving it. "Trace always wants to go out, to get a babysitter."

Anne finished operation move-the-sushi and set down her chopsticks, gazing off across the restaurant again, watching as the older couple left their table and made their slow way towards the exit. "Does she? Is that what she wants, or what she thinks you want?"

I hadn't thought of this. I recalled the brief time I'd spent at Trace's a few days ago, and felt guilty. I had kept a good five feet away from the playpen at all times.

Anne continued. "It could be that she's over-parenting because she feels overwhelmed and alone. You say the father doesn't seem to be much use. So perhaps you could offer to come over once a week and spend an hour with the kid. Trace will hover. Maybe it won't amount to anything, but eventually she might be able to relax and trust you. Then she could do things like keep the laundry going or take a shower while you're keeping an eye on the little one. From what I hear, that's the kind of relief new mothers need."

I considered this. It seemed like good advice. I poked at the pile of ginger left on my plate with my chopsticks. "There's one problem," I said. "Trace isn't talking to me.

Anne waved a hand. "Oh, come on. Friends fight. Friends get over it. All she needs is an apology."

My phone let out a tone in my purse.

Anne gave me a little grin. "Maybe that's her now."

I fished out my phone and looked at the screen. The text wasn't from Trace. It was from Nora. It said, "Guess who asked to teach your lesson again tomorrow?"

Chapter 8

"We're going to try something a little different today."

Clint said this from his position next to the shoulder of a lean black horse that was tied in the aisle next to one of the empty stalls. Clint was snugging up the cinch as I watched the slow, smooth movements of his hands.

The horse was the only horse in the barn. It stood quietly, one hip cocked, ears drooping.

I had just walked in, and now came to a stop near the tack room door. Dots walked over to sniff my leg. She looked up at me, and her tail wagged once. Surprised, I almost crouched to rub her ears. Then I remembered how Clint had touched her at the party. I stooped instead, running one hand down her back, trying to imitate Clint's gentle but solid kind of touch. I stopped after one stroke, and straightened. Dots gave another single wag of her tail and trotted off to investigate something near the hay.

I looked back at Clint and felt my face heat up. He'd finished adjusting a stirrup and was watching me, his expression intent. He'd clearly observed my interaction with Dots. I thought he was going to say something. But he didn't. He kept his eyes on me a moment longer, then walked around to the other side of the horse.

"Something different?" I tried to make my tone both confident and casual. It came out wobbly and unsure.

"This is one of my bridle horses." Clint said this without looking at me, occupied with the other stirrup.

I understood the term. Nora had explained on one of our longs rides that her family followed a training tradition that had developed in another part of the country, and had its roots in classical Spanish horsemanship. She'd explained that their horses went through a particular set of phases that took six or seven years to complete, and when the horses were "finished" they were called "bridle horses," because they wore an elaborate sort of bit that allowed the rider to communicate complex movements with only the tiniest adjustments of hand and seat position.

I had gotten the impression that bridle horses were a rare thing in today's world. They took a real investment of time and skill to create, and were a sort of work of art in and of themselves. I knew, of course, that there were bridle horses around the Tipped Z. But they were a bit hard to tell from normal horses when no one was riding them.

I looked at the tied gelding with more interest now. He was almost solid black, with one narrow ring of white around a hind ankle.

"His name is Rascal," Clint added, coming back around the horse's rump and looking at me as if he expected a response.

I looked at the horse's profile. "Hi, Rascal."

Clint was looking at me again. The briefest of smiles lit his face before it vanished so quickly I wasn't sure I had even seen it.

"You're going to ride him."

"Try crossing your arms. That will help you keep them a little quieter."

It was ten minutes later. We were in the round pen. I was on Rascal's back, and although Rascal was supposedly a bridle horse, he had nothing on his head whatsoever.

The round pen at the Tipped Z was the largest round pen I'd ever seen. The sides were high, and made of solid wood: impossible to see over unless you were on a horse. The gate was shut. Clint was standing in the center, hands resting on the top of a flag, its handle set in the dirt.

My task had seemed deceptively simple at first. I was to ride Rascal at a walk around the edge of a pen. When I was ready, I was to turn him around and walk the other way.

But there were no reins. I had no reins in my hands. I was to accomplish this using legs and seat alone.

"The horses you've been riding are safe." Clint had said by way of explanation when I'd gone all quiet and goggle-eyed at the news I'd be riding Rascal.

He had not elaborated further until I'd said, "He's not safe?" nodding towards the dozing black horse.

Clint had waited a moment before answering, as if weighing possible responses. He'd settled on, "He's light as a feather."

This had not done much to clear the question up for me, but Clint had said no more. He'd untied the rope and led the horse out of the barn.

Now, on Rascal's back, I crossed my arms. I tried to relax, tried to feel the horse's steps as Clint had instructed. I was supposed to time up with the inside front foot and feel for when it left the ground, then tip that foot in with my outside leg while I pushed the haunches under with my inside leg.

I did all this. Or tried. Rascal, instead of turning off the fence, began to trot.

Alarmed, I uncrossed my arms and clung to the horn. Despairingly, I looked at Clint. He was smiling. "That's okay," he said. "You forgot to shift your weight, and your timing was wrong. Just tell him you want to walk."

I was feeling flustered and powerless, I was riding a bridle horse with no bridle on, and he was trotting. Just how I was supposed to tell him to walk was beyond me. "Rascal," I said, "please walk."

"Hips, Erin." Clint's tone was amused. "Ask him with your hips."

It was possibly the most distracting thing he might have said. I immediately thought of some questions I might ask Clint with my hips.

Annoyed with myself, I pushed those thoughts out of my mind. I focused on Rascal's trot. To my surprise, the longer he trucked along, the less need I felt to cling. His gait was smooth and rhythmic. I rose into a shallow post and found it no trouble to time up with him.

I went for about half the circumference of the round pen, then took a deep breath and stopped posting, slowing my hips to a walk.

Rascal dropped the trot, downshifting more smoothly than Anne's Lexus.

"There," Clint said.

Gooseflesh rose on my arms. I had to resist the urge to flop forward and throw my arms around Rascal's neck.

Clint gave me a moment to revel in my success. Then he said, "Now let's try for the turn again."

An hour later, I was feeling like the champion of the world. We'd progressed from turning to the inside of the pen while moving forward to stopping and turning to the outside. From there we'd gone on walk-trot and trot-walk transitions, leaving the fence and trotting across the center of the round pen, trot-halt transitions, and rollbacks. With some of the faster maneuvers, Clint came over and used the flag to drive Rascal's front or hind until I got the hang of asking with my weight and legs. But after a while, I didn't need his help anymore.

The longer I rode without reins, the more comfortable I felt. Rascal was smooth with everything he did. All it took was a little shift of my weight to influence his direction or speed. It was an incredible feeling— as if we'd forged a telepathic link.

It was a warm morning, and we had to be close to the end of the lesson. The heat was rising. My shirt was soaked in sweat. We'd finished a rollback and I was walking along the rail again, waiting for instructions.

Clint was in position at the center of the arena, his hat casting a shadow over his face. As I looked at him inquiringly, he glanced at his watch. "I guess we're about out of time, but why don't you go ahead and lope him before you step down."

My newfound relaxation vanished faster than the sweat was evaporating off my skin. I wanted to turn and gape at Clint, but I had learned to keep my eyes on where I wanted to go. "Lope?" My voice came out in a squeak.

"It's a three beat gait, canted, with one front and one hind leg reaching further forward each stride."

Forgetting about keeping my eyes looking ahead, I turned to Clint, dumbfounded. That little smile was playing around his lips again.

He was *teasing* me. This was Clint being playful. I blinked and looked away, unsure what to say.

There was a beat of awkward silence that made me realize I should have laughed. Clint went on. "Ask him to pick it up nice and easy whenever you're ready. Go into the trot first, if that's more comfortable for you."

My hand gave a spasm, wanting to cling to the horn again. I resisted the urge to fling myself out of the saddle to save myself the embarrassment of falling.

I wasn't sure how to ask a horse for the canter without reins. I asked for the trot, and started posting.

We trotted. I licked my lips. Sweat was running down the back of my neck, collecting in my already soaked collar.

"Whenever you're ready," Clint said again. "Keep your eyes looking ahead."

I looked up at the landscape visible past the round pen walls. I sat down, and squeezed.

Rascal rocketed into the canter with so much force I was thrown backwards as he nearly shot out from under me. I choked down a small scream. For one horrible moment, I thought I *was* going to fall.

But I didn't. The saddle's cantle caught me and scooped me forward. Rascal's pace was fast but fluid. As I relaxed into riding, he slowed down. Soon we were loping an even, if fast, pace around the outside of the round pen.

"Good," Clint said. "Now stop and go the other way. And ask him with about 90% less energy than you used last time."

I called everything Clint had said about stopping into my mind. I picked a stride and sat, hard, crunching my abs and saying, "Woah," even though Clint and Nora had both told me their horses weren't trained to respond to verbal cues.

Rascal stopped. He stopped hard, slamming to a halt from the lope so quickly, I bounced forward and hit the pommel.

Working hard to stay calm and centered, I used my outside leg to step Rascal's front around, then asked him to walk in the other direction.

"Good," Clint said.

I asked for the trot. A few strides in, I tried for the canter again. This time I just thought about the gait, imagining lifting the horse into it with my hips.

Rascal picked up the smoothest, most balanced canter I had ever felt.

We went three laps. By the time Clint said I could stop, I was grinning from ear to ear.

"Boswell, Norman. Here."

I was pushing through the front gate, my arms full of two bags of laundry and my overnight bag. Surprised, I peered around my load to see the two Bull Terriers halt their mad dash to oversee my entrance into their domain. They looked over their shoulders at my mother, as if to assess whether or not they'd heard what they thought they'd heard.

My mother did not repeat her command. She stared at them with as fierce an expression as I'd ever seen on her face.

The two dogs turned as one and walked over to her, stopping to flank her like a pair of breathing bookends.

I pushed the gate closed behind me, astounded. My mother must have read my expression. She said, "The party was embarrassing. Dots was the picture of good manners while these two," she gave her two darlings a look full of daggers, "were roving around like lawless bandits. Nora gave me some training pointers."

Boswell sighed and glanced again in my direction, his expression pleading.

"Don't look at me," I told him. "You made your own bed."

"What's all that?" my mother said as I started across the patio, seeming to register the load in my arms for the first time.

"The laundry room at my complex hasn't had water for a week. I'm on my last clean bra."

My mom took one of the bags of laundry. We went together into the house. It was Thursday afternoon. Something remarkable about Thursday that I had somehow failed to notice in my life up to this point is how far away it is from both Tuesday and Sunday.

The week had been a struggle. The phrase "driven to distraction" had taken on a whole new meaning for me lately. I couldn't seem to focus on anything.

After speaking with Anne, I had decided to write a letter to Trace. But so far all I'd managed to do was sit down at my desk and write her name on the top of a piece of paper.

It was Clint. I couldn't get him out of my mind. My ride on Rascal had escalated things to a whole new level of infatuation. I was even prepared to try to convince myself I was not infatuated, that I knew Clint well enough to like him, and that I liked him quite a lot.

Everything I saw, everything anyone said, everything I heard, reminded me of him.

I was turning into a head-case.

"Your dad is picking up a frozen lasagna for dinner. I hope that sounds okay?" Mom had followed me into the laundry room and watched as I dumped my first load into the washer.

"Sounds great." I folded up my empty hamper bag and reached for the detergent.

"Have you told the management there's no water in the laundry room?"

"It's the talk of the complex." I set the cycle and dropped the metal lid closed, then turned. My mother was blocking my way out of the room.

"But does the manager know?"

I looked at my mom. There was something a little strained about her expression. "Is everything all right, Mom?" I mentally double-checked that I had seen both Boswell and Norman on my way in.

She turned then, walking back towards the kitchen with a wave of her hand. "Oh, they're sending your father to Iraq again. He has to leave in the morning."

I listened to the water fill in the machine behind me. "I'm sorry," I said. "Should I go back to my place?"

The front door opened as if on cue. Dad walked in, grocery bags dangling from his hands. "Erin!" he said. "I hope you're staying for dinner."

I looked at my mom. Her expression was unreadable. She walked around me and went outside to help unload the groceries.

"But you just got back." I poked at the remaining lasagna on my plate, separating the noodles from the cheese and the cheese from the meat.

It had been a tense evening. Two things had emerged after my dad had gotten home. One, my mom was angry to have my dad leaving again so soon. Two, my dad had no desire to engage with her on the subject. To him, my presence was a godsend, a great excuse not to have to get into it. To her, it was a hindrance, something preventing her from airing her uninhibited views.

It had seemed like they were sending my dad abroad more often. For many years he'd gone once every six months, as promised. But lately it seemed a lot more like once every two or three months. And this time he'd barely been home two weeks.

The worst part of all of it was he couldn't talk about why. He couldn't explain what he was working on, couldn't inform us about the great work he was doing and why it was indispensable to national security or improved the lives of hundreds of thousands of people. He just had to go and come back, leaving us with only the vaguest idea of what he did while he was away.

"Maybe I should ask that cowboy to stay with me while you're gone." My mother said this apropos of nothing, as far as I could tell. She was looking at my father with a hard expression. "He could protect Boswell and Norman from thieves, no doubt, and help me train them at the same time."

"You mean Clint?" I couldn't imagine my mother was serious, but when she was in this sort of mood you never quite knew what she'd set her mind on. I thought she was trying to get a rise out of my father, get him to show some flicker of jealousy or discomfort at the thought of her living with an attractive young ranch hand.

Instead, my dad looked up from his plate. "If you think that would make you feel better. It wouldn't have to be him though, if he has better things to do. Maybe Erin could stay with you while I'm away."

They both looked at me. Dad's expression was inquiring, Mom's was unreadable. I felt that my response was central to some larger question I wasn't aware they'd been arguing over. "Of course, I could stay here." My tone was uncertain.

"Oh don't be ridiculous, Carter," Mom said, standing up and picking up her plate. "Erin is a grown woman. She has better things to do than keep her lonely mother company." With that, she went to the kitchen. She wasn't exactly storming out, but a moment later we heard her go into her workshop and close the door.

Dad gave me a guilty look. "She's unhappy I've been called on to go again so soon." He said this as if it wasn't obvious.

"I suppose you can't blame her." I kept my tone neutral. Behind me, Boswell or Norman whined at the workshop door. It was opened to admit the two dogs, then closed again.

Dad set down his fork and scooped more lasagna onto his plate. "It's something I have no control over," he said. "Hopefully she doesn't fillet me before I can reach retirement age." Before I could respond, he shifted gears. "So what about that cowboy then?"

I tried to keep an impassive exterior as the blood in the veins lit like napalm. "What about him?"

My dad gave me a sly look. "Oh come on, Erin. He's attractive, reserved, good with animals, of suitable age, has a fun, friendly sister. You can't tell me you're not at least a little bit interested."

I could try to deny it, but it would be no good. I could feel the heat rising to my cheeks. "He's been asking Nora to teach my Tuesday lessons instead of her. Today he let me ride his bridle horse. That's a big deal." I added the last part when my dad's expression revealed he had no idea what a bridle horse was.

Dad let out a low whistle. "That sounds promising." He reached across the table and tipped more wine into my glass. "And how did it go?"

⊙

I pulled up next to the mailbox and rolled down my car window, hesitating a moment before reaching out with the envelope and dropping it into the slot. I rolled my window up again and drove away a little faster than necessary, as if resisting the impulse to go back, feed my arm through the narrow box mouth and fish the letter I'd just sent Trace out from among all the other mail.

It was sent now, and there was no un-sending it. I felt as if a small weight had been lifted from my shoulders. I turned onto the main road and punched the radio on, hoping to lose myself in some music. I turned if off again a moment later after flipping through eight channels and finding nothing but obnoxious morning shows.

It was Monday, and the morning was cool. The summer heat had broken. It looked like we were in for some pleasant weather. Yesterday, I'd ridden with Nora again. It had been cool all day, and we'd ridden for hours. She'd taken me out to one of the far pastures. Our job had been to check the cattle and the fence. Everything had been in order, so it had amounted to just a long, long day of riding. I'd been on Paul, who liked to get out and explore. He was an unremarkable-looking bay horse, with good gaits and a willing disposition. I'd enjoyed riding him, but found myself wishing to be astride Rascal more than once that day. It wasn't that I could find any fault with Paul. He was well mannered and polite. But he wasn't Rascal. There was something missing. Something I couldn't quite put my finger on.

I pulled into the gallery parking lot, stopping in an empty spot on the far side. I gathered up my purse and left my car, heading for the entrance to the central patio. As I walked, I noticed a black truck zip out of a parking place near the exit and pull onto the main road. Some little intuition caused my skin to prickle.

Sure enough, as I stepped through the little archway and wound my way through the lush arbor the owner of the strip mall cultivated, I saw them. What started as a bright splash of color among all the green soon revealed itself to be a huge bouquet of yellow and orange and pink roses, set right on the mat in front of the gallery.

Grumbling under my breath, I stepped around the blooms to unlock the door. Not knowing what else to do, I took the vase inside.

I set the massive bunch of flowers on the floor inside the door and did my normal morning circuit. I turned on the lights and the air compressor, sorted the mail, picked the spammy faxes up off the office floor and put them in the recycling bin, and checked the answering machine. All of this took approximately five minutes, and all that time the knowledge of the flowers loomed larger and larger in my mind.

Finally, there was nothing for it. I made my way back across the quiet gallery. Our current featured artist was a metalsmith who made tiny tableaus of people in ridiculously small, dreamlike settings, crafting alloys and patinas and enamels to make vivid, detailed scenes. These were set on slim, upright pedestals dotted throughout the gallery floor. I had to wend my way around them to get back to the flowers.

I passed the last sculpture and looked down, glaring at the blameless roses as if they had chosen to disrupt my morning of their own volition. With even more reluctance than I'd dropped Trace's letter into the mailbox, I stooped and fished the little card from where it was tucked between two stiff stems.

They were from Ben, of course. The message was brief, but he'd written it himself. "Please let me explain. Then I will respect your decision."

I resisted the urge to kick the flowers over. I stared at the note for several minutes, reading the two sentences over and over. Feeling defeated, I picked up the flowers and carried them to Anne's office, setting them on her desk. I considered making a counterfeit note and leaving it to replace the one Ben had left me. Something like, "To Anne, for being such a fabulous boss."

But it seemed too disingenuous. I left them there, devoid of note, and retreated to the frame room in search of something to calm the frantic scrambling of my mind.

"Erin?" Anne's voice sounded from her office. I looked up from the mat I was cutting, no doubt wearing the expression of Rapunzel's father caught in the garden.

I waited. I'd heard Anne come in a few moments before, heard her go into her office. Now I heard her footsteps draw near the frame room. A moment later, she appeared in the doorway, her upper body obscured by the bright array of roses. She gave me a look and said in a mock serious tone, "These seem to be missing a card."

I looked at the flowers. I still couldn't get over the sheer size of the cluster. Ben must have spent a fortune on them. I dropped my gaze back to the work bench. "Ben left them for me."

Anne walked through the doorway and set the flowers on the side table. "But you thought he meant to leave them for me?"

I pointed at the card, which I'd left sitting on the edge of the work table. She picked it up and read, eyebrows knitting as she absorbed the two lines. "When was the last time you talked to him?"

"Talked?" I said. "Let's see, that would be when he was leaving a pair of expensive cowboy boots on my doorstep."

Anne leaned against the doorframe. She was wearing all black again—black slacks, black top, black boots. "But you didn't talk to him, right? He gave you the boots and left?"

I thought back, nodding.

"And you didn't talk to him when you went to his house to return the letter?"

"I talked to his wife, Anne. His *wife.*" I found myself starting to feel defensive and frantic for some reason. I set down the straight razor I'd been using to scape some dried out tape residue off a piece of glass.

Anne held up a hand as if to defend herself from my accusing expression. "I'm not trying to persuade you of anything. But look at the facts. First, you date this guy for several months. He never mentions his wife. He takes you out in public a lot. He makes a point to show his face at your place of work. He meets your family. At no point does he hesitate to be seen with you in any capacity. Then you discover he has a wife, and instead of slinking away, he keeps trying to reach out to you, saying he can explain. Who knows? Maybe his explanation is something that doesn't sound good to you, like he has an open marriage. But maybe, just maybe, there is something he could say that makes the circumstances better than they appear."

I glared at her across the table. "You think I should forgive him."

Anne shook her head. "I think nothing of the sort. I want to know what his story is. Don't you?" She grinned at me as she said this. "And plus, right now he has power over you. He feels you owe him a chance to tell you the truth. That leaves you in a defensive position. If you let him say his piece and then reject him, he has no ground left to stand on." She nodded at the roses. "And he'll have less incentive to keep leaving you these reminders of his existence."

I stared at the bright flowers. They were arranged to perfection, every single bloom in that not-quite-open state that would make it last the longest.

"And at the very least," she said, turning to go back to her office, "it'll make for a better story if you know the real facts."

I punched in the gate code and sat as the mechanical arm rotated, taking the gate with it and opening my path onto the Tipped Z. I waited until there was space for my Hyundai, and eased my booted foot off the brake.

It was Tuesday morning, and I was a nervous wreck.

The night before, I'd gone home after work and created another high school worthy diary entry, pouring my heart out onto the page. I had written about Ben and Clint and my father going back to Iraq. I ended up falling asleep across my notebook like I used to collapse into slumber when I was a little kid who didn't know when to stop reading.

I'd decided Anne was right. I had to talk to Ben, if only to give myself closure. I'd promised myself I'd text him today, after my riding lesson, and see when he wanted to get together.

So that was one thing to be nervous about. The other thing was I hadn't heard from Nora on the subject of who was going to be teaching my lesson this morning. This fact made me approximately a million times more nervous than the prospect of seeing Ben again.

The thing was, I was aware of what a big deal it had been for Clint to put me on his bridle horse. I was aware that trainers like Clint did not usually suffer amateurs around their mounts. For some reason, he'd gone off the beaten path with me, decided to let me feel something special.

The question was why? I didn't get the feeling that Clint had many (or any) students. I didn't get the feeling that, in general, he sought the role of teacher. But he was going out of his way to teach me. That had to be a good thing?

But I hadn't heard from Nora about today's lesson, hadn't gotten a text saying Clint would be teaching me again today. Which meant one of three things. 1) Clint was busy with something else. 2) Clint was teaching me but Nora hadn't felt the need to mention it. 3) I'd done something horrible during my last lesson and Clint would never teach me again.

I was aware that number one was by far the most likely option. But still, my mouth was as dry as if I'd been sucking cotton balls when I came around the bend and saw an empty parking area before me.

The notable absence of Nora's truck sent my heartbeat ratcheting up a few more notches.

I parked my car. Pulse racing, I sat behind the steering wheel and took a few deep breaths. It was ridiculous, really, that I was this wound up over the simple question of who would be watching me make a fool of myself on horseback today.

I stepped out of my car and looked towards the barn. Three wire-haired dogs stood in the doorway, their half-perked ears at attention. Dots was among them. I had learned to associate Dots with Clint's presence. As I walked towards the dark doorway, I tried to remember if she'd ever been in the barn when he had not.

I felt faint. I squared my shoulders, and stepped inside.

The hay room was empty except for the hay. The large bay doors were open, letting in the weak morning light. I walked around the corner and looked into the aisle between the stalls. That space was empty as well.

My heart sank a little, like a hot air balloon allowed to release some heat. Nora must be running late.

Then I noticed the dogs. All three of them had trotted over to the bay doors. I turned in that direction and heard the unmistakable thud of a horse stamping its foot.

I followed the dogs. When I stepped out of the barn and looked to my right, I saw Clint at the hitching post, adjusting Paul's bridle while Rascal stood quietly behind him, hip cocked.

Clint looked up when he saw me. His face broke into a smile.

"It's such a beautiful morning," he said. "I thought we might ride out, if that's okay with you."

"When they get out of balance it's usually because they aren't using their hindquarters properly," Clint said. "It makes them heavy on the forehand, which means they are tripping a little and falling forward with every step."

I looked down at Paul's head. Clint and I were trotting side by side along the bottom of a wide, smooth wash, flinging sand up behind us. The bay gelding was distracted, his head pointing off towards the east as we went.

"When that's happening," Clint continued, "they try to compensate by going faster and faster. That's why they can feel like they're running away from you even when you're at a low pace."

Paul was in a bit of a mood this morning. On all our previous rides he'd been willing enough to go, but docile and even lazy at times. This morning it was cool, the night's chill still clinging in the low places and the shadows. The temperature appeared to have a stimulating effect on Paul. Every gait I put him in, he wanted to go faster.

"So instead of pulling back on two reins," Clint said, "make him think a little. Tip his nose one way and push his haunches back underneath you with your foot. No, just one rein. Loosen up on the other. Don't forget your foot. Push his haunch under you, harder, harder. A little more with the nose. There. Release. Release."

I let the reins out, feeling a softening in Paul's body. For about three strides, he felt like the horse I was used to: soft and balanced and smooth. Then he began to pick up the pace again.

"All right," Clint said. "Now do it again. Use the other rein and other heel this time. You can't do this too much. It'll make him soft to your hand and your leg, and keep him from getting ahead of you all the time."

We had ridden away from the Tipped Z on a trail I'd never taken before, heading south and passing through a series of gates. Now we'd dropped into a wash that ran between two ridges with large cottonwood trees lining the edges.

It was beautiful country. I wished for one sour moment that Paul would calm down a little so I could enjoy the scenery. I pushed this thought out of my mind and tried again to do what Clint was asking. It was easier the second time. Paul's nose tipped to the right. I felt his hindquarters step up beneath me. "There," Clint said. "That one was nice."

I felt a thrill run up my spine. I had to consciously prevent the muscles in my face from breaking into a dopey grin. Clint seemed to catch my sentiment anyway. He looked across at me from Rascal's back, holding my eye for a second and smiling. I felt fire shoot through my veins again. "And make sure he's trotting at the speed you're riding him, not vice versa."

We kept going, trotting around a series of large boulders scattered in the wash-bed. Clint pushed Rascal ahead to lead us through a section where a cottonwood had dropped a great branch in among the rocks. Then, just as I was clear of the obstacles, he pointed Rascal at the bank and pushed him into a lope. They surged up the sandy incline with me hot on their heels.

At the top, Clint slowed to a walk. We continued deep into a thicket of cottonwood trees. The air was cool and sweet, the ground littered with yellow leaves. The trunks were pale and smooth. There was no sound but the thud of hooves and the rustling of the branches above.

We wound our way into the grove and up to a series of tumbled rocks. Here, Clint swung down, let Rascal's cinch out a couple of holes, unhooked a set of hobbles from the back of his saddle, and buckled them around his horse's front ankles. He accomplished all this in the time it took me to realize we were taking a break. I scrambled off of Paul's back. As I imitated Clint by letting the cinch out, he came up behind me, leaving Rascal standing in the shade. He unhooked another pair of hobbles that had been hanging on the back of my saddle. He was so close for a moment I could feel the fringe of his chinks brushing my pant leg. Then he drew away again, and knelt to buckle Paul's hobbles in place.

We stepped away from the horses and walked towards the pile of rubble. I noticed the stones were laid out in a rectangular formation. As we drew near, this emerged as the leftover footprint of a one-room house. A fireplace and doorway were visible along one wall.

Clint stopped, propping his boot up on a stray stone. "This is the original Tipped Z."

I halted next to him, looking down at the outline of the structure. It would have had an interior about the size of my parents' kitchen. "Really?"

"Ranch headquarters." Clint kicked the rock as if it could somehow corroborate his story. "Back when everything came and went via horseback or mule train. They moved to where we are now when there came a need for a real road."

I looked around the cottonwood grove. A ridge reared up on one side, the wash ran on the other. It would have been a sheltered place. It was quiet now, even though the hum and rumble of modern life couldn't be more than ten miles away. I glanced at the horses. They stood in their hobbles, side by side, relaxed, and happy for the breather.

Clint shifted, moving his boot off the rock and somehow ending up a lot closer to me. I felt the hairs on my arms rise, scoping towards him as if pulled by an electrical current. "I used to ride out here all the time when I was a kid," he said. "I tried to rebuild that corner over there. Had a tarp stretched over the top for a while. It was my hideout."

His voice was a low rumble beneath the sigh of the cottonwood leaves. My eyes followed his gesture. I could see now that the far corner had been shored up a little with smaller stones of the type a boy could lift and carry without help.

Clint was close, and he was looking at me. His eyes were soft, his expression open, as if he was waiting for something. My heart gave a little thrill, a sort of clenching that sent a delicious tremor of anticipation through my body. I said, "Seems like a pretty good place to get away to."

Clint took another step, closing the last gap between us. I felt him take my hand in one of his, felt his rough fingers on my palm. His voice was right next to my ear when he said, "I thought you might like it here."

I turned my head. For a second our faces were separated by only a breath.

Then he kissed me.

I had thought I knew what kissing Clint would be like. I'd thought about him so often while kissing Ben, and while not kissing Ben, that the reality of his mouth and his hands and his scent took me by surprise.

It was not what I had imagined, but something even better.

It was the sweetest, most perfect kiss—firm enough I didn't have to reach for him, but smooth and slow and gentle. It was a kiss of exploration, of seeing how we fit together.

Time seemed to slow down. Somewhere in the distance, a woodpecker rattled against a tree trunk. One of the horses sighed. The breeze stirred my hair. The place seemed to wrap us up in its quiet, in its waiting. I wondered how many kisses these trees had seen, how many triumphs and tragedies had played out around this little stone house.

Clint drew back, letting the kiss end and looking me in the eye. He held my gaze for a second, his expression quiet, centered, certain. His smile flicked into brief existence. He ran a thumb along my jaw, turned away from me and, still holding my hand, said, "The well was over here."

My phone rang, making me jump. I'd been sitting at my kitchen table for at least fifteen minutes since I'd finished my sandwich, gazing out the window in a rose-colored haze. I blinked a few times, my mind returning to reality.

It was Trace's ringtone. I scrambled out of my chair, following the sound towards my bedroom. I'd all but forgotten about my letter to Trace in all the insanity with Ben's roses and Clint's kiss. Now my heart gave a jerk—half guilt, half nerves.

My knees felt a little wobbly as I walked. I was still giddy with the events of the morning. Clint and I had spent about half an hour exploring the old cottonwood grove, then we'd ridden back to the ranch. He'd kissed me again, briefly, when he'd walked me to my car. That was all. But it was enough to make me feel like a schoolgirl with my first reciprocated crush.

My cell phone was plugged in on my bedside table, charging. I sat down on my bed and picked it up. It said, "Trace," across the screen, overlaid on a photo I'd taken of her at Disney Land when we'd driven to California on a lark, to celebrate her breakup with the terrible guy she'd dated before Andrew. She looked young in the photo. Thunder Mountain was in the background and she was holding a Mickey Mouse shaped chocolate pop.

I swiped the green phone icon. "Hi, Trace."

There was a long silence on the other end. For a moment, I thought she'd pocket dialed me. Then I heard a long, shuddering sigh. "I got your letter," she said. "And you're right about everything. What are you doing? Could you come over?"

I decided to ride my bike to Trace's. It was far enough that it would be murder in the summer. But today a low bank of clouds had settled around the mountains and the air was almost cool as the day progressed to afternoon. Plus, it would give me time to think, to get my mind out of giddy post-first-kiss territory and into the zone where I could repair things with Trace and learn to be interested in Olivia.

The first part of my route wound along the bike path, going past Julio's and continuing along the wash. I remembered my ride home, weeks ago now, when I'd fantasized about Clint riding his horse up the bank and leaping into the path to accost me. Shivers ran up my arms as the reality of the kiss in the cottonwood grove sank in further.

Clint had kissed me. *Clint*. He'd taken me to his childhood hideout, his most secret place in the world, and he'd kissed me.

I wondered, suddenly, why Clint was single. He wasn't lacking in the looks department. He also wasn't proving to be shy in terms of moving things with me forward. I realized I didn't know a thing about his relationship history. Or even where he lived for that matter. I thought he lived on the ranch. Did that mean he lived with his parents?

I reached the end of the bike path and had to navigate my wending way through an older neighborhood, coasting over speed humps and being barked at by bored dogs in fenced yards. I made a few twists and turns, crossed a large, humming street, and was back on another bike path. This one wound around the perimeter of Trace's subdivision and would take me (albeit indirectly) to her street.

I was only lightly sweat-slicked by the time I stepped off my bike and pushed it to her front door, leaving it leaning against the wall that encircled the back yard. I spent a moment smoothing my hair before I rang the bell.

Trace answered quickly, opening the door and stepping back to let me in. She looked disheveled, her normally perfect hair a bit rumpled. "Olivia's napping," she said. "Let's go sit in the back."

We walked through the house. I had to resist the urge to tip-toe like a cartoon character. In the past, such antics would have made Trace laugh. But now more than ever I was aware we were entering new territory. Our friendship was going to have to evolve if we wanted it to last.

Trace eased open the sliding glass door. We went out back. The yard was mostly dirt, with a few small shrubs that would eventually grow into something resembling landscaping placed strategically along the perimeter. The yard was walled, with six feet of stucco cutting us off from the neighbors. It gave me a claustrophobic feeling. I situated myself so I had a view of the mountains as Trace set her iPad down on the little table between us. On it was a black and white image of Olivia sleeping in a crib. I pointed, amazed. "Is that live?"

Trace nodded, but she seemed distracted. She was picking at her cuticles—something she hadn't done since we were sophomores in high school and she'd been going through her parents' divorce. I got a prickly sensation on my neck of a very different sort than the one I'd felt before Clint had kissed me. I tried to look her in the eye, but she kept her gaze down. "Trace," I said. "Are you all right?"

"I think I need to divorce Andrew." It came out in the barest hint of a whisper.

I leaned forward, not sure I'd heard her correctly. "Say that again?"

She shook her head, as if once had been all she could manage. It hung there in the air for a moment. I felt tired. Here I'd had hopes of telling Trace about my day with Clint.

I felt guilty for even thinking such a thing. I kept my eyes on Trace's downcast profile, intent on rising to the occasion. "What makes you say that?"

Trace contorted herself so she could fish a tissue out of her jeans pocket. She dabbed at her eyes. "He just...." She stopped, chin trembling.

I waited for her to go. She did not. "But you love Andrew," I said. I could well remember their giddy courtship, how happy he'd made her.

She shook her head. "I loved the Andrew I married. Now...." She broke off again.

I waited. I could hear the sound of young voices calling and the happy cries of playing children far enough away to not be irritating. Trace took another shuddering breath. "What you said in the letter, about not making an effort to get to know Olivia, about thinking of her only in terms of how she changed things between us." She paused, dabbing at her eyes again. "That's exactly how Andrew seems to think of her, too. It's like he resents her because she takes so much of my time."

I reflected that letters are not an ideal means of communication. It is so easy to sit alone at one's desk and examine one's soul, to reflect honestly and openly on your relationship with a person and write it all down. It's quite different to realize the person you were thinking of in the abstract has actually read what you wrote, absorbed it, and can now repeat it back to you.

"That doesn't sound like a great quality in a father." I noticed a black smudge of chain grease on my calf. I tried to rub it off without success. "But does that mean you need a divorce? Wouldn't it make sense to try to fix things first?"

"I have been trying to fix things," Trace said, her voice gaining some volume. "He's never home. And when he is, he won't talk to me. I think he might be having an affair."

I sat back, stunned. Trace and Andrew were a *good* couple—one of those rare pairs everyone agrees is a perfect match. They had been one of my bastions of hope, one example that kept me believing people could find suitable partners in real life. I didn't want this to be true.

"Okay," I said, trying to regain some control of the situation. "It seems to me we have two distinct problems here. First, Andrew's relationship with Olivia. Second, his relationship with you. Granted," I said as I saw Trace preparing to argue, "they are connected. But I think it's worth thinking of them separately."

Trace rubbed her eyes in a weary way that made me think the "logical discussion" approach was not what she needed right now. "I was actually wondering if you could talk to him for me."

I stared at her. "Talk to him? Me?"

"Yeah." Trace looked up. Her eyes were red-rimmed and tired. "You both like beer. He has that microbrewery where he hangs out practically every night after work. Maybe you could meet him there, try to get some idea of what's up with him. Would you do that for me, Erin?"

I looked away, gazing blankly at one of the stunted shrubs in the corner of the yard. I felt increasingly that in spite of the fact that I was ostensibly an adult, my life felt less and less under my own control. "Of course, Trace. I'll go today."

Chapter 9

"Hi, Erin."

I looked up from the Kindle app on my phone to see Andrew standing next to my table, a pint in one hand and a pained expression on his face. I made a gesture to indicate he should sit down, and put my phone away.

I'd been sitting alone, nursing a pint for about half an hour. Being alone hadn't bothered me for once. It was preferable to the alternative in this particular circumstance.

I was not thrilled at the prospect of talking to Andrew about his relationship with Trace, and he looked about as happy as I felt. Behind him I could see a table full of other guys about Andrew's age, some of whom were craning their necks in my direction, as if trying to catch a glimpse of an elusive animal through the bars at the zoo.

Andrew sat and took a sip of his beer. It was something dark and malty. He seemed to look at everything in the room but me. I could hardly blame him.

I'd always liked Andrew. He was pale skinned, with reddish hair and a slight build. But he spent enough time in the gym to have broad shoulders and contoured forearms. Usually he was quick to smile, friendly, and engaging. I'd heard from Trace that he was good at his job, managing to motivate and inspire the team of designers and programmers whose work he oversaw.

Today, he looked at a loss for words for the first time I could recall. That was bad, because I was not known for my skills navigating awkward conversations. He cleared his throat. For a moment I thought he would say something. But he took another sip of beer and lapsed back into silence.

"How's it going?" I managed, realizing even a difficult conversation can start with pleasantries.

"Fine," Andrew said, grasping at my lame attempt at conversation like a drowning man clings to a water-soaked log. "How've you been? Seems like I haven't seen you in a while."

"Seems like you haven't seen much of anyone outside of work in a while." This answer shot back before I could consider the pros and cons of straying from niceties to the actual meat of the issue.

Andrew looked startled. He rotated his pint glass between his palms. "The workload at a startup can be overwhelming."

"But you have a lot of time to hang out here." Even as I spoke, I realized I was likely approaching this from the wrong angle. Getting people defensive was rarely a good way to encourage them to spill their guts.

Sure enough, Andrew's face hardened. He looked directly at me for the first time all day. "What is it, precisely, that you're here to say, Erin?"

I realized Trace must have phrased her texts to make him think this was *my* idea. I was willing to do a lot for a friend, but letting her husband think I was proactively interfering in her marriage was not on that list.

I backpedaled, trying to rewind, to start this the right way. "Look, Andrew. I'm sorry. Trace asked me to talk to you. She...." I paused. Andrew's friends had stopped looking over at us and the place was quiet otherwise. I leaned forward and said in a low voice, "She thinks you're having an affair and she might need to divorce you."

Andrew rocked back in his chair as if I'd dropped a pipe bomb in his lap. His blue eyes were wide and bright and startled. "What?" His voice came out in a desperate hiss. "What? How could she?" He made a desperate gesture with his hand as if to somehow summarize everything he couldn't put into words. He swallowed and rubbed his forehead, keeping his eyes closed for a moment.

"She says you're not the man she married." I decided since I was dropping bombs, I might as well empty my arsenal and get it over with.

He said something from behind his hands, too muffled to make out.

"Sorry?" I said.

He sat up a little straighter and let his hands fall to the table. "I said, she's not the woman I married either."

I looked at Andrew. He seemed to be vacillating between annoyance and exhaustion. I wondered how good an actor he was. I'd never pegged him as someone practiced in deceit. But you never knew with people. Still, if he was having an affair, he was handling my accusations like a pro.

"Trace says you don't show any interest in Olivia, that you...."

The look on Andrew's face stopped me in midsentence. He had leaned forward. For the first time all day, he looked furious. "Don't show any interest? Don't show any interest?" His voice had risen a notch. He made a visible effort to bring it back down. "Erin, you've seen her. She's insane. If I even try to hold my own kid, she's standing there right over my shoulder, hovering like I'm going to just forget that a baby is a living creature and set her down on the table and walk away. I can't get near Olivia without being spied on and micromanaged. I tried to change her diaper once. Trace redid the entire thing because I did up the little sticky tab thingies in the wrong order. The wrong order!" He let out a sort of groan and dropped his face into his hands again. I sat in silence, too surprised to talk, processing this new information. "Do you know," Andrew said after a minute, "she sets an alarm to wake her up every hour, all night, so she can go check on Olivia? And usually Olivia is sleeping fine. And half an hour later, Olivia does wake up and starts to cry. Trace goes to her, of course. I don't know if she's gotten more than an hour of consecutive sleep since Olivia was born."

"Wow." I took a sip of my beer. It was cold, the flavor sharp.

Andrew was rolling now. He also sipped his beer, and continued. "You know why I've been working so late? It's because I stay after to nap. I'm so exhausted, and I know I won't get any sleep at home. I literally have a sleeping bag in my office. I go in early and sleep for an hour, then stay late and try for another nap. Then I come here because I know as soon as I go home, Trace is going to be watching me like a hawk, waiting for me to go near Olivia so she can criticize the expression on my face when I look at her."

A couple walked into the bar, the man setting his hand on the small of the woman's back as he followed her between the tables. She looked over her shoulder and gave him a quick smile. I could remember when Trace and Andrew had been that happy.

"Andrew," I said, thinking. "Everything you've said, that's all pretty weird? Extreme behavior, I'd say. Wouldn't you?"

Andrew shrugged. His anger had faded. I could see the fatigue lines etched around his eyes and mouth. "I've never been around a mom with a newborn before. I don't really know what's normal."

I reached back into my purse for my phone. "No," I said. "This isn't normal. I think something is wrong."

"Have you ever heard of postpartum depression?"

I was in the kitchen at my parents' house. It was Wednesday night, and I had invited myself over to cook for my mom. She was sitting at the kitchen counter, flipping through a book on dog training.

She looked up when I asked this question, peering at me over her reading glasses. "Of course, I've heard of it. I had it."

"Oh." I paused in the act of chopping an onion. Given that my mother had only had one child, there was no mystery as to who had been the cause of her downswing. "Sorry about that."

My mom made a little scoffing sound. "It wasn't your fault. You were just a baby."

I set the chopped onion aside and started on the red pepper, enjoying the sharp edge on my dad's good chef's knife. I knew I'd been an unwanted child. In my new quest to educate myself about postpartum depression, I had read that unplanned pregnancies were more likely to trigger the disorder, which made sense for all sorts of reasons. "Well, I think Trace has it."

My mother marked her page and let the book close, but made no comment.

I went on. "Andrew and I had a long talk the other day. Trace is overprotective and paranoid and has hardly left the house since Olivia was born. She's fired dozens of babysitters, sets an alarm at night to wake up every hour to check on Olivia, won't let Andrew do anything to help, and then gets mad at him for not helping."

"Sounds like an extreme case. How old is Olivia now?" My mom picked a few pistachios from the mixed nuts, eating them one by one. My father hated it when she did this. He was a "eat a whole handful" kind of guy. But he wasn't there to chide her.

"Nine months." I dropped the onions and peppers into a skillet and began slivering mushrooms.

Mom looked up, startled. "That's old. My depression only lasted a few weeks. Trace needs to get some treatment."

I paused as a piece of mushroom escaped the cutting board and fell to the floor. A month ago, it would have been immediately devoured by a white, four-legged garbage disposal. But Boswell and Norman had lost kitchen privileges. They no longer walked past the stools where my mom sat. They were currently curled up by her legs, not showing any interest in what I might be doing in the kitchen. I stooped to retrieve the errant fungi and tossed it into the sink.

"I know," I said. "Tomorrow, Andrew and I are going to talk to her, stage an intervention, try to convince her she needs help. The problem is, she thinks it's everyone else who has the problem."

My mom ate another pistachio. "Most depressed people do." She was quiet for a moment. The kitchen was still except for the clicking of the oven heating up. "Maybe we should have them over for dinner," she said. "All three of them. I haven't seen Trace in a while. I think one of the biggest helps with postpartum depression is just getting out of the house."

I looked over at my mom. Usually, she was the one who preferred to stay in, to slip off to her studio, to avoid people and social situations. She really must be missing my dad.

"Sounds great," I said.

I ducked my way past a couple waiting by the server's podium and peered into the dining room, moving forward with some trepidation when I saw Ben seated at a small table by the window. He saw me coming, and stood to wait for me. When I was only a few steps away, he said, "Erin." His face was grave. I had the idea he was thinking about a hug. I must have stiffened visibly. He settled for pulling out my chair.

I sat down, trying not to process the fact that Ben looked good. His golden hair was mussed to perfection. He was dressed a notch up from usual, his striped shirt tucked into a pair of slacks that showed off his hips and had the look of having been custom tailored.

Ben had suggested a five star restaurant for our conversation. I had countered with Julio's. We'd compromised on a little bistro called The Stone Table. It was Friday night, and it was busy enough that most tables were full. I had arrived right on time, but there was already a bread basket and an open bottle of wine on the table.

Ben stood one moment longer, gazing at me like a marooned sailor catching his first sight of land. "It's good to see you. Thank you for letting me talk to you."

I felt a strange twinge of guilt, as if I'd drawn this out on purpose to make him suffer. The truth was, I'd had a lot going on. Not dealing with Ben had been easier than dealing with him. The boots he'd given me were still shoved in the back of my closet. The flowers, I'd left in the gallery, where they were growing less perfect by the day.

I unfolded my napkin and set it in my lap as Ben sat down. He reached across the table to pour me a glass of wine. "I hope everything is okay with you? With your family?" His cufflink glittered in the light from a candle set above us in a sconce on the wall. I was wearing a somewhat worn pair of chinos and a plain top. I felt underdressed.

"Look, Ben, I appreciate all this," I waved a hand to indicate the environment as a whole, "but I'm having trouble understanding how a charming dinner conversation can do anything to ameliorate the fact that you're married and you didn't feel the need to mention this to me before we started doing things like going out on dates and sleeping together."

Ben's smile faded. He set the bottle back on the table. The server appeared then, and asked if we would like an appetizer. I shook my head, but Ben ordered the baked brie. I consoled myself with the knowledge that I had the right to be unimpressed with his explanation. I could storm out at any time.

"Okay," Ben said when the server left. "I'm so sorry, Erin. You're right. I should have told you. But I didn't at first because..." He paused and took a small, shapely roll from the basket, setting it down on his bread plate. He swallowed, then stalled. "I want to say something up front here. I know I haven't been honest with you, and that's caused problems. So today I'm going to be honest, even if it means I don't come off sounding great all the time."

He looked at me, as if waiting for permission to continue. I gave a small nod and took a sip of wine. It was dark and spicy. I resisted the urge to rotate the bottle around so I could read the label.

Ben gave a short sigh and tore his bread into bite-sized pieces, leaving them on his plate. Steam from the still-warm interior drifted up, scenting the air with a sweet, crisp smell. "Okay," he said. "I didn't tell you about Kim at first because it seemed like too much information. I wasn't looking for anything serious. I wanted to get out a little, get my head around the idea of being single again."

"Single?" I paused in the act of reaching for my own loaf.

Ben looked across the table more intently. "Yes, single. You didn't think we're still together, did you? We filed for divorce months ago."

I felt as if someone had placed a cold, heavy stone in my stomach. I picked up a piece of bread and broke it open with my knife. I reminded myself that people can lie, that Ben had possibly lied to me before, and that he could be lying to me again right now. "But you're still living with her?"

Ben's expression was somewhere between defeated and pleading. "It's the house. We're underwater. Kim is," he stopped, his poise leaving him for a moment. He rubbed his forehead with his hands. "She's unemployed."

"Uh huh." I did my best to inject these two syllables with a healthy dose of sarcasm.

Without a word, Ben leaned down and reached into a slim briefcase I hadn't noticed sitting by the foot of his chair. He pulled out two official-looking documents. They both bore seals and an array of signatures. He set these on the table, scooting the butter dish and wine bottle to one side to make room. With some reluctance, I looked down. One paper said, "Application for Divorce." The date on that was from late June. The other said, "Divorce Decree" at the top, and printed on the lines underneath their signatures were Ben and Kim's names. The date was from Monday—the day he'd dropped off the flowers.

I licked my lips, my feeling of having the higher moral ground fading.

Ben picked the papers up again, tucked them back into his briefcase, and moved the butter dish and wine back into the gap. He went on. "After what happened with you, I realized we'd both been dragging our heels on hammering out the particulars of our separation. She's moved out. The divorce is finalized. We still have to sell the house, but we agreed we can't wait any longer in terms of moving forward with our lives."

He said these last two sentences softly. I remembered what Anne had said a few days ago, about how there could be an explanation that would make his behavior acceptable. I felt myself slipping dangerously off my conviction that Ben was a total sleaze-ball. I ate a piece of my bread. The butter was sweet and creamy and the bread was warm, but I hardly tasted it.

"We'd agreed to see other people. She knew about you." He gave a big sigh, running his hands through his hair. "I didn't know how to tell you about her. Every time I saw you, I told myself I would. But I was so afraid...."

He broke off as the server appeared with the baked brie and more bread, setting the steaming wheel of cheese in the center of the table. He asked about entrees. I said I would be sticking with wine and appetizers. A little grimace crossed Ben's face, but he didn't protest. The server withdrew.

Ben sat up straighter, gazing at me until I grudgingly met his eyes. He picked up where he'd left off. "I was so afraid *this* would happen."

I ducked my head and attacked the cheese, less out of desire to eat it than a need to look at something other than Ben. Disjointed thoughts were chasing each other around my head like hamsters on a sugar rush. I smeared brie on a baked sliver of bread, then set it on my plate.

"Erin." Ben's voice had a plaintive quality. "Say something."

I realized I'd uttered less than three complete sentences since I'd arrived. I nearly apologized. But I stopped myself. I was not the one with things to apologize for. I reminded myself of this while trying to think of some response that wouldn't absolve him. I settled on, "It's a lot to take in."

Ben made no reply. We were silent for a minute or two, sipping wine and eating cheese. The brie was excellent, as was the wine. I felt myself relaxing by degrees in spite of myself.

"You know," Ben said, sitting back in his chair and swirling his wine in his glass, looking off across the restaurant. "When I met you I thought you were cute and fun—someone who would be really great to hang out with for a while." He shook his head as if to indicate the unmeasurable folly of this previous version of himself. "But the more I got to know you, the more that changed." He trailed off and looked up at me. His bright eyes held mine for a moment. I felt a little rush of something—surprise and discomfort—force heat to my cheeks. "I fell for you, Erin. I never felt that with Kim." He dropped his eyes to the table and fiddled with the brie knife. "We had a scare, early on. We'd only been seeing each other a short while. She thought there was going to be a baby. She wanted to keep it. I didn't want to try to change her mind. So, I proposed. We went down to the courthouse the next day."

There was a long silence. I felt I had reached some sort of capacity and had stalled. My processor was overloaded. I would not be able to respond to anything more Ben said tonight. Around us, the room was filled with the quiet murmur of conversation overlaid by the clinking of silverware and a tasteful light-jazzy Parisian soundtrack low enough to soften the other sounds without interfering with intimate conversation.

Ben continued. "The pregnancy ended itself naturally in the first trimester." He was quiet for a moment, still staring at the table. His voice was low when he added, "I'm told that's common."

It was once again my turn to say something. I knew there were all sorts of sensitive, appropriate ways to acknowledge the fact Ben had just told me about a life-changing series of tragic events. "I'm sorry," I managed. "How did you and Kim meet?"

"That's how this gets even worse." He took in a deep, slow breath, as if preparing to dive down and pick something heavy up off the bottom of a pool. "We were coworkers. We'd been friends for years. We both went through bad breakups at the same time. We thought we'd have a casual fling, that it would be fun. But then there was the baby thing, and suddenly we were married. It seemed we should at least try to make it work. We bought a house and moved in together and, you know, it was okay for a while. Good, even."

The server came by and refilled our wine glasses. The wine was starting to win out over the circumstances. I was finding my mindset shifting from defensive and righteous to sympathetic and interested.

"So then something happened at work. Something bad, and it was my fault. We were in different departments, but I was the senior of the two of us and had a much better salary, not to mention opportunity for advancement. Before I could do or say anything, Kim fudged the records and took the blame. She made it look like it had been her fault. She resigned as a result of the mistake. She did this so I could keep my job. I love my work, but she'd never been all that happy at our company. So it made sense to her." Ben pushed his cheese plate away, as if its contents had become too rich for him. "I never would have let her do that for me if she'd have asked. Ever since, it's left me feeling responsible."

I thought of the Kim I had met—the electric blue nails, the top-heavy, tanned figure. She hadn't struck me as the sort of person capable of that kind of selflessness. I nodded to show Ben I was following his story.

"That was three years ago. She's been unemployed ever since. At first she job-hunted a little. But the economy is bad. She took a break, which turned into a really long break. Our relationship went from fine to kind-of-bad by degrees. I wanted out, but, well, how could I kick her to the curb? She was married to someone she didn't love, she'd had a shot-gun wedding, and she'd lost her job, all because of me." Ben kept his eyes downcast as he delivered this list of his sins, like I was a holy person capable of handing out absolutions.

I was experiencing an unpleasant sense of vertigo—a shifting of the foundations upon which I had built several assumptions that had been shaping my recent life. If Ben's story was true, he was not only a decent guy, but an *extra* decent guy. If I wasn't careful, I was going to agree to start seeing him again. But that couldn't happen because of Clint. Clint had taken me out to his childhood hangout. We'd ridden there on horseback, and he'd kissed me. It had been an amazing kiss, a kiss of the kind that can send sparks shooting down your spine just remembering it three days later.

But Clint hadn't *said* anything. I didn't know *why* he'd kissed me. Maybe Clint was a casual kisser? Maybe it meant nothing at all? And here was Ben, pouring his heart out to me, telling me he'd made all these changes in his life, just so he could be eligible. For me.

"I need to go." This burst out of me of its own accord as my thoughts wound themselves around each other, colliding and ricocheting until I felt a sudden, intense need to no longer be in this cozy restaurant. I rose, pushing back my chair so quickly it scraped and wobbled.

Ben sat up straight, looking alarmed. "Are you okay?"

"It's just ... I need some time to think about this, to take it all in."

Ben rose too, signaling the server. "Let me walk you to your car."

We stepped out the front doors of The Stone Table a few minutes later. The cool, dark night was a relief. The breeze stirred the hair at the nape of my neck. Downtown was alive. Trucks cruised by with their windows down, country music blaring, then fading as they moved on.

I took a few deep breaths, trying to calm myself down. Ben didn't know about Clint, I reminded myself. He wasn't trying to be impossible. He was doing what any reasonable person would do in the same circumstances. "Where did you park?" Ben was glancing around the small wedge of a parking lot for my Hyundai.

I felt a twinge of embarrassment as I remembered I'd parked several blocks away because I'd been early and I hadn't wanted to be the one to get there first. "Um, over near Maloney's."

Ben gave a sad little smile, as if he'd been reminded of some dear friend from his childhood. "Because you were early?"

I nodded. For a second he looked like he was going to do something like lean forward and kiss me. I turned and started walking. He fell in step beside me, closer than I would have liked.

We walked in silence for a while. The doors of restaurants and bars opened as we passed, spilling light and noise outside for a moment, then falling closed, leaving the street seeming darker and emptier.

We reached the end of the block, and turned left. Up the street I could see my car, tucked in against the curb. The sight of it relieved me somehow. *Almost there.*

I stopped as soon as I reached the trunk, turning to look at Ben. "Thank you for your honesty," I said, trying to sound sincere. And suddenly, I realized it would be cruel to leave him hanging any longer, to do anything other than cut him loose now. I had to tell him about Clint. "There are some things I need to tell you, too."

Ben reached down and took one of my hands in both of his. I had to resist the urge to snatch it from him. "It's okay, Erin," he said. "I understand how overwhelming this must be. I can look back and see how it must have felt to you, like you never really knew me. It seemed to me that if I didn't tell you anything about my life, I wouldn't be lying."

I struggled not to be diverted. I had to tell him about Clint. Now. "Yes, but...."

Ben leaned forward and gave me one slow, tender kiss on the lips, withdrawing before I could pull away or protest. He shook his head and gave my hand a squeeze. "Let's leave things where they are. You think about everything. Take your time. I understand that if you give me another chance, it will be a step backwards." He stopped, eyes leaving my face and shifting to the street behind me. His eyebrows creased.

"What?" I said, trying to turn. But he was still holding my hand.

"Nothing," he said. "It looked like one of those girls was going to call to you. But she must have thought you were someone else. They're moving on."

I tugged on my hand. Ben released it with obvious reluctance. I turned around. The opposite sidewalk was full of groups heading to Maloney's. One was a cluster of six or seven girls, all dressed in tight jeans or short skirts, clutching tiny purses and looking precarious on their tall heels. They were a little distance away, bathed in the garish red light from the Maloney's sign. From the jumble of their backs, I couldn't pick out anyone familiar. I turned back around.

Ben said, "I appreciate that you gave me this chance and heard me out. I know I may have done something irreparable."

As he said this, it struck me as the sort of thing someone says when they're certain you'll forgive them. I looked up at him. I was going to say something a little cutting. But his expression was so hopeful, the sharp words died on my lips.

"You know when I really fell for you?" His voice was tender and smooth. I could smell his aftershave. He was standing very close again.

I shook my head, feeling claustrophobic. I took a tiny step back. My calves bumped into my Hyundai.

"It was the night by the bike rack," he said. "When you kissed me that night, it was something else. Something special. No one, ever, in my whole life, made me feel the way you did that night."

I felt sick. Physically ill.

Ben misread my expression. He took a step back, giving a short nod as if making an agreement with himself. "Okay, I'll give you some time and space. I promise. I'll wait to hear from you." He hovered there for a moment, his hair extra golden in the yellow glow of the streetlights. He looked like he wanted to touch me again, but thought better of it. "See you soon, I hope." Then he turned and walked away, his excellent figure making a strong silhouette against the street.

"Post-partum depression?" Trace said the words in a dull tone, as if reading a particularly uninteresting headline in the paper. She shook her head. "No," she said. "I love Olivia." She reached out to give her daughter a little pat on the back.

It was Saturday afternoon, and I was at Trace and Andrew's house. Trace was on the floor next to the colorful blanket laid out for Olivia, who was sitting there in a pink onesie, flinging her toys off the blanket and watching her mother retrieve them.

Andrew was seated on the couch behind them, looking tired. I was in the armchair on the other side of the room.

I waited to see if Andrew would say something. He did not. Apparently, I was going to have to do the majority of the intervening. "Post-partum depression doesn't always have as much to do with how you feel about your baby as how you feel about the rest of your life."

This seemed to penetrate a little. Trace cast a guilty look in Andrew's direction.

Olivia flung a toy that rattled when it hit the ground. She released a sharp, high sound that I recognized a moment later as laughter.

Trace looked back at Olivia, retrieved the toy, and we all sat in awkward silence for a moment.

This was stage two of the intervention. Stage one had happened this morning. I'd come by before work and told Trace that I'd spoken to Andrew, he was most definitely not having an affair, and that the two of us wanted to talk to her together that afternoon. Then I'd gone and done my Saturday half-shift at the gallery. Now I was back, this time with Andrew in attendance. We were trying to convince Trace she needed help.

After my night with Ben, I'd driven home in a sort of numb state, crashed into bed and slept until my alarm had pulled me out of the sheets. Since then it had been Trace and work and Trace again. My head was starting to feel like some sort of compression chamber, filled way past capacity with things that needed my time and attention. But instead of taking them out and airing them, I kept pushing more in on top.

I kept talking. "The more I've read about it, the more I think you're manifesting a lot of the symptoms. It's the kind of thing that's hard to recognize and cope with alone, but it's treatable. All you need is a little help."

I said this last bit delicately. Trace had always prided herself on her strength of character. I was afraid she was going to react to this nudge with a violent denial that she had any kind of problem.

Instead, she said nothing. Olivia threw the toy again, laughing as it rattled. Trace retrieved it and dropped it back into her daughter's lap.

Andrew spoke. His tone was halting, as if he was picking every word off an approved list before incorporating it into his sentence. "I searched for someone who specializes in mental health for families. I made us an appointment for this afternoon."

"Us?" Trace turned to look at Andrew, her face going a little hard.

"All three of us," Andrew said. "If you'll go with me, that is. If not, Olivia and I can go without you."

I sat forward, alarmed. This was not a tactic we'd discussed.

Trace stiffened too, her spine going poker rigid. "You can't just take her." Her tone had gone from disinterested to combative in half a heartbeat. I resisted the urge to groan and drop my head into my hands.

But Andrew responded in a tone that was both gentle and firm. "She's my daughter too, Trace."

That was all he said, but the statement seemed to fill the room with a tense sort of expectant energy.

Olivia threw her toy. It rattled across the floor, and lay still.

Trace was staring at Andrew as if he'd sprouted cloven hooves and horns. "But you don't...." She broke off, glancing at the toy, her voice seeming to fail her.

Olivia laughed, and clapped her hands.

"I don't what?" Andrew said. His tone was still gentle. "Don't know how to put a child in a car seat? Don't know how to change a diaper? You didn't know any of those things nine months ago, either, remember? There are men a lot less competent than me taking care of their own children."

Trace slumped, her body language defeated. "Okay," she said, her voice barely above a whisper. "We'll all go."

As Trace leaned forward and reached for the rattling toy, Andrew caught my eye and gave me grim smile.

I inhaled the smell of hay, smiling at the sound of Nora's voice drifting in from the aisle between the stalls. She had a tendency to chat with the horses she was tacking and grooming when no one else was around.

It was a fine, cool morning. The sun had yet to spill over the mountains, and the Tipped Z was quiet. Only one dog had appeared to watch me as I stepped out of my car. Dots was not in evidence. While this was disappointing, at least it made me a lot less jittery as I walked past the hay and into the aisle, stopping next to Paul to pat him on the shoulder.

"Hey, girl." Nora was just straightening from picking Sally's feet, her face flushed from bending over. "How was your week?"

I thought back over the recent insanity that had been my life. "Weird." I rubbed at a little patch of dried sweat behind Paul's ear with my thumb. "Weird and busy."

"Oh yeah?" Nora stopped to look at me. There was something in her tone and expression that was a little bit hard. Coming from the sunny, relaxed Nora, this was a definite departure from normal.

Before I could ask her if something was up, there was the clatter of hoofbeats in the yard, and a man's voice gave a shout. Startled, both Nora and I looked towards the bay doors. Two mounted men rode into the hay room at the trot, stirring up a lot of dust before coming to a stop at the mouth of the stall aisle. Though they were backlit, I recognized Clint and his father.

"Nora, we need you." Hank's voice was all business as he stepped down from the back of his horse and tossed his get-down over his horn. "The north bull got himself caught in the fence. We're going to need to get him cut out and doctored." He stopped at the door of the tack room, taking me and the two almost tacked horses in with a sharp glance. "Bring Paul, and reschedule your lesson. This isn't a job for green horses, or people either."

With that, he disappeared into the tack room.

Clint had been riding Rascal. He dismounted as well, walked up to me, and took one of my hands in his. His hand was warm and rough as he looked down at my face. "I'm sorry, Erin," he said. "This wouldn't be safe for you."

"It's okay." I gave a glance over my shoulder at Nora, who was oddly still looking at me and Clint, her expression even flintier than it had been a moment before. I hesitated, feeling there was something happening here that I was missing. "I can put Sally up, if that would help."

Their father reemerged from the tack room, carrying a set of long-handled clippers and a red clinking bag with a white cross screened onto the site. He thrust the bag at Clint, who had to drop my hand to take it. "Let's go, Nora."

Nora unfroze. She hurried to Paul and slipped his bridle on while Clint said, "Sally goes in the south pasture, the one with the blue gate. Thank you, Erin."

He stepped away from me, affixing the red bag to the back of Rascal's saddle. Nora finished with Paul's bridle, moved the coiled rope from Sally's saddle to Paul's, and swung on board. "Sorry," she said in a low voice, then trotted Paul out after Clint and her father, who had already disappeared back into the bright day.

I stood there a moment, alone with Sally, feeling dazed. Even the dogs were gone. The dust the horses had kicked up hung in the air around the hay. I thought of that day I'd watched Clint stacking the bales. It seemed like a long time ago.

I took my time untacking Sally, making sure I got everything tidied the right way and stowed in the right place. Nora's mare led quietly back to the pasture and followed me through the blue gate without protest. After I turned her around and took her halter off, she ambled towards the water trough.

I picked my way back through the yard, scanning the horizon for signs of the three riders as the sun came up to spill down over the broad, scrubby pastures. But all I could see were the blank yellow hills and the blue mountains.

Chapter 10

"I thought we could go for a walk." Trace said this brightly, shortly after letting me into her house. I had followed her from the entryway into the living room, where Olivia was in her playpen, chewing on a plastic cow. It was 5:15 on Monday. I'd just gotten off work. We'd had another big job from the bank, and so I'd been standing all day, framing. My feet were sore. I thought wistfully of Julio's and a cold beer.

"A walk sounds great."

Trace gave me a small, hesitant smile, as if she was relearning how that expression fit on her face. She scooped Olivia up and carried her to the garage while I trailed after. I watched as Trace secured Olivia into her stroller with an elaborate belt-harness mechanism that looked modeled after those used for holding astronauts into their seats through the rocky departure from the earth's atmosphere. Olivia didn't seem to mind the precautions, though, so I made no comment.

Trace packed some things into the zipping pouches on the back of the stroller, and finally began to push the weighted-down thing towards the open garage door. I fell in step next to her as she rolled Olivia out into the sunlight.

It was a fair evening, if a little warm for late September. Trace punched a code into a keypad next to the garage, and the large, beige door slid closed behind us with a dull rumble that ended in a click.

"How was Saturday?" I asked this in a casual tone, half feeling I shouldn't pry but also aware that I had staged an intervention. Along with that came the responsibility to follow up.

We reached the sidewalk, and turned left. Olivia giggled and flapped her hands at a cluster of colorful rings that were attached to the upright post of the stroller. The top was foldable and could be pushed forward to provide sun protection. Right now it was pulled as far forward as possible so Olivia was entirely in the shade, even though the sun was well advanced in its descent towards the horizon, and weak.

Trace looked at me. Her eyes were misty. I felt suddenly afraid she was going to tell me she'd given Andrew the boot, after all. "Erin." Her voice was trembly. "I can't thank you enough. You were exactly right. I had no idea...." She stopped, reaching into one of the zipping compartments at the back of the stroller to pull out a tissue. "Saturday was amazing. It was like Dr. Dresden could read my mind. She knew all these things I'd been thinking, all the inadequacy and fear." Trace drew in a long, shuddering breath. "She helped me talk to Andrew, helped us both understand what I'm feeling and why."

In front of us, two boys on bikes were pedaling up the sidewalk, their knees sticking up comically as they sat on seats far too low for them. As the space between us closed, they left the sidewalk for the road, one of them hopping down the curb, then up again, then back down, standing on his bike and balancing on his two wheels without going forward for a moment. The other boy said something. The two of them pedaled off, laughing.

Trace had been watching this with wide eyes. "I'm so glad I had a girl."

We walked a moment longer. Trace's voice had gained some strength when she continued. "Anyway, I know these things don't change overnight. I know I have a lot of work to do, to repair things with Andrew and learn to relax about Olivia. But knowing that what I'm going through isn't uncommon, that it's a medical condition and it's treatable." She stopped talking again, looking over at me with shining eyes. "It's huge. It makes all the difference, really."

We walked a while longer. For the first time in what felt like ages, it felt comfortable to be with Trace. Olivia was cooing happily in her cushioned seat. Trace's phone was nowhere in evidence. The light was growing richer on the fronts of the houses we passed, the shadows lengthening. We'd have to turn back soon. But for now it felt good to be out walking with a friend. My feet had even stopped hurting.

"So what's new with you?" Trace said.

My phone beeped. Feeling a little sheepish, I pulled it out of my pocket and checked the screen. My heart gave a little lurch when I saw it was from Nora. The first part set my heart to thumping with anticipation, while the second part crushed my hopes flat. "Gotta cover a shift for a friend. Can't make lesson tomorrow. See you Sunday?"

I pulled up to Ben's house, letting my car coast to a stop next to the curb and inevitably thinking of the last time I'd been here. The front of the house looked no different. The garage door was closed and impassive, the gravel of the front neat and freshly raked, free of weeds or the drift of fallen mesquite leaves. I allowed myself a moment to sit in the car and take deep breaths.

Ben had invited me over for dinner, wanting, perhaps, to prove that he now lived alone. I had accepted because I was determined to end things, determined to find a gentle but firm way to explain that I was no longer available and never would be again. The boots were in their box on the back seat of my car, waiting to be returned to their rightful owner.

I sat, listening to the clicking of my car's engine as it started to cool. The street was empty, the sun sliding out of sight behind a house in front of me. Finally, I could put it off no longer. I opened my car door and stepped into the street.

I had made a deliberate effort to dress casually while also doing my best not to look like a slob. The result was a pair of white capris and a green tank top. I'd left my hair back in a ponytail. As I made my way up

Ben's walk I entertained the conviction that he'd be wearing a suit and tie.

As it turned out, he answered the door in only jeans and a t-shirt. His feet were bare. He held a glass of white wine in one hand. The smell of simmering garlic wafted out of the house behind him, and a light indie soundtrack was playing inside.

Ben grinned, looking magazine-model casual. He stepped aside to gesture me into the house. "Hi, Erin." His tone was relaxed. I realized with a little stutter-skip of my heart that he thought we were all better—that things were repaired between us.

"Come on in." Ben led the way across the tile floor of the entryway back towards the kitchen. I took in the granite counter-tops and the high-ceilings, the well-stocked bar along the far wall. Ben's house was massive and well turned-out. It was easily larger than my parents'.

I drifted after him. The music moved with me as I walked, pouring out of invisible speakers that must dot the whole house. It was a band I recognized but couldn't place. The lead singer's familiar voice teased the edges of my memory.

Ben went into the kitchen and took a second wine glass down from a cupboard above the stove, holding it up to the light to inspect the shining crystal for dots left by drying water. He polished one spot with a white dish cloth he had draped over his shoulder, poured some wine, quickly stirred a sauce that was bubbling on the stove, and came back to me to hand me my drink. "Make yourself at home," he said, noting my rigid, uncertain posture with a look of concern. "Do you want the grand tour?"

Two glasses of wine later, we were installed at a cozy table set into a sort of nook at the edge of the kitchen. Through the windows, we had a view of a lighted pool glowing a pale, bright blue in the dark outside.

We'd had the grand tour of the house and yard, then we'd returned to the kitchen while Ben had put the final touches on the meal. It had turned out to be a seafood dish over delicate pasta, topped in a light home-made sauce that would have impressed my father. Now our plates were empty, and we were sipping the crisp wine.

I was managing to sit quietly at the table while Ben carried the conversation. Now that the cat was out of the bag, he appeared to want to compensate for never having told me much about his life by telling me everything. He detailed the divorce agreement and the awkwardness of it all. He explained how it felt so horrible because he and Kim had been good friends before they'd started sleeping together. Now with the divorce, things had gone a little sour. He felt bad about how it had ended even though he was happy to be able to move on.

When he delivered this last statement, he looked at me, eyes shining under his shock of blond hair. I couldn't help but think again how incredibly good looking he was even as a voice in my head said, *Do it. Do it now.*

Ben seemed to realize he'd been doing most of the talking. He cleared our plates off the table and took them to the kitchen, returning with the wine bottle. He topped up our glasses, sat back down, and affixed me with his most earnest look. "You've been quiet this evening." His tone was kind and interested.

I looked down at my fingernails. There was a hangnail developing on my ring finger. I resisted the urge to pick. Numerous ways to tell Ben about Clint fluttered around in my mind, bumping into each other like a cluster of awkward moths flapping around a lamp.

"Ben." I paused, half hoping for a phone to beep, the doorbell to ring: anything to save me from having to do this. I looked up and saw him leaning forward, face open and eager. My courage failed. "Thank you for dinner."

Now why had I said that? It implied the exact opposite of what I wanted to communicate.

Ben's perfect smile lit his face. "You're welcome." He reached across the table and took one of my hands. Unlike Clint's, his palm was smooth "Thank you for coming."

I felt too warm. I felt I was in an impossible situation. I wanted to run away. But at the same time, I didn't want that. The wine and dinner and music and sumptuous surroundings had dulled my conviction, leaving me uncertain.

After all, Clint had kissed me. He'd kissed me once on the lips, once on the cheek, and he'd taken my hand in his. That was all. That was all I had from him. What if it meant nothing?

I thought back to that conversation I'd overheard so long ago, the one I'd typed out on my computer and later read to Nora. She'd told me Clint had been talking about his horse.

But what if Nora was wrong? What if there was a side to Clint his sister didn't know about? Clint, as far as I knew, didn't even have my phone number. He'd never asked me out, certainly never cooked for me.

I thought back on the kiss in the cottonwood grove. It had seemed so magical then. Now it felt surreal. Impossible, even.

"Penny for your thoughts?" Ben was still looking at me, his expression soft. I had to hand it to him. He'd been more than patient with me.

For one wild moment, I almost told him. The phrase, "I kissed someone," hovered on my lips. But then I thought how his face would change if I said that. I thought about how cruel life was. Wouldn't breaking things off with Ben be the best possible way to ensure Clint never kissed me again?

"I'm just...." I stopped, fiddling with the base of my wine glass. The top of Ben's table was a deep polished tone, made of small, interlocking pieces of triangular wood that varied slightly in hue. "It's so strange to be in your house, finally."

Ben ducked his head, like a schoolboy reprimanded for squirming. "It's great to have you here."

"So what do you think about this crazy forecast?" Anne wandered into the workroom, cup of coffee in one hand, newspaper in the other. Although she had a smartphone, Anne picked up the paper on her way to work at least twice a week. Now, she set Friday's weather page on the work table, tapping the headline that said, STORM SYSTEM TO CAUSE SEVERE FLOODING.

I looked up from a French mat, to which I was applying a wash, long enough to shrug. "If it's anything like hurricane Nora, we should plan a BBQ."

Hurricane Nora was something I vividly remembered from my childhood. The entire population of southern Arizona had been in a state of near panic for days over a hurricane coupled with an El Nino year. Schools had shut down, flood warnings had been issued. The forecast had included a 100% chance of rain.

Not a drop had fallen.

Anne gave a little laugh and leaned against the table. She was wearing linen pants and a dark brown jacket with half sleeves and a big collar. She looked bright and perky this morning. I wondered what she did most nights. Cook dinner for herself? Go out on hot dates? Read books in the bathtub?

A smile still hovering on her lips, Anne looked at me with a curious expression. "So how are things with you? Have you talked to Ben yet?"

Inking French mats was by far the most technically demanding part of my job. It was an intricate process, done using loose ink and a ruling pen. My first attempts had been so embarrassing I'd destroyed them before Anne could see. But now I was a passable hand at the process.

Still, I felt the need to finish the final line on the mat and set down the ruling pen before answering Anne's question.

Because the trouble was, I'd left Ben's house without breaking up with him. I had, in fact, let myself kiss him for a little while.

At the time, it had seemed like the rational thing to do.

It had happened one slow step at a time. After Ben and I had finished another glass of wine and I'd said I really needed to go, he'd leaned in for a kiss by the door. With my wits softened by the wine, I'd made a split-second decision. I'd decided to kiss Ben without pretending he was Clint, and see how that felt.

It had been purely an act of research: a means of collecting evidence the better to make my final decision.

In truth, the kiss had been very good. But even "very good" had turned out not to hold a candle to kissing Clint. (Or even kissing Ben whilst pretending he was, in fact, Clint.)

Still, it had been nice. I had let it go on for a bit longer than strictly necessary for data collection alone. Finally, I had extricated myself and said goodbye. As soon as I'd gotten into my car and turned on the engine, I'd begun berating myself for my utter failure to do what I had planned.

"I, um ... I actually went over to Ben's last night." I said this in a low voice, squinting down and watching the ink on the mat seep in and stop glistening.

"Did you?" Anne was all interest now.

I summarized what had happened since I'd last filled her in, from Ben's story about his wife, to his bringing his divorce papers to dinner, to me going over to break up with him only to end out in a brief but undeniable make-out session.

By the time I was done, I felt even more horrible than I had when I'd started. Anne, however, was looking nothing if not amused. "I don't know why you look so horrified," she said, picking up my mat and examining the corners where the lines joined. "It sounds like the ideal outcome. Nice job on this, by the way."

I put the lid back on the ink and cleaned the ruling pen, my ears so hot they felt like they were going to start smoking. "Except I kissed Clint too."

Anne set the mat down again, looking shocked. "Last night?"

I placed the French mat tools back inside the old shoebox where they lived and stowed this on the shelf behind me. "What? No! Of course not. A week ago Tuesday."

"And?" Anne brushed a few dried clumps of ink off the work table, swiping them into her hand and carrying them to the trash can.

"And what?"

Anne stopped in front of the window, her expression exasperated. "And then what happened?"

So I told Anne all about Clint, too, and added almost in spite of myself that last Tuesday was the first time he hadn't taught my lesson in over a month. As I said this, I felt my stomach sink at the thought that since the kiss, I'd hardly seen or spoken to him.

Anne was quiet a moment when I finished, her expression thoughtful. She'd walked to the wooden chair in the corner and was leaning against the back, gaze directed at the window. "So to sum up," she said. "Ben is an attractive, decent guy who makes good money and is really into you. He'd commit in a heartbeat if you let him. Clint is an unknown quantity with communication issues. He lives with his parents, and he may or may not have any intention of getting serious."

My skin prickled as the truth of this summary impressed itself upon me. I felt restless. I pulled a piece of tape off the roll we kept affixed to the table and taped over a small tear in the brown paper covering my work area. "I guess that about sums it up." I was able to keep my voice from wavering.

"My advice," Anne said, leaving the chair to step towards the door, "don't cut Ben loose until you're sure of Clint. Be sure he wants you, and be sure you want him. And take this from an old pro: wanting him to want you only goes so far."

With that, she strolled out, leaving me to chew on my problems and wait for my mat to dry.

I looked at the clock on my dashboard before killing the engine. 6:30, on the dot. We had moved my lesson start time back an hour, due to the sunrise getting later.

I had parked next to Nora's truck. I now stepped out of my car. It was a cloudy morning, and dim, the first of the forecasted storm clouds beginning to pile up on the horizon. It was Sunday, and I didn't know what Nora had in mind for my lesson.

I'd spent Friday evening and Saturday studiously trying not to think about Ben. I'd decided, more than anything, I needed to see Clint again. Ben's position was clear.

I looked around the quiet barnyard as I moved away from my car. When I was still a few steps from the barn, Dots appeared, her brindled face and shoulders just visible inside the open door. She looked out at me with interest, ears perked.

The mere sight of her sent a searing stab of anticipation through my nervous system. My heart clenched, then started beating at twice its usual rate.

Dots meant Clint.

I stepped into the barn and knelt next to the small dog to run my hand down her back. She gave me a wag of her tail and looked over her shoulder as if to indicate I should follow her gaze.

I straightened, and saw him.

Clint was standing in the middle of the hay room, utterly still, and looking in my direction. He was carrying a bridle in one hand. His aspect was startled, as if my appearance had taken him by surprise.

I was about to say hi, to walk up to him, maybe even do something incredibly bold like kiss him on the cheek.

Then I noticed his face. His expression stopped me cold.

His eyes had a stony look to them, overlaid with something close to pain.

I took a step in his direction. Something hung on the air between us, something bad. I scrambled to understand this change. The last time I'd seen Clint he'd been holding my hand and smiling.

Could he possibly know what had happened with Ben? Could he be so perceptive that he'd picked up on it like a mind reader?

No. That was impossible. I tried to reassure myself I was imagining things. I took another step forward and said, "Hi, Clint." My voice sounded small in the huge room.

Clint turned away from me, rotating on one heel like a cutting horse. He gave a short whistle. Dots sprang after him with one backwards glance in my direction, her expression almost apologetic.

Shaken, I stared at Clint's receding back until he'd disappeared. A moment later, I saw him pass by in front of the open bay doors, riding off towards the hills on Rascal. A moment after that, Nora appeared, leading Paul and Sally. She saw me, grinned, and launched into the tale of the work drama that had had her working more hours than usual lately.

I drifted after as she walked into the stall aisle, glad her exuberance made any response from me unnecessary. Only half listening, I watched as she tied a deft release knot to secure each horse. Sally and Paul stood side by side, ears drooping, giving off no indication they would be inclined to go anywhere even if they hadn't been tied.

Nora went into the tack room and came back with the grooming tote. She handed me a curry. "We've got a special job to do today."

I moved to Paul's shoulder. I worked the brush over his short coat in smooth arcs. I thought of the day Clint had watched me tack Duke and felt another surge of hot confusion over the scene that had just played out. I'd never seen Clint be rude to anyone. There was no way he could have overlooked me or not heard when I'd said hello. I tried to tell myself there could be an explanation. Maybe he'd been in a really big hurry?

But even as I tried to convince myself this was the case, I knew it wasn't true. Clint was a man of few words, but his body language was anything but opaque. Something had changed between us. Something fundamental in the way he thought about me had undergone a shift. And not in a direction that made me happy.

Nora gave me a quizzical look from her position at Sally's flank. I made an effort to uphold my end of the conversation. "What's that?"

"We need to bring in the team."

"The team?" I said this with a great deal of uncertainty. For some reason, all I could picture was a squad of cheerleaders in frilled skirts and sleeveless tops with the Tipped Z brand emblazoned across their chests.

"Yep. It's this doozy of a storm system. When things get flooded, the four-wheelers turn useless. If a fence goes down, or you got to haul hay, or do anything else that amounts to moving heavy stuff over a long distance in a raging monsoon, no machine we have is going to cut it. So we've got a couple harness broke Shire crosses that were bred to be bucking horses but didn't have the temperament. Mostly they hang out with the east herd. But Dad wants them up here closer tonight in case he needs them. You ever ponied one before?"

I had, in fact, never ponied before. Although Nora assured me there was nothing to it, I spent most of the long ride out to the east pasture worrying about what was going to happen on the way back. For one thing, I didn't know what a Shire cross would look like. For another, I had not realized people bred horses just to be buckers. In my hazy approximation of how things went at rodeos, I'd assumed the horses in the bronc riding displays were rogue creatures that, having proven themselves unwilling to carry a rider, were induced to buck through goads and pinching straps. I hadn't put much thought into how they were moved around or maneuvered into the chute in the first place. But I'd figured if they did it with bulls, a half-wild horse couldn't be much harder to handle.

But as we rode out into the desert under the threatening sky, I learned this was not the case. Nora told me that bucking horse lines were bred and nurtured as carefully as racehorse stock, trained to buck from a young age, and guided through their careers by owners who had every reason to want them to live long, useful lives. As we trotted out through the pasture, she told me all about the ranch where they'd gotten their team and how the stud there had earned hundreds of thousands of dollars and won title after title in his prime. Now he was retired and, as Nora put it, "Docile as a kitten unless you got on his back."

Initially, Nora's tale had been little more than a welcome distraction from the sting of Clint's brush-off. But by the time we topped a low ridge and looked down to see a small cluster of horses below, I was curious to meet the team.

The east herd was a small group of horses that were in various states of retirement or recovery. A handful were bridle horses too old to continue to work. A few were mares who'd had complications during their last pregnancies and were getting a year or two away from the stud.

As the sound of our horses' footfalls reached the herd, a number of heads popped up, one of which had massive, fuzzy ears. I stared for a moment. "Is that a donkey?"

"That's Zeke." Nora seemed utterly nonplussed. "He's a guard donkey."

Before I could figure out whether or not she was joking, she moved Sally down to a walk and said, "Now don't stare too hard. These guys kind of do their own thing out here. We'll circle around the side and try not to get them to feel like we want them to go anywhere. But if they do move, we want them to move towards the ranch, not away. We'll see how they're all feeling. If they're too fresh we might have to bring the herd in. But a lot of times they're in a friendly state of mind and you can just ride in and halter whoever you want."

I dropped my eyes from the spectacle of the shaggy-headed donkey among the sleek, round contours of the Quarter Horses. We circled the herd. While a couple of them kept their eyes on us with evident uncertainty, most of them went back to nibbling at the brush and undergrowth.

"Okay," Nora said. "Untie your halter and we'll ride into the herd and fetch the two we want. These guys are easy to halter from horseback because they're so tall." She gave a quick laugh.

My mouth was strangely dry as I did what I was told. I fumbled with the rope halter Nora had secured behind my cantle. I eyed Nora, at an utter loss for understanding how she intended to ride one horse while haltering another. She caught my look, then looked judiciously back at the watchful herd. "Actually," she said, "it'll be simpler if just one of us goes in. Will you pass me that halter?"

I passed over the halter and watched as Nora rode off on Sally. Feeling a mix of relief and embarrassment, I gave Paul a pat on the shoulder.

There was no question as to which two horses Nora was after. The bulk of the herd was made of typical Quarter Horses in their standard array of browns and reds. Then there was the donkey, who watched Nora with his massive ears held straight and stiff. And then there were the bucking horses.

They were both black, with broad white faces, tall socks, and a small number of random white markings on haunch and belly. One of them had a single blue eye and a bit of white in his tail. They were impressive physical specimens, both easily a hand taller than the rest of the herd, with well-muscled chests, large feet, and long, shaggy manes.

Nora and Sally slipped into the herd like a hot knife into butter, moving as fluidly as if they were one animal. The way Nora rode made me think disjointedly of the way Clint had crossed the space between us before he'd kissed me. I shut the thought down as soon as it popped up, and squinted at Nora as if the day was too bright.

It was only a few minutes before she had both of the large horses haltered. I admired her technique. She rode up to each horse in turn, side-passing Sally close enough so she could rub an itchy forehead or scratch a jaw, then eased a halter into place. She left the herd moments later, two ropes dallied around her horn, the massive team shambling along beside Sally's smooth haunch.

I dropped my purse by the door and wrapped both hands around the door-knob, engaging in a brief wrestling match. I nearly fell onto my rump when the wind gusted, changed direction, and the door slammed shut with a bang that reverberated through the entire house.

"Is that you, Erin?" My mom's voice sounded from a distant room as I picked up my purse. Boswell and Norman were watching me from the entrance to the den, trying to decide whether or not the pets they would receive were worth the bother of coming over to say hello.

"Yep." I hung my purse on the coat rack and kicked my flip-flops off as the already dark air gave a flicker. A roll of thunder rumbled and boomed.

It was Sunday evening. Nora and I had gotten the team back to the ranch without incident. With a little coaching, I had indeed found ponying to be no problem. Paul and the bucking horse, whose name was Chip, were both old pros. Neither one gave me any trouble as we trotted along behind Nora on Sally, leading Dale.

Back at the barn, we'd had our work cut out for us. Chip and Dale's heavy, wavy manes and tails had been full of sandspur burrs and foxtails. We'd spent over an hour grooming them. They'd proven to be sweet, docile animals with gentle expressions and a slow way of bending their heads around to sniff at your back while you worked a comb through their manes.

After the horses were restored to some semblance of tidiness, I'd helped Nora unpack the harness and hook the team to a flatbed cart. We'd driven them around the barnyard long enough to determine horses and cart were in working order. Then we'd unharnessed and turned the team out in the closer pasture where Sally and Paul and the horses in regular work spent most of their time.

The entire undertaking had consumed the vast majority of the day. Fortunately, the tasks had been engaging enough and Nora's constant stream of information had been interesting enough that I'd had only a few scattered moments to gaze at the horizon and wonder where Clint was. These lapses were always brief. There was always some change in task or conversation topic and my attention would return to where it belonged.

This had held true until I'd left the Tipped Z. But almost immediately upon getting into my car, my brain had gone into Clint-fueled overdrive. The scene from that morning set itself to play on repeat in my mind. I groped for something I had missed, some detail I had overlooked that would explain the whole thing and reveal how to get me and Clint back onto the giddy plane of hand-holding and kissing we'd inhabited so briefly.

I'd gone to my apartment, but it had only taken a shower and half an hour of restless pacing before I fled my solitude and headed for my parents'.

My mom appeared in the open doorway that led to her workroom, holding a pen in one hand and looking at me over the top of her glasses. "Is it raining out there?" She took the cap off the end of her pen and clipped it into place over the felt tip. She looked at the clock and stretched in a way that indicated she'd been sitting for quite a long time.

"Not yet, but wow there's some wind." I redid my ponytail, smoothing the fly-away strands back into order.

"Your dad's supposed to fly in tonight." Mom's tone was distant. I was used to this. It always took her a while to fully return to the world the rest of us inhabited from whatever mental space she occupied when she worked.

"Oh, that's good." I walked into the kitchen and peered into the fridge, suddenly aware that I was ravenous.

"Unless the storm shuts down the runways."

As if to punctuate my mother's point, another roll of thunder sounded. We heard the light patter of rain on the roof. I closed the refrigerator door and looked out the window. I could see an approaching sheet of darkness—a line of heavy water-filled air advancing towards the house. The term "storm front" took on new meaning for me.

"They say there's going to be major flooding," I said. The weather warnings I had dismissed so flippantly when I saw them in the paper seemed a good deal more likely to be apt now that I could see the shifting sheets of heavy rain bearing down on the vegetation across the yard.

My mother came to join me in staring out the window. "Let's just hope the bridge doesn't go out."

The bridge my mother was referring to crossed a wash that lay between the new subdivisions and the older, less dense neighborhood where my parents lived. It was a two-lane affair, with a sign on either end that said, "Narrow Bridge." The wash it crossed wasn't much of anything, usually, but in extreme weather it could come to life. Once every five to ten years, the storm waters rose with unusual force, sweeping the bridge away. And with the bridge out, there was no way into or out of my parents' neighborhood unless one had a kayak and a sense of adventure.

I could remember the last time this had happened. I'd been in high school and had missed several days of classes. The event had caused a flurry of local rallies for more robust infrastructure in the area. But the bridge had been replaced with one everyone agreed was no improvement. In the words of my parents' partially deaf neighbor, Walter, it was only a matter of time before the whole scenario repeated itself.

The storm reached the house. There was a sudden increase in the sound of the rain on the roof. The noise matured from a patter to a roar, intermixed with occasional thunks. "Is that hail?" I looked up at the roof as if I could see through the ceiling and the shingles and assess the relative density of the water falling from the sky.

My mother didn't answer. She was staring out the dark window. I took in her tight jaw and the tense way she fiddled with the clip on her pen. She didn't like it when my father had to fly. She liked it even less when he was in the air during bad weather. I concluded a distraction was in order. "Have you eaten?" I moved towards the refrigerator again, this time with purpose. "If you're going to be driving through a storm in the middle of the night, you'll need some sustenance."

The thing about life is you can never anticipate the turning points. That evening, as I whipped up the fanciest dinner I could manage with the ingredients on hand, I didn't seriously believe anything untoward would happen. I didn't guess the downpour that had just reached our house would turn out to be the most violent storm to strike Southwestern Arizona in decades: that it would not only wash away the little bridge leading into my parents' neighborhood with as little effort as a stream carrying away a twig, but it would take down power lines and burst damns. That water would overrun the greater Tucson area like a wet, liquid plague. I never guessed my mother would be one of the last people to cross that old bridge, that the tires of my dad's Ford Explorer would trundle across that trembling concrete probably less than an hour before it gave way. I would be in bed by that time, having found sleep and escape from worries about Clint via mothering my mother and the medicinal qualities of several glasses of wine.

When I woke, it was still dark. I couldn't at first figure out what had lifted me from sleep. My room was preternaturally still. The air was heavy with humidity but the storm had passed. I thought at first I was only noticing the absence of the roaring rain. But it dawned on me as I rolled over in bed that this was a deeper silence.

The house had gone still. It was warm in my room, but there was no drone of the swamp cooler. The fan on my dresser had stopped with its oscillating and humming. I rolled back over and glanced at the clock I kept on my desk across the room. The green digits that usually glowed in the darkness were notably absent.

It was not unusual for the power to go out in my parents' neighborhood. They were one of only a dozen or so homes back in a valley that had once belonged to a single ranch. Even a mid-level monsoon often disrupted things for an hour or two. So, I was not unduly alarmed. I sat up and punched my pillow a few times, staring around at the darkness and trying to guess what time it was. I'd drawn my blinds. Even if dawn was starting to break, I wouldn't know.

My phone beeped. I'd left it on the bedside table next to the lamp. I picked it up, remembering my father's midnight flight.

The text was from my mom. It was one of several I had missed. The first, she had sent quite soon after leaving the house. I had gone to bed around eleven and must have fallen right to sleep. The timestamp on her message was 11:12. "Pulled over storm is crazy."

I felt a twinge of guilt. It was not unlikely my phone's modest beeping had been all but inaudible over the sound of the rain and hail. But still it seemed to reflect poorly on my competence as a daughter that I'd not woken up when this had come in. Why didn't phone carriers have a way to weight the importance of any given message? One like that should automatically be deemed critical, and therefore trigger the kind of persistent, penetrating chime that would interrupt even the most intense of slumbers.

The next message had come half an hour later. "Flight diverted to Dallas everything flooded - at the Comfort Inn on Houghton."

The final two messages were from this morning. The first had come three minutes ago, at 5:49am. "Bridge is out." The last had just arrived, and it said, "Do you have hidden apt key?"

I sat up, staring at my phone with bleary eyes, trying to piece together the series of events laid out by my mother's brief messages. I knew the Comfort Inn on Houghton. My apartment manager had put me up there once when I'd had to leave for a night due to a gas leak in my kitchen. It was less than ten minutes away from my parents' house.

My mother had left the house, driven a few miles, and pulled over because of the weather. Then she'd heard my father wouldn't be coming in after all and gone to a hotel rather than drive home through the storm.

My mother was not a timid driver.

I texted back. "Sorry I don't but the office opens at 7. They should be able to let you in."

I left my bed and walked to the window, pulling open the shades. I half expected to look out on a scene from a sci-fi movie: a water-world of muddy desert floodwaters, the bushy crowns of the mesquite trees just protruding above the surface.

Instead, I saw a normal view. The landscape was dim with the pale pre-sunrise dawn. I could make out the small wash that skirted my parents' property-line. It was full and raging. The strange phenomenon my father referred to as sandfish bloomed as narrow humps in the middle. Meanwhile, clumps of white foam accumulating in the eddies.

My phone beeped again. This message contained a rather long and detailed set of instructions for feeding Boswell and Norman. Resigning myself to the reality that I would not be climbing back into bed, I went to my dresser and surveyed my meager array of clothing options. I selected an old pair of U of A sweatpants that had a wildcat on the butt, and a plain red tank-top.

As I dressed, I heard a quiet snuffling noise—the sound of a dog trying to get a whiff of something through the crack at the bottom of a door. This was further evidence that not all was as it should be. Boswell and Norman were independent animals and I was not their Person. My mother was their Person. My relationship with them had always been a bit cool on both sides. They were not at all in the habit of caring whether or not I was behind any given closed door.

The dogs were waiting in the hallway outside my room. Boswell was sitting, his dark eyes intent. Norman had been the one doing the sniffing. They both began wagging and grinning when they saw me. They were eager to follow me across the house and escape into the yard.

I followed them out onto the patio. The desert had that scoured feeling that comes after a heavy rain. The sky was clear, growing brighter with every minute. The sand between the mesquites was smoothed and sculpted into little layer-lines where water had run. Boswell and Norman raced around wildly, noses to the ground, ecstatic over the feast of new scents brought down by the storm.

"I'm afraid the helicopters can only accommodate people. We don't have the capacity to deal with pets."

I gave a small, thoughtful nod, as if to indicate I agreed this was an utterly reasonable way of structuring an evacuation. I glanced at Boswell and Norman, who were now crashed out on the patio in the afternoon sun. Their white coats were stiff and discolored with drying sand and mud. They had spent all morning romping in the storm-ravaged yard, showing particular interest in the low corner where the wash had overflowed and formed a shallow pool.

"I'm afraid I'll have to stay here then. Thank you for stopping by."

I was speaking to a young man wearing a dark uniform and a serious expression. His hair had the look of having recently been under a helmet. His face bore the expression of one who takes himself rather too seriously. He'd come in through the front gate a few minutes before, introduced himself as James, and told me I needed to prepare for evacuation.

"We can't guarantee we'll be able to make it back before your food and water supplies run out." He said this in a frustrated tone. I guessed some other neighbors were also showing reluctance to abandon pets and homes to an uncertain fate.

According to James, the storm had brought down something close to the apocalypse. Roads and bridges were out all over town. Rescue crews were short-staffed trying to move the stranded to safety.

"Look, I'm fine here. I'll be fine for a while." I said this with more conviction than I felt. In truth, I wasn't sure how long I'd be fine. I had plenty of food. My parents had their regular refrigerator plus an old freezer out back that was stocked with frozen meals and meats. My father also kept a full ten gallon water cooler stashed in the back utility area because the well that supplied my parents and their neighborhood required electricity to run. No power meant no water. Which meant I had the water in the pipes and however long ten gallons would last a person and two dogs. And then I *would* be in trouble.

But this guy's manner had irritated me, and it seemed premature to abandon ship. I had texted Anne to let her know I wouldn't make it to work. She had texted back to say of course that was fine. Then I'd turned my phone off to conserve batteries.

James looked at me, perhaps guessing he had come at this from the wrong angle. He made an attempt to smooth his rumpled hair. "Look, I understand you don't want to go without your dogs. But I'm not sure when we're going to be able to get back here. It could be days."

"I'm sure the power will come back on before then." I said this in as optimistic a tone as I could manage, which only made me sound vapid and complacent.

James' mouth tightened around the edges. He snapped back to all-business mode. "Okay. If you refuse assistance, I'll need you to sign here." He produced a metal-reinforced clipboard and extracted a form from its interior compartment, clipped it into place, and circled an X next to a line. He offered me the clipboard and pen.

I felt suddenly uncertain. Without power, I had no television, no internet. My phone had been off for hours. I didn't know the extent of the damage, or even the forecast. The article Anne had shown me had predicted a series of violent storms, not just one.

I wanted to ask him to wait so I could call my mother. Better yet, I wished my mother was there. We could either sign together, our righteous indignation making our upwards strokes crisp and decisive, or agree to go, leaving Boswell and Norman with enough food and water to hopefully get them through their newest ordeal.

Still, while it was easy to think about going inside, grabbing my purse, and returning with James to his helicopter, it was harder to think of facing my mother. I'd have to tell her I had abandoned the two dogs who had so recently returned to her against all odds and left them in another high-stakes situation.

I accepted the pen and signed. James gave a quick, irritated sigh, extracted the form from beneath its clip, and handed me the yellow carbon copy. "Good luck." He said this without venom, only a certain weariness. He strode to the gate on the hunt for more willing cargo, leaving me to my folly.

I turned to look at the dogs. They were still sprawled in positions of utter contentment. "You guys don't even appreciate what everyone does for you."

There is something slightly romantic about being stranded, about refusing rescue for selfless reasons, about holding to family loyalty in the face of extreme weather events. I enjoyed this sensation for nearly three hours.

But as the sun began to fall, the house remained encased in its eerie stillness. As I set out on a search for candles and flashlights, my attitude shifted in the direction of self-pity.

In normal circumstances, there would be all sorts of ways to distract myself from the reality of my situation. I'd be able to watch TV, or a movie. I'd waste time on the internet or work on my novel. But none of these options were open to me. I had no electricity. I had plenty of books to read, but I was having trouble concentrating. It was maddening. I found myself quashing the urge to turn my phone on approximately every fifteen seconds.

But by 6:00 in the evening, I felt it was time. I set the last group of candles I'd unearthed from a storage closet on the kitchen counter, and reached into my pocket. I'd kept my phone near me throughout the day, despite the fact of its offness. I walked into the living room and flopped onto my parents' leather couch, pressing and holding the power key. I waited for the opening ditty to play, for my phone to latch onto the cell signal and give me one, tenuous connection to the world beyond the wash.

My message notification sounded. There were two texts from my mother, relaying a brief but colorful story of the lengths to which she'd had to go to convince my apartment manager to let her into my apartment. There was one from Ben asking if I was okay, one from Trace asking the same thing, and one from my father, saying he hoped I was okay and that if I was offered the chance to evacuate, I should take it.

That last one made my stomach sink. I'd spent part of the late afternoon removing the ravages of the wet morning from Boswell and Norman's coats and feet. The two dogs were now lying on the living room rug, sleeping as if they had not spent the vast majority of the day doing just that.

I sent Ben and Trace the same message. "I'm fine. Stuck at Mom and Dad's." There was no need to burden either of them with the pesky reality that I could die of dehydration by the end of the week if the city didn't get the power back on.

I wrote my mom back and said I was glad she had gotten in, then stared at my dad's message for a minute or two, all the while feeling the remaining seconds my phone had of life tick by at an alarming rate.

I couldn't think of anything to say. I didn't want to lie. But I also didn't want to tell him I'd already sent the helicopter man packing.

I closed the message from my dad and opened a new text to Nora.

I'd been hoping there would be a text from her, saying Clint had asked to teach my lesson tomorrow. But there was no such reprieve. Whatever had happened to make Clint turn his back on me was still real. I sighed and tapped out a brief message. "Stranded at parents'. Just me and the dogs. No electricity. Won't let dogs on helicopter. The point: I won't make lesson tomorrow. ☹"

I reread the message a few times before hitting send, hoping it didn't seem too whiney.

I waited for another minute or two. No one got back to me. I wrote my dad, two words. "Thanks. Okay."

I waited another moment, hoping for some reply. I was about to power down my phone when my father wrote. "Hang in there. Expect another storm tomorrow. Love you."

Chapter 11

○

"They haven't come back." I sent this message and waited impatiently, staring at the battery indicator in the upper corner of my phone's screen. Over the course of the day, it had progressed from green to yellow to red. I was down to 8% battery life.

It was midday on Tuesday, and the reality of my situation was starting to sink in. I'd woken up that morning with hope, but a quick glance at my dead clock had revealed that nothing had changed. There was still no power.

I'd passed the day in restless agitation, trying to ration my phone's batteries but still turning it on more often than was strictly necessary. Just now I was on the back patio, pacing around like a caged tiger.

My dad got back to me right away. He'd made it to Tucson and he and my mom were both now installed at my apartment, which was strange for all sorts of reasons. As the day had passed and he'd gotten increasingly mystified as to why no helicopter had come to our neighborhood, I had confessed I'd declined to evacuate. But he was convinced I'd get a second chance. His reply was practical. "When you go, leave the dogs outside. Put the closed food bag on the porch and dump the open one out. They'll rip the closed one open if they get hungry enough. Put water in the shade, in the deepest container they can reach the bottom off, to minimize evaporation."

I read these instructions with a sinking heart. I wrote back. "Hopefully it won't come to that."

I looked at the dogs. In spite having a reputation for being keen animals—supposedly in tune with the subtlest emotional nuances of their human masters—Boswell and Norman had not picked up on my anxiety. They were currently engaged in their favorite pastime of basking in the warm sun. They had enjoyed another fantastic morning romp in the still-damp yard and were now sleeping off their excesses.

In the short period of our internment, they had started to warm to me. They now frequently came over for a pat on the head or a scratch on the shoulder. They looked up and wagged their tails whenever they heard my voice.

The battery indicator on my phone dropped to 7%. Reluctantly, I shut it down. Then I stared angrily down at the fence line. The small wash that skirted my parents' property had stopped running, but the ground was so waterlogged it would only take a minor rainfall to set it going again.

I found myself blinking around tears of frustration. It seemed so unfair. What kind of civilized society were we, that we would save people from natural disasters only if they agreed to abandon their animals to an uncertain fate? I knew my father was doing everything he could, pulling every string he had access to, attempting to call in outstanding favors. But there was too much damage, not enough resources, and more storms on the horizon. One girl stranded with two dogs was not enough of an issue to get anyone's attention.

I was still staring off into the distance, wondering if I could hike out and swim across the wash, when I heard it. The snort of a horse.

I stood up straighter, looking down past the fence. I thought I saw a flicker of movement behind the mesquites. Then there was the thud of a hoof and the soft clink of metal on metal.

Boswell and Norman sat up in unison, bullet-shaped heads oriented towards noise.

And then I saw him.

Clint emerged around a clump of Palo Verde scrub, riding Rascal. Paul was following along behind. A rope ran from Paul's halter to Clint's horn. The two horses crossed the smoothed sand of the small wash, picking their way around debris and leaving furrowed hoof prints in their wake.

Clint rode up to the gate and stopped, looking towards the house. He saw me staring and held up one hand in a silent greeting.

I stood, frozen in place, my heart pounding. I wondered if isolation and stress could cause vivid hallucinations.

Clint's hand dropped. I waved mine in a quick, spastic response.

I shoved my phone into my pocket as the dogs surged to their feet, bounding down the yard, tails wagging. I called their names. They stopped and looked back over their shoulders with evident reluctance. I took a page from my mother's book and glared at them. They came skulking back while I found my flip-flops by the door and slipped them on.

I was still wearing the horrible sweat pants. I was in a different tank-top—blue instead of red. I, of course, hadn't showered since the power had gone out. I was aware I was not at my most alluring. But I hurried forward anyway, unable to contain the utter joy I felt not only at seeing Clint but at the hope of rescue. The Tipped Z was most definitely on the other side of the raging Rio Oro, which meant he had crossed with horses and could cross back to the other side.

By the time I made my way off the patio and started down the slope, Clint had dismounted, opened the gate, and led the horses through. I was close enough now that I could see the sweat in their coats. It was a warm, humid day, the air already heavy with the threat of the coming storm. The horses both came to a grateful stop as Clint closed the gate behind them.

He was wearing his chinks and his hat. He looked so good I felt a brief spasm of irritation at his perfection. I tamped this down and approached him at what I hoped was a brisk but relaxed walk, trying to think of something to say.

I was only a few feet off when he glanced over at me. He'd been untying some bags that were strapped to Paul's saddle. "I heard you were stuck." He said this the way another person might say, "I heard you were having a party," or, "I heard you'd be in town tonight."

"Yeah," I said. "Stuck, stuck, stuck." I winced internally as I said this. What was it about Clint that reduced me to the conversation capacity of a two year old?

To distract myself from feeling ridiculous, I examined the horses. Their feet and legs were mud spattered and soaked. I wondered how they'd gotten here. I'd driven out to the wash that morning to marvel at the presence of so much seething, filthy brown water occupying a place where usually there was no water at all. The flood was so high you couldn't drive a hummer across. There was no sign of the bridge that used to span the Rio Oro at all. Had the horses been able to swim that?

Sensing my mystification, Clint explained. "You go up high enough and the wash splits. It runs over rock, gets wide and shallow. I found a place even a dog could cross safely." He was busy pulling a canvas sack from the saddle as he spoke. From that he produced a bag of grain. He tipped his head back to glance at the sky. "There's another storm coming, so we can't waste time. It's a roundabout trail, so its hours to get back. I need to get these two fed and watered. If you have some jeans, maybe you could put those on. Then we need to get moving."

Paul picked his way around a pile of mesquite branches and beans that had piled into a drift across the trail. He was compliant today, content to follow Rascal at a polite distance, never offering more speed than I asked for.

I shifted in the saddle. We were an hour into our journey. The jeans I had on were not ideal for riding. They had bling on the pockets and were of a cut more suited to shaking your booty on a dance floor than sitting in a saddle. They lived at my parents' because they had never fit me well.

I glanced down past Paul's shoulder. Boswell and Norman had started our excursion in high spirits. They'd been in awe of the horses, ecstatic about the adventure, and overwhelmed with the treat of going past the fence without leashes. They'd raced around, sniffing one new object after another, lagging behind, then sprinting to catch up. Clint had watched them with a slight frown. "It would be better if they would conserve their energy." This had been his only comment.

Now I understood what he meant.

We were still going up.

For the first fifteen minutes of our ride, we hadn't been on a trail. I'd followed Clint as he'd chosen a path through the desert, going in what I knew to be the exact opposite direction of the Tipped Z. He'd routed around clumps of cacti and bulges of rock. Finally, we'd encountered the trail we were on now. It had skirted the base of the ridge that humped up behind my parents' house and had delivered us around the other side of a peak we'd used to hike when I was younger, that I knew got steep and rocky at the top and was impassable on horseback.

Since reaching the trail, we'd been trotting, heading ever upwards and towards the mountains.

The terrain got more rocky and less vegetated as we rode. The trail hardened from sand to clay. The dogs were beginning to be less thrilled with the adventure. But they kept up, only stopping every now and then to sniff something particularly fascinating.

Clint was not talking. He hadn't said anything at all for at least 45 minutes. Right when he'd arrived, he'd said quite a few things. He'd asked for water and some kind of bucket to put the grain in. We'd emptied my dad's emergency cooler, letting the horses and dogs drink their fill after we filled the canteens that were strapped to the saddles of both horses. While the horses had eaten their grain, Clint had handed me the pair of boots I'd worn that day at the Tipped Z, before I'd gone with Nora and gotten my own.

I had hurried inside to change, my heart a drumbeat in my chest. I'd texted my parents to let them know what was happening and turned my phone off before they'd had time to reply.

Now that we were moving, Clint seemed disinclined to say anything more. I could feel the strain between us, that block that had made him turn away from me without saying hello in the hay room. I wondered dismally if we would go the rest of the way without exchanging another word.

I was ricocheting between relief and agony. Relief that I'd been rescued. Agony that Clint was proving to be as frosty as the last time we'd seen each other. It was as if the kiss in the cottonwood grove had never happened. Or worse, that it had happened and Clint was dead set on never repeating the experience.

The trail grew steep for a short section, with the rounded surface of a massive rock protruding out of the clay. I felt Paul's large haunches working beneath me as he hauled himself up the slope. Then the terrain flattened, and his stride smoothed out again.

I gave him a pat on the neck, and he stopped suddenly. I looked forward, startled, to see Clint and Rascal had come to a halt. Clint was dismounting. I looked around in confusion. We were not at the Tipped Z, nor anywhere near it.

Clint went to the pack tied behind Rascal's saddle and pulled out something that looked like a plastic disc. He did something with his hands and it flipped open, turning it into a shallow bowl. He poured water from the canteen into the bowl and carried it to Rascal's nose.

I took the opportunity to dismount as well, opening my own canteen and taking a drink. I could feel some tender places on my inner thighs where the ultra-low-rise jeans were starting to chafe. I tried to ignore this and watched as Rascal and Paul both refused the water.

Clint knelt and gave a whistle. Boswell and Norman ran to him. He let them drink while he ran his hands over their broad, white backs. It occurred to me that Dots was not along for the ride. Somehow, this made the situation a little more serious and even more real.

I took another drink and tied my canteen back onto Paul's saddle. "How much longer do we have to go?" Part of me was loathe to be the one to break the silence. But a larger part of me needed to know.

Clint looked up at the sky when I asked, as if the question had descended from on high, not come from my mouth. But I knew what he was looking at. Dark clouds were building along the horizon. The sunlight was growing wan. "At least two more hours," he said. "Assuming the dogs can keep up the pace."

I nodded, trying not to let trepidation show on my face. I'd been caught in storms on horseback before, but never out so far into the unpopulated foothills, and never in an already waterlogged desert.

Clint, unlike Boswell and Norman, seemed to pick up on my anxiety. When the dogs were finished drinking, he collapsed the water dish and stowed it once again in the saddle pack. Then he walked over, pausing to adjust the brow-band on Paul's headstall. His eyes scanned Paul, taking in the saddle placement, the cinch, the bags tied behind the cantle. Finally, they came to rest on me.

I felt a little shock as our eyes met, as if the alignment of our pupils allowed a subtle electrical current to pass from his body to mine. I felt the pull of that current and had to resist the urge to step forward.

It seemed we stood that way, looking at each other, for a long time. A cactus wren cried from a clump of cholla next to the trail. One of the dogs gave a sigh, the tags on his collar rattling as he scratched an itch on his neck. "You holding up all right?" Clint said this in a gentle tone, as if he really cared, as if he hadn't turned his back on me just a few days ago, walked out the door and ridden away when I'd said hello.

I felt the thrill in my veins shift to a sort of frustrated throbbing, which changed unexpectedly into a flash of irritation. Who was this guy, to think he could toy with me like this? What kind of person kissed a girl one day and shunned her the next? I dropped my eyes and looked at the worn toe of the borrowed boot on my foot. "I'm fine." I realized I sounded sulky—like a child denied their first choice of dinner options refusing all reasonable alternatives just to be difficult.

Clint drew back, stepped away from Paul, and swung onto Rascal's back without another word. Taking care to keep my wincing internal, I too hauled myself back into the saddle.

Forty minutes later, I was beginning to entertain the idea that Clint was a psychopath. He'd lured me out into the desert in the guise of a rescuer to make me trot until I literally expired.

It seemed we had been trotting for approximately a week, and the trot kept getting faster. The longer we rode, the more often Clint glanced up at the sky. Every time he did this, he and Rascal accelerated.

Rascal, it turned out, could trot at a pace I'd never before experienced on horseback. I had to work to get Paul to keep up. Once I'd urged him ahead too strongly. He'd broken into a canter. Clint had slowed down and turned in his saddle. "Try not to let him lope," he'd said. "We need to conserve their energy."

So Paul and I were exploring the limits of the long trot, and neither of us was enjoying it.

Nevertheless, I could understand Clint's urgency. The sky was growing darker by the moment, and we had not yet crossed the Rio Oro wash. You didn't have to be a seasoned desert survivalist to know crossing a flooding waterway in a monsoon was a good way to end up dead.

We were racing the storm. I understood that. But that didn't make it any less uncomfortable.

The dogs were flagging as well. Boswell had taken to running ahead and lying down in the trail, sprawling in the damp areas under the brushy mesquites and trying to cool himself by coating his belly with mud. Norman was proving more dogged. He had installed himself at Paul's flank. Eyes blank, tongue lolling, he was going whatever pace Paul went.

I could see the wash on our left now. It would emerge between the trees and rocks, sometimes a raging flood of clear water over rock, sometimes a dark band of slower-moving seepage over sand. I had seen several places that seemed crossable—places where the floodplain grew wide and the flow branched into channels of forked waterways. But we passed all of them, following the trail higher and higher until I was sure we were going to crest the mountain at any moment. I was perplexed about this until we passed a particularly clear expanse of wash and I could look across to see the barbed wire fence that ran along the opposite bank, the bottoms of the posts submerged in some places. Then I understood. Man and nature were conspiring to make this as difficult as possible.

An unmeasurable amount of time after my revelation on this topic, the sound of Rascal's footfalls changed. He walked for a moment, then stopped. Clint swung down from his saddle and looked back at me, his body-language tense. Paul and I had come to a grateful, sweat-sodden stop as soon as Rascal had slowed down. He said, "We'll want to lead them across."

I gazed at Clint, my discomfort once again coalescing into irritation. He looked like he always did. Sure, there was a stressed air about him, deeper creases at the corners of his mouth, the distracted way he kept glancing at the sky. But all in all, he looked fine. He didn't appear fatigued. He was sweaty, sure, but his legs weren't shaking beneath him, as it turned out mine did as soon as I stepped off Paul's back.

Clint went to Rascal's head and led his horse forward, leaving the trail and disappearing around the back of a huge boulder. Paul and I followed, the dogs at our heels. Finally, I saw where we were going to cross.

It was a large expanse of smooth rock, interspersed with deeper grooves and areas of sand. It was wide and the slope was slight, so the water ran in a shallow sheet over the rock. Clint stepped into the flow without hesitation, glancing back and saying, "Take your time. Give Paul plenty of space. Let him choose his own way."

I let Clint get a horse-length ahead, then stepped into the water. My boot grew cold, but my foot stayed dry.

Most of the rock was coarse, evidently not usually under water. The areas around the deeper grooves were more slick. I worried Paul would put a foot into one of these.

I took my time. I gave Paul plenty of space and let him choose his way. For his part, the horse took his job seriously. He picked his path with care, never refusing to cross anything, but not hurrying either.

I managed to stay reasonably relaxed about the situation until we were about halfway across. That's when the dim air flickered with lightning. A thunderclap came hard on its heels. The crash was loud enough to make Norman yip.

I froze in my tracks, reviewing what I knew about lightning. Lightning tended to strike the highest organic object in any given area. It was attracted to water and metal and living beings. Which meant, in theory, it would be particularly enticed by two large living creatures standing in shallow water and wearing various pieces of metal.

I started to feel truly panicky for the first time all day.

Clint was still ahead of me. He looked back again, as if he could hear my internal dialogue. We were more than halfway across the water-slicked rock. Turning around would be no safer than going on. "Don't rush now," he said. "Take your time."

More thunder rumbled. I wanted to close my eyes, open them again, and wake up in my apartment, slicked in nightmare-induced sweat but otherwise unharmed.

I closed my eyes and opened them to no effect. I could still feel the current tugging at the cuffs of my jeans, still feel the course horsehair reins in my hand. I kept walking, Paul following along behind.

The dogs didn't appear to mind the water at all. Both of them had waded in with enthusiasm, sides heaving, pink skin visible where their haunches met their torsos. They lapped the water and stood in the deepest areas they could find, the current washing some of the grime from their legs and chests.

I kept my eyes on the rock in front of me, close enough to Rascal's hind legs to be sure I took the same route he did. Behind me, Paul slipped. There was a heart-stopping clatter of horseshoes on rock as he scrambled to keep his feet beneath him. I turned and watched, powerless to help. But he recovered and kept on walking as if nothing had happened.

"Almost there now." This came from up ahead. Clint and Rascal had crossed the final deep rivulet and were walking a bit faster across the last stretch of coarse rock. I had to resist the urge to hurry, to encourage Paul to go faster.

Then Clint was out the other side, stepping up onto a higher slope of rock that led down to the most welcome expanse of dirt I'd ever laid eyes on in my life. Boswell and Norman scrambled up behind him. A moment later, Paul and I followed. The damp soil clung to the bottoms of my soaked jeans, but I didn't care. My fatigue lifted, my sore muscles eased.

I was across the Rio Oro! I was no longer the prisoner of insufficient infrastructure funding. And I'd escaped without abandoning my mother's dogs. I wanted to fling my arms around Clint's neck and kiss him. But he was still looking at the sky, his face grim. "I'm sorry, Erin," he said as he led Rascal forward enough to give me room to mount. "There's no time for a rest."

Ignoring the fact that just hearing Clint speak my name sent a little surge of adrenaline through my veins, I settled for giving Paul a quick hug around the neck and climbing back into the saddle.

Riding after the crossing was easier for a time. Although the sky continued to darken, the rain held off for another fifteen minutes. We trotted down a gentle sandy slope that led away from the mountains and angled towards the scrub-brush plains I knew made up portions of the Tipped Z's pastures.

Only a few minutes after crossing the wash, we came to an intersection of fences. One was the barbed wire fence I'd seen across the wash. The other was smooth wire. Where they met there was a gate and a sign about the permit you needed to enter State Trust land. A trail was visible on both sides. On ours, it went straight up towards the mountains at a steeper angle than how we'd come down. On the other, it headed down and away on a similar trajectory to the one we'd been following.

Clint trotted up to the gate and worked the latch from horseback. At the gate's bottom was a solid metal bar about a foot off the ground: a technique for keeping ATVs out of the mountains. Paul stepped over the bar without protest, Boswell and Norman close behind. Clint closed the gate, then unrolled a pair of waxed canvas slickers from behind his cantle. He passed one to me and waited to see that I put it on. He donned his. We set off again at the trot.

My newfound optimism and energy at surviving the crossing lasted for approximately five more minutes. Then the realities of my aching legs and chafed toosh began to intrude again. We were trotting a little more slowly now, but the gait was not different enough to provide riders, horses, or dogs any measurable relief. Still, I kept on, trying to ride well, taking care to steer Paul around fallen cactus pads and branches that had made their way into the trail. I had even gotten back into a sort of dull rhythm.

Then the rain hit.

It came at us from the side, sweeping over a ridge to our left with gale-force winds, flinging cold pellets of hard water over our faces. I blinked. Paul tried to turn. I heard Clint call, "He's going to want to put his back to the wind. Don't let him."

Therein followed a brief battle of wills with Paul. I asked him to straighten out and follow Rascal. He refused.

In Paul's defense, he was tired. I could feel it in his body, in the lack of elasticity in his trot. Nevertheless, throwing a tantrum now wasn't going to help anyone. I tried to remember everything Clint had ever said about being firm but fair. I pointed Paul's nose towards Clint and Rascal and gave him a solid thump with the leg he was trying to turn into.

He stayed stiff for one more second. I applied one more thump. He gave in. Ears tipped back against the blowing rain, he dropped his head. We went on.

I could sympathize. The rain blew against the side of my face, flinging itself into my eyes and making me blink. My hair, face, and jeans below the slicker were soaked through in exactly 1.5 seconds. As I felt a trickle of water run down my back, I flipped the slicker's collar up and eyed Clint's flat-brimmed hat with new comprehension and envy. He seemed to feel my gaze on him. He turned. He had to raise his voice to be heard over the sounds of the storm. "I'd give you my hat," he said. "But it's too big. It'd blow off your head."

I felt suddenly horrible, like the worst sort of dependent greenhorn. "That's okay," I called back, annunciating my words as if we were shouting from the deck of one ship to another. "I'm fine."

We trotted on. The slicker was roomy on me, its interior rough against the bare skin of my arms. But I was more grateful for that flapping canvas than I'd ever been for any article of clothing in my entire previous life. The horses were rain-slicked within a few minutes. The dogs were drenched as well. They had both fallen in behind Paul now, squinting against the water-filled air, lacking the energy to even cast reproachful glances up at me.

We trotted and trotted. Thunder crashed and rumbled around us. The dim air flickered and flashed. My focus narrowed to two things: keeping Paul's nose aligned with Rascal's rump, and making sure Boswell and Norman were still behind me.

The trail twisted as it went. When the wind was at our backs, things weren't so bad. The horses perked up and we all got a brief reprieve. But when the trail bent back or the wind shifted and flung water into our faces, we all suffered.

I lost track of time. I kept shifting my attention forward, back, forward, back. Rascal, dogs, Rascal, dogs, Rascal ... no dogs.

I sat down, asking Paul to stop. He'd apparently entered the same sort of mental tunnel I'd been occupying. He ignored me. I had to give a little tug on the reins to get his attention. But as soon as I did, he sagged gratefully to a stop.

I turned around in my saddle, blinking the water out of my eyes. Norman was standing a ways back up the trail, tail between his legs, ears flattened. He was halfway between me and the small white smudge in the distance that was Boswell.

I looked forward, ready to call out to Clint, but saw he was already stopped and turned around, guiding Rascal back in my direction.

Boswell was walking, but at a slow pace. His sides were heaving beneath his rain-slicked coat. He was all but tottering on his feet. I wondered for the first time if I had made the right decision, subjecting them to this adventure.

Clint rode Rascal up next to the dog and swung out of the saddle. With a sort of gentle scooping gesture, he laid the dog on his side. Boswell appeared surprised to be off his feet and tried to scramble up again. Clint held him down, hands gentle but firm. After a few seconds of being pinned to the ground, the dog relaxed. In a series of quick, deft movements I couldn't follow, Clint produced a set of leather thongs and bound Boswell's feet in front and behind, then turned and heaved him onto Rascal's saddle. He did the same thing to Norman, startling me when he stood and swung the dog up to hang as a warm, soaked presence between my hips and the saddle horn. I expected him to squirm or protest in some way. But he just hung there, panting. I realized Clint had needed to let them get this tired so they would hold still on horseback.

Clint mounted up again as a swaying mesquite branch sent a spray of wet beans clattering down over the top of us. He turned Rascal and started back along the trail, but he did not pick up the trot again.

I finished wiping the sand off Paul's bridle and hung it where Clint had shown me. Not in the tack room, but next to Rascal's headgear and the two soaked saddles in one of the empty stalls that was outfitted with a selection of saddle horses and hooks. Here, I gathered, the soaked gear would be able to dry without infecting the entire tack room with dampness.

I slid the stall door closed behind me and walked over to another stall, peering down at the two pale shapes just visible in the gloom. Boswell and Norman were installed with enough food and water and wool blankets to last them a week. My mother's Bull Terriers were already dead to the world—collapsed into sodden, exhausted heaps.

I resisted the urge to open the door and collapse next to them. I could not remember a time I had ever been so tired. My legs felt like putty, and I was certain the removal of my jeans would reveal life-threatening chafeage. The slicker I was still wearing had protected the bulk of my body from the wet, but my head and hands felt water-logged and chilled.

Clint had gone back out into the storm to return the horses to their herd. He'd been gone a bit longer than seemed necessary to complete that task. But then, I was willing to admit my sense of time had abandoned me.

I left the aisle between the stalls and headed for the hay room, approaching the large bay doors to stand just beyond where the rain blew in and fell on the packed dirt floor.

The storm was still storming. Lightning crashed and flickered. The air was dark with clouds. It could be high noon for all you could see of the sky. I squinted towards the gates that led to the pastures but could only make out the dim outlines of the water tanks and one or two shapes that may or may not have been horses.

There was a tread behind me. I spun around. Clint was entering through the small door that led in from the parking area, water streaming off his hat and the ends of his slicker. He saw me by the bay doors and stopped walking.

And there we were, standing in the same places we'd been the last time we'd seen each other, our positions switched. For a moment, I felt certain he was going to turn around and leave, abandoning me to a night sleeping on the hay or in with the dogs.

It was an uncharitable thought. I instantly felt bad for even thinking it. This man had just spent six hours riding through extreme conditions to save me from a situation I'd signed myself into.

Still, that thing was in the air between us again, that block, that obstruction I'd felt for the first time on Sunday. We stood for a long time, looking at each other as the rain pounded on the metal roof of the barn.

Finally, Clint took a little step forward. "Nora can't get in. The ditch on Ray Ranch Road is flooding and there's a truck stuck."

I processed this. If Nora couldn't get in, that meant Clint and I couldn't get out.

"Should clear up as soon as the storm lifts, though." Clint added this in a reassuring tone, as if afraid I would conclude I'd been rescued from one trap only to find myself in another.

I sensed it was my turn to say something. "Good," I managed. "And thank you, Clint, really I...." He turned away from me before I could finish my sentence. For a moment I thought I'd been wrong, that he was going to leave me out here after all.

But he spoke as he headed for the door. "You best come on up to the house."

I scrubbed at my wet hair with a towel and stared bleakly into the mirror, wishing for a make-up kit. Or at least a comb. With a sense of resignation, I turned the light off and ducked out of the bathroom to scurry across the hall, back into "my" room. There was no way I was going to look like anything other than the victim of a shipwreck, so there was little point trying.

I was wearing a pair of black sweatpants that were rather too large and a t-shirt that was a little too tight. It had seemed the best compromise I had available. Clint had provided me with a selection of clothing options, some pulled from his own closet, some brought down from the room at the ranch house Nora still stayed in with some regularity. All the bottoms from the Nora pile had turned out to be tight in areas that made them both uncomfortable and revealing, and all the tops from the Clint pile made me feel like a bag lady. So I'd rolled the waistband of Clint's sweatpants over itself a few times to make them shorter, slipped into the largest shirt from the pile, and resigned myself to my fate.

Back in the room, I looked at the clock on the dresser and realized with a sinking feeling that there was no way I could hide from Clint for the rest of the evening.

It was 5:30. It felt like it should be midnight. It felt like we had ridden through the dark stormy desert for at least eight hours. In reality, it had been a little over three. The chafing that had felt life-threatening while I was still riding turned out to be two modest streaks of red skin, utterly disappointing in how mild they looked.

I paced around the bedroom a few times, stopping to stare out the window. The storm was beginning to let up; the sky was getting brighter in a sort of faux dawn. But the sun was beginning to drop in the west. We were likely in for the sort of spectacular sunset that populates the sorts of calendars they sell in the airport.

Clint, I had learned, did not live with his parents. He had his own house tucked on the other side of a little hill that rose behind the Tipped Z proper. His driveway left the Tipped Z parking area and wrapped down and around and back towards the pastures. His location was invisible from the barn but not actually far away.

The little house was a splendid adobe structure with a covered front porch and a yard encircled by a low wall. The floors were all tile, and the walls were dominated by large windows. The living room featured a massive fireplace and opened into a kitchen with copper countertops and an island with a built-in cutting board.

We'd trooped in together, dripping and sand-covered. He'd directed me to the guest bedroom and bathroom, then disappeared towards the opposite end of the house.

I'd taken my time with the shower and the changing, but I was running out of delay tactics. I took one final look at my reflection in the mirror, went to the dresser where I'd set my purse (which Clint had brought in from the saddle bags), fished out my phone, and ventured forth with the mission of asking for a charger.

My phone had proven unwilling or unable to turn on. Which meant my parents still thought I was riding a horse through a monsoon with Boswell and Norman in tow. I felt a bit bad about that. As I padded my way down the short hallway and peered into the main living area, I reflected I maybe should have tried to get in touch with them before the shower.

The house seemed empty. The hallways connected to the living room with the fireplace. Past that I could see into the gleaming kitchen and the entryway. It wasn't a large house, but the open architecture made it feel spacious and also a little intimidating. I crept in, keeping close to the wall like a mouse venturing into the cat's domain. I headed for a little nook in the entryway that seemed to house a phone and answering machine. Once there, a quick scan of the plugs and wires revealed a cell phone charger. I plugged my phone in, heard it beep, and felt a little bit better.

I gave the phone a moment to charge, peering around the dim house. The wall space that wasn't occupied by fireplace or windows held black and white photos of horses and cattle, most of them abstract in some way.

I stepped away from the phone nook to examine the nearest one. It was a study in contrast. The bottom of the photo was an unbroken billow of white dust. The top was a black sky. In the middle appeared the shapes of horses and riders, rising from the dust like mythical creatures riding the crest of a wave.

"My late wife took that photo."

Clint's voice made me jump. I spun around to see him standing in the doorway on the opposite side of the living area, the one I assumed led to the master bedroom. He was wearing a pair of sweatpants a good deal like mine, but his t-shirt fit him a lot better. It was strange to see him in anything other than his ranching get-up. His hair was wet and stuck up in all directions, as if he hadn't thought to look in a mirror before coming out into the house.

"Easy," he said when he saw me twitch in place. "Storm's outside, not in here." He cracked that little smile. But then he looked away from me, his eyebrows knitting as if he'd remembered something painful. His face lapsed back into the mask it had been since the day he'd walked away from me in the hay room.

I tried to steady myself, taking a few deep breaths to calm my racing nerves. Why did this man have this effect on me? I was a grown woman, for crying out loud. I should not go all to pieces just because I was alone in a house with the sexiest cowboy who had ever walked the earth.

"I borrowed your charger." I blurted this out like a child confessing a raid on the cookie jar. He gave a little nod, as if to suggest he was not surprised but wasn't going to hold it over my head.

Then I realized what he'd said.

He'd said *wife*. And he'd said *late*.

Wife meant wedding ring.

Late meant dead.

I turned back towards the photo, searching the silhouettes of the riders. Now that I was looking, I could recognize them. There was Clint, his flat-brimmed hat pulled low over his eyes. There was Nora, a partial profile, laughing at something. And there was their father, throwing a perfect loop towards a plunging calf.

I turned back to Clint. He was staring at the floor, his mouth a tight knot. For once, the correct thing to say rose to my lips unbidden. "It's a beautiful shot. I'm sorry for your loss." I felt proud of myself after I said this, as if I'd passed some sort of test.

"She was a photographer." He said this in a wistful tone that was hard to hear. My newfound conversational alacrity abandoned me. I could think of nothing more to say. He went on after a moment's silence. "I've got a phone call to make as well. You have everything you need?"

I nodded He turned around, disappearing back the way he'd come.

Heart pounding, I returned to the desk, where I felt a disproportionate surge of relief when my phone powered on without a hitch. I waited as it searched for a signal, managed to register one tiny bar, and downloaded a deluge of messages from my mother along with one or two from my dad. Instead of reading them all, I texted them back. "Safe at the Tipped Z, but stuck for the night. Boswell and Norman are fine."

I hit send, and went back to my list of messages, noticing one from Nora mixed in with all the ones from my mother. I opened it. "Feel free to borrow any of my clothes," it said.

I stared at my screen for a moment. It occurred to me Nora had not been entirely on the up and up in her matchmaker role. Why hadn't she told me Clint had been married—that he'd suffered such a loss?

I wrote her back. "Thanks. Currently inhabiting one of your old shirts."

I sent this, and continued to think. Nora had seemed like the sort of person who told everybody everything. But clearly her propensity for chatter didn't mean an indiscriminate spewing of information.

On impulse, I composed another text. "Can you think of any reason Clint might have been cool towards me since Sunday?"

I sent this and waited, glancing behind me at the door to Clint's room as if it might disgorge an angry bull at any moment. I wanted to take the phone charger with me to my bedroom so I could text behind a closed door. But that seemed both rude and forward.

I waited for what seemed like an eternity but was really less than one minute. My phone beeped. The text was from my mom. "Finally!"

The next one was from my dad. "So glad to hear it honey. Rest well tonight. Love you."

Before I could start a reply, Nora wrote back. "Sorry. Probably shouldn't have interfered. I told him about your other guy. He's kind of fragile. He seemed so into you. Didn't want him getting hurt."

I texted back, righteous indignation flooding my veins. "My other guy???" Then I waited, heart pounding, staring at the screen until it lit with Nora's reply.

"I saw you downtown last week, kissing by your car."

A crushing wave of realization swept over me. I knew what she was talking about. That night Ben had taken me to dinner, he'd walked me back to my car, and stolen that kiss. He'd looked behind me at a group of girls. He'd said it had seemed like one of them was going to call out to me, but then had moved on.

I wanted to bang my head against the wall. I wanted to text Nora back and tell her Ben was nothing, he was no one, things were over between us.

But then I remembered how I'd made out with him just a few days ago. In reality, I'd had ample opportunity to end that relationship. And I hadn't.

I had nothing to say in my own defense. Clint had kissed me, and a few days later Nora had seen me out on the town with another guy.

Nora texted again. "You're the first girl he's shown any interest in since his wife died four years ago. I thought he should know. Didn't think he'd take it quite so bad."

I wrote back, feeling shaky and ashamed. "Thanks for telling me."

Chapter 12

"Erin!" My dad said my name with a huge smile, pushing open the low gate in Clint's patio wall to step up onto the porch and wrap me in a warm, enthusiastic hug. It took me a moment to hug him back, mostly because I was having trouble processing his presence.

Sensing my confusion, he released me and stepped back, holding me at arm's length to survey my face, still beaming. "Your mom's up at the barn with the dogs. Clint sent me down here to find you."

Indeed, my father's mud-spattered Ford Explorer was parked a short distance off, the driver's side door hanging open.

"How did you get in?" It had been only an hour since I'd texted them. Clint had reappeared from his room a few minutes after my exchange with Nora and said he was going back out to check on the herds and the fences now that the rain had stopped.

I'd spent the last hour giving myself a pep-talk. I had an opportunity here, I'd decided. An opportunity to spend an evening with Clint and repair the damage that had been done the night Nora had seen me with Ben.

Except here was my dad, standing in the failing light in Clint's puddle-spotted driveway, ready to be my latest rescuer.

And it was good to see my dad. He looked a bit thinner than when he'd left, his hair perhaps a little more gray. But he was beaming at me with such happiness, my answering smile soon shifted from forced to genuine.

"It was a bit of a maze, let me tell you," my dad said in response to my question. "We had to string together a bunch of neighborhood streets and cross one or two pieces of terrain that aren't precisely meant to be driven on. But your mother wasn't happy about the dogs spending the night in a horse stall, and we both couldn't wait to see you."

"Thanks for coming." I managed to get the sentence out without giving away my dismay. "Let me go grab my stuff."

My mother was waiting in front of the barn when my dad and I followed Clint's looping driveway up past the ranch house and stopped in the parking area. Boswell and Norman were with her, sitting on either side of her and blinking around at the twilight with bleary eyes. She came over to give me a hug when I stepped out of the car. When she released me, she said, "Thank you for getting them out, Erin. Clint said it was a hard ride but you did really well, and he couldn't have gotten them both back without your help."

Surprised, I glanced around the parking area. Now that the storm had blown over, the evening was still and quiet, the normal activity of birds, small animals, and insects on pause as the desert's inhabitants began a waterlogged recovery. It occurred to me for the first time that I could have declined to go with Clint, or sent the dogs with him and staked my hopes on the return of the helicopter.

"Where is Clint?" I was adjusting to the idea that I wasn't going to spend the evening in Clint's house after all. I couldn't decide if this was a relief or a disappointment. Still, I didn't want to leave without saying good-bye.

"He rode off somewhere." My mother made a vague gesture with her hand. "He said he wouldn't be back until after dark." She moved to the back of the Explorer as she spoke and opened the rear hatch so Boswell and Norman could hop up.

A wave of weariness washed over me. After it had seemed the entire universe had conspired to get me and Clint alone together, cut off from the outside world, thrown into an intimate situation, it had changed the set-up at the last minute. I spent one more moment staring out towards the darkening pastures, as if Clint might materialize, riding out of the twilight to ... do what? Ask me to stay anyway? Ask for my hand in marriage? Maybe my problem with relationships was I didn't even know how to fantasize about romantic outcomes.

My mom shut the tailgate and climbed into the front seat. On horseback, up in the mountains, I'd been scared but intrepid. I'd risen to the occasion, walking through a rushing sheet of water in a lightning storm, handling Paul's tantrum when he didn't want to walk into the wind, steadying Norman in front of me in the saddle as we endured a deluge. Now I was relegated to the back seat, just like when I'd been a kid, to stare out the side windows and watch the moon rise as my father patched together a winding route back to my apartment complex.

"She lives!"

I looked up from the mat I was cutting to see Anne standing in the workroom doorway, wearing a flowing linen suit and a delighted smile. One thing about getting stranded by a natural disaster for a few days is it sure makes everyone happy to see you.

I smiled back, finished my cut, and set the mat aside.

It had been a busy couple of days. When I'd arrived with my parents back at my apartment complex, I'd learned my father had had the brilliant idea of asking at the office if there was an unoccupied apartment they could rent for a week or two. Before they'd come to get me, my parents had moved my father's suitcase and my mother's meagre array of possessions out of my domain and into their temporary accommodations. Which meant I did not have to share my one-room apartment with my parents and two dogs. This had been more of a relief than I would ever admit to anyone.

It was now Thursday morning. Anne had insisted I take Wednesday off to, "Get reoriented," which had turned out to mean alternately pacing around my apartment and walking over to check on my parents.

Anne was grinning at me, one shapely eyebrow cocked, her face amused. "And you got rescued on horseback? By a cowboy?"

I felt myself begin to blush. To cover this, I cut a fresh piece of brown paper off the roll and taped it down over my work area, saying, "Clint rode in with a horse for me."

Anne was still beaming. "That is the best story I've ever heard. I hope you gave him an appropriate thank you."

I had to admit it did make a good story, as long as you omitted the part where I'd blown my opportunity to express my gratitude via overwhelmed kisses or amorous, lingering, embraces.

Ever since my parents had driven me back to my apartment, I had been busy imagining all the ways in which I could have used my time with Clint to advantage. I could have, say, flung my arms around him when he'd first arrived at my parents' house. I could have orchestrated a sodden but romantic make-out session once we'd made it back to the ranch. I could have boldly invaded his bedroom after I'd showered, or at least smoothed down his spiked hair and thanked him for saving me.

I'd done none of these things. As far as I could recall, I hadn't even said thank you. I certainly hadn't delivered the obligatory kiss required from any rescued damsel in distress.

I flicked a piece of lint off the surface of the clean paper. "Yeah, I'm afraid I blew it in that regard."

"Blew it?" Anne said, coming into the room and leaning against the other side of the table. "What do you mean?"

"I found out Nora saw me downtown with Ben and told Clint. Now Clint thinks I'm with Ben, and was with Ben the whole time he and I sort of had a bit of thing. So even though we were together for hours, he has basically stopped talking to me. I think he's not interested after all." It was painful to sum things up so succinctly. But as the words flowed from my mouth, they had the ring of truth.

Anne looked skeptical. "But he'll still ride through a monsoon to rescue you from a flooded neighborhood."

I reached for the artwork for the frame. It was a small lithograph of a single rose in a vase standing in front of a window. I flipped it over and lined it up on the backing board. "His sister obviously made him do it. She'd probably have come for me herself, but she couldn't get to the ranch." The more I thought about the rescue in this light, the more it made sense. Clint had been holding back the whole time, keeping as much distance between us as possible.

But then I remembered what he'd said to my mom, about me doing well on the ride, about how I'd been helpful.

Anne was watching me, her eyes growing narrow as she seemed to pick up on my inner turmoil. "Erin." Her tone would have been stern if her eyes hadn't been so playful. "What are you not telling me?"

"He had a wife." I said it fast, staring at the back of the artwork. "She died."

This surprised even Anne. She was quiet for a while, fiddling with a stray piece of backing paper, folding it into halves, quarters, eights, then flattening it out again and repeating the process. I thought about how still Clint was in comparison to Anne. Clint never fidgeted. Every time he moved it was deliberate and calculated, efficient and smooth.

"What do you want in a relationship?" Anne said this in a firm tone. The question surprised me so much I didn't have an answer. She waited a moment while I scrambled around internally, coming up with nothing.

When I failed to answer, Anne strode across the room impatiently, tossing her scrap of paper in the trash can. "I mean," she said, coming back to the other side of the table, "does the damsel in distress role appeal to you? Is that how you want the balance of power to play out? Are you the helpless girl who needs rescuing? Or are you a partner who can tow the line: help him when he needs it?"

It seemed like a no-brainer to me, but as I prepared to answer I could see Anne wasn't done. She went on. "In spite of supposedly being liberated, so many woman still act helpless. They refuse to take initiative, they wait for the man to make a move. But what it seems like here is that Clint needs help. He expressed an interest in you. It sounds like he's not much of a talker, but he's gone out of his way to show you he cares. He rescued your mom's dogs once, then he rescued you and the dogs a second time. He's holding himself back because he's been through a lot and he doesn't know how *you* feel. For all he knows, you're in love with Ben."

I looked at Anne in some surprise. She seemed angry all of a sudden, like I'd done something to personally offend her. My tone was uncertain when I said, "So what do I do?"

Anne looked at me, her expression shifting back towards her more typical look. "You either let him go or you make a move. I'd say it's your choice."

She left then, her heels ringing on the tile floor as she strode towards her office. I stood, staring down at the back of the lithograph for a long time. Penciled on the back, it said, "Rives BFK, University of Arizona print shop, limestone, traditional etching." The words seemed to swim in front of my eyes. I moved away from the table so I wouldn't cry on the artwork.

Anne was right. I was behaving like the heroine in a bad piece of historical romance. Clint had made his moves. Several of them.

It was my turn to act.

I watched with some dismay as Olivia swiped at the plastic tray in front of her, sending a spray of cheerios flying in every direction while she laughed and followed up with a hand gesture I had recently learned meant "more" in sign-language.

I looked across the table at Trace. She gave a little shrug as she poured a few more cheerios from the box. She said, "Sometimes I wish we had a dog."

"I should have brought Boswell and Norman. They are not loving apartment life." I took a sip of my beer and tried to ignore the butterflies in my stomach.

It was Friday night. I was at Trace's house, attempting to get my courage up. I was determined to end things with Ben. Now. Tonight. Ben had wanted to take me out to dinner. I'd said I had plans, but wanted to drop by for a few minutes around 6:30.

It was a tricky business, planning to break up with someone. I hadn't wanted to say anything too foreboding and then leave him worrying all day. But on the other hand, it had seemed equally cruel to let him think we were going to have a fabulous evening that would result in more of the making out that had occurred the last time we'd seen each other.

So I had a plan. I was going to drive over to his house, give the boots back, and explain we were through.

I'd invited myself over to Trace's first, partially to save myself from my parents (who were almost as restless as Boswell and Norman in their temporary accommodations), and partially because I hadn't seen Trace all week. I was curious to see how she was doing.

"Are you sure though?" Trace said, picking up the thread of the conversation we'd been having before Olivia scattered her food. I'd been busy pouring my heart out, explaining my situation in detail. "You could go to Clint first, before you end things with Ben? That way if he's not into you, you have a fallback plan."

I shook my head as Trace shifted in her chair and picked a cheerio out from underneath one of her legs. "I need to end things with Ben, one way or another. I really like him. Just not in the right way."

Trace gave a sympathetic nod. Before Andrew, she'd been the queen of brief, flamboyant relationships. She'd broken a lot of hearts, sometimes dumping guys I thought she was into.

"Plus," I went on, corralling the stray cheerios on the table-top into a little pile with my hands, "I need to be able to tell Clint it's over. He can see through a lie like I can see through a window."

Olivia gave a shriek and picked up her sippy cup to bang it several times on the tray in front of her. Trace gave her daughter an absent smile.

The change in Trace since the last time I'd seen her was nothing short of remarkable. She hadn't turned into a lax parent, by any means, but she had gained a sort of equilibrium that had been lacking before. She was seated in the chair across from me with a glass of wine, leaning against the back with her legs crossed. Gone was that poised look she'd had for so long, the sense that she was ready to spring to action at any moment, to wage war on any stuffed animal large enough to smother, or plastic toy piece small enough to choke.

The house was looking more normal too. There was a bag of groceries on the counter. I could see a bag of tortilla chips protruding out the top and the outline of a jar of salsa next to it. It wasn't that the place was a mess, but it had lost the over-polished, pristine look that had suggested a certain over-amplified attention to cleanliness.

Trace looked better, too. The lines of strain around her eyes and mouth were diminished. She'd even laughed several times since I'd been here.

"What are you going to tell Ben?" Trace asked as Olivia scattered cheerios again, laughing like a maniac. According to Trace, Olivia had just been introduced to cheerios. To me it appeared she was getting a lot more mileage out of launching them than putting them in her mouth.

I rubbed at my forehead with one hand. As much as I recognized the necessity of what I had to do, the actual doing it part was not something I was looking forward to. "Just that I'm not into him, I guess."

Trace looked up, an expression of horror on her face. "You can't tell him that." She sounded as if I'd said I intended to bash his knees in with a length of pipe.

I began to add the latest scattering of cheerios to my pile. "Why not? It's the truth."

Trace was shaking her head. "You have to be nicer about it: pad reality for him. Getting dumped is hard on the male ego."

"So what would you say?"

Trace looked thoughtful for a moment, leaning forward to flick a stray cheerio into my pile. "Say you met someone right after you found out about Kim, and things are going well with the guy."

I shifted in my chair, giving Trace my most skeptical look. I tried to imagine saying this to Ben. It was not difficult to envision the crestfallen expression on his face, the hurt look in his eyes. "You think I should tell him there's someone else?" To me, that seemed unnecessarily cruel.

"It closes the door." Trace said this in a tone of authority, rotating the stem of her wine glass between her fingers. "It destroys his ability to keep hoping you'll change your mind. That, my friend, may seem mean. But it's the kindest thing you can do when you're dumping someone who doesn't want to be dumped." Trace rose as she finished her speech. "Will you keep an eye on her for a second?"

She left the kitchen. I heard the bathroom door close a moment later.

I looked over at Olivia, who was busy trying to pick a single cheerio up between one thumb and forefinger. She moved like a lobster who had only recently been converted to human form, pinching at the cheerio with a look of extreme concentration on her face.

I leaned forward, picked up the cheerio, and tried to hand it to her. Her fingers were soft and sticky with a mix of cheerio dust and baby saliva. Three cheerios were stuck to the bare skin of her forearm. She kept up with the pinching motion. I couldn't help but laugh as the hand-off failed several times in quick succession.

I had finally gotten the cheerio transferred from my hand to Olivia's when Trace returned, walking back into the kitchen just in time to see her daughter laugh, hold the cheerio up in front of her face, and shove it into her mouth.

I left my apartment, turned to lock the door, and headed towards the parking area. Instead of going down to my car, I turned left and continued halfway around the arc of the lot, turning up the walkway that had the offices and the pool on one side and apartments on the other. It was dark out. The solar lights threw their pale, mild light around them in pale puddles.

I knocked on the door of Unit 1. It was only a moment before I heard the clicking of toenails on the other side of the door and the snuffling sounds of dogs. But there was no immediate response that sounded human.

As I waited for the door to open, I realized I never knocked when I went to my parents' house. I always walked right in and said hello.

The night was cool. A breeze stirred the decorative shrubbery around the paths. I crossed my arms. A dove was calling somewhere nearby. I wondered what about birds allowed them to be so satisfied with making one noise indefinitely.

I was beginning to worry my parents had decided to go out to dinner when I heard the sound of the dead bolt turning. My father opened the door. He was wearing a bath robe, and his hair was dripping wet. Boswell and Norman crowded around his legs. Their tails began to wag when they saw me.

"Sorry, hon," my Dad said. "I was in the shower."

He walked away from the door so I could come inside. I stepped around the dogs, pausing long enough to pat their backs.

The apartment my parents now occupied was one the complex kept vacant but furnished for two reasons. They used it to show off their fanciest model to interested parties. But it also served to house other occupants of the complex in the event of broken water pipes, malfunctioning stove tops, backed up plumping, or any of the other eventualities that could render a small space temporarily uninhabitable. I had not stayed here during my gas leak adventure because two apartments had been impacted by that problem, and the other one had housed a family with two young kids and a dog.

The floorplan was much larger than mine. The kitchen was its own independent space, with a dedicated dining area. There was a good-sized living room, three bedrooms, and a small patio out back. It was populated with the kind of furniture that looks nice from a distance but upon closer inspection turns out to be both cheap and worn.

"Where's Mom?" I followed my dad inside and shut the door behind me. I'd not yet gotten over the strangeness of seeing my parents in this place. My dad's phone sat on the kitchen counter. Boswell and Norman's shiny new food and water bowls stood on the tile near the patio entrance.

My dad was rubbing his hair dry with a towel. "She's out shopping. She's been putting off buying any real clothes. But she's meeting a potential client tomorrow, so she needs something reputable."

I would have thought this was strange, except it was classic Mom. She always made a point of shopping at off hours, darting into places before they closed, knowing she'd be one of the only people in the store.

My mother disliked crowds of strangers, most particularly when she was trying on clothing.

My dad disappeared into the bedroom and came back a moment later wearing jeans and a t-shirt. He looked at me, still hovering in the entryway, and said, "Is everything all right?"

"I broke up with Ben." This had been on the tip of my tongue since I'd arrived. It was strange to say it out loud, to tell someone else about the scene that had just finished playing out.

My father looked confused. "Come on in and sit down," he said. As we adjourned to the living room, he added, "Forgive me for being out of the loop, but I thought you broke up with Ben some time ago?"

I collapsed onto the couch. Norman came over to set his heavy, bullet-shaped head on the cushion beside me. I ran my thumb along the ridge in the center of his skull as he gave a happy sigh.

Dad settled into the chair opposite me. I filled him in on all that had transpired in my recent romantic history, adding the part where I had gone over to Ben's house with the box of still unworn boots, given them back, thanked him for trying so hard, and told him it wasn't going to work out.

I almost hadn't taken Trace's advice. On the way over to Ben's, I'd decided not to. But Ben had tried to refuse the boots, tried to tell me it was fine, we didn't have to hurry, he understood it might take a while to get back where we'd been before the Kim misunderstanding.

Then I'd seen what she'd meant. As long as it was just me not caring enough, Ben would think there was hope, some chance he could find the right switch to flip and get us back on the course we'd been on before.

So I'd told him about Clint after all. Not everything about Clint, of course. Or even Clint's name. I'd explained I'd met someone, fallen hard for him, and that was that.

And as Trace had predicted, Ben had changed. He'd closed up, his face going a little hard. I'd set the boots on his coffee table and said I was sorry again. He'd walked me to the door.

I'd come home, spent five minutes in my empty apartment, and come in search of parental support.

My father took my story quietly, absorbing every detail. When I was finished, he leaned forward and squeezed my knee. "You did the right thing, honey." He said this in his warmest, most paternal tone.

I was surprised to feel the sting of tears behind my eyes. I nodded, looking away from him at the dark window. "Thanks, Dad. Now can we talk about something else?"

My dad sat back in his chair, eyes twinkling a little. "I have some news, too," he said.

Norman gave a little groan and slid from his half-propped pose to lie next to me on the floor, setting his warm jaw on top of my foot. For some reason, this little act of fidelity caused one of my not-quite shed tears to escape from my eye. I wiped at it discreetly while I waited for my father to go on.

He straightened in his chair, assumed his "I'm going to tell you a long story" expression, and began.

"Six months ago, I agreed to take on a higher-risk, higher intensity series of jobs. I can't tell you much about them, but they meant more travel, more responsibly, and more time spent in less stable areas. It was one of these if/then/maybe sorts of deals that pop up in the military from time to time. Basically, if I agreed to do this work, my supervisors would recommend me for early retirement, and maybe I would get to leave five years early."

I looked up from the baseboard I'd been squinting at, my urge to cry passing.

My dad went on. "I didn't tell you and your mother because I didn't want to get anyone's hopes up. But...." He paused, grinning. "I heard today. No more trips overseas. My last day will be December 31st."

I stood up, thoughts of Ben banished to the backburner. Dad stood too. I gently dislodged Norman's head so I could walk around the table and give him a huge hug. "Does Mom know?"

We stepped back from the embrace, beaming at each other. He shook his head. "I got the final word on all this today. She was mad at me this afternoon because I've had to stay late at work all week. She left to go shopping almost the moment I got home." He winked at me. "I figured I'd tell her when she got back."

I glanced towards the door as if I could summon her by pure force of will. The clock on the microwave said 8:41. "Stores will be closing," I said. "I bet she'll be home soon."

⊙

I shifted in my chair, scooching more to one side so the encroaching shadow of the mesquite tree did not fall across my page. Not that I was getting a whole lot of reading done. I seemed to be averaging about one page every ten minutes.

I was sitting on the little patio in front of Clint's house, occupying one of his deck chairs. His truck was parked in front of the house. I knew he was around, but there had been no response to my knocking. I assumed he was out on horseback. Which was what I'd expected. I'd settled in to wait.

It was a beautiful, soft desert evening with a smattering of clouds across the sky. The breeze had a cool underbelly, and I'd thrown my most stylish woolen pull-over in my car in case I got cold waiting.

As much as I wasn't making much progress with my book, I was also surprisingly not nervous. After my mother had gotten home the night before and we'd celebrated my dad's retirement with a toast, I'd headed back to my place in a kind of happy fog. Today, I had planned my next move. While I should have been riddled with anxiety over what I was about to do, instead I felt calm, centered, and confident.

I was taking Anne's advice. I was going to make a move. And I comforted myself with the knowledge that things with Clint could not possibly get any worse. A little initiation on my part might even make them a whole lot better.

Of course, there was also the other possibility. After today I might never want to show my face on the Tipped Z again. But I tried not to dwell on that outcome.

Clint's house was a peaceful place. With the hill at its back, it managed to attain the feeling of being totally isolated, of having its own little bubble of spacious solitude. The sagebrush plains fell away in every direction, now blurring pink at the horizon. I could make out the dotted shapes of cattle in the far distance and the distant lowing of a herd making their evening migration.

But so far, no Clint.

I sat up straighter, shifting around and closing my book. My stomach gave a grumble. I shushed it. Today was about the plane of emotion, the higher matters of heart and spirit, not the base needs of the body.

My stomach was not swayed by this logic. It growled again. I wondered if I had a granola bar in my car.

I was about to go check when I heard the jingle of a spur.

I went still, staring through the fading light at where Clint's driveway wrapped and descended around the side of the hill. A cottontail rabbit made its lazy, hop-wise way across the packed dirt, but I could see no other sign of life.

I heard the jingle again and turned in my chair in time to see Clint strolling around the other side of the hill. Belatedly, I realized there was a narrow path there—a more direct route between his house and the barn. It led to a side door I'd not noticed before. With a stab of consternation, I realized he was going to go straight inside without seeing me.

I stood, thinking I should call out, do something to get his attention. My previous calm had vanished like mist in the desert sunrise. My heart was hammering out a frantic baseline in my chest, but I stayed silent.

Dots saved me. She was walking at Clint's side, her small, pale form a bright, delicate outline in the failing light. When I stood up, she went stiff, the wiry hair all along her back rising. She stopped walking and growled.

Clint had been gazing off at the cattle, but Dots' alarm brought him back to the present. He stopped walking instantly and he looked down, checking the terrain around his feet for snakes.

I took one little step closer. Dots gave a single bark, hopping on her front paws as she did so, as if the force of her warning was so great it caused a brief lift-off.

Clint looked up, and he saw me. He set a reassuring hand on Dots' head. The dog went still. We all went still. The desert seemed to suspend its normal activity in anticipation, as if it had been waiting for the finale and was watching how this scene would turn out with great interest.

I made no other move. All the pretty phrases I'd practiced on my drive over vanished from my brain. I'd promised myself I wouldn't be tongue-tied and awkward. I would be firm, eloquent, persuasive, and collected.

Clint changed course. As he set his hand on the side gate that led onto the patio, I was none of those things. I was as still as the wall behind me. I was a life-sized cardboard cutout. I was sure I'd even stopped breathing.

The latch on the gate gave a click. A hinge squeaked as it swung open. Clint came through, waited for Dots, and closed the gate behind them.

We were now separated by only a small expanse of flagstone.

Dots trotted up to me, sniffed my pant leg, gave a little wag of her tail, and went to lie on the welcome mat.

Clint waited a moment, staring at me with a face I couldn't read. He walked forward until he was only a few feet away. Then he stopped. He was wearing his hat. It cast a long shadow over his face, but I knew him well enough now to see the tension in his stance. Was it possible he was as nervous as I was? That he was so quiet and closed and still because he felt as shaky as I did?

I'd been determined to speak first, but I failed at that. He said my name, setting it free in the blushing night like a toy boat pushed onto a lake. "Erin."

There was a pause as my heart attempted to batter its way free of my rib cage.

Clint spoke again. "Did you forget something?"

I glanced towards Dots, who had set her head on her paws with the patient air of one accustomed to waiting. At first I didn't know what he meant. Then I realized he must think I'd come back for a stray item— some small but vital object that had escaped my purse and fallen behind the dresser or been kicked under the bed in the guest room.

"No," I said, managing my first word of the evening.

The outline of Clint's hat gave a small, uncertain nod.

I tried to rally. I'd come here to make my position and my feelings clear, not to gape at him like a schoolgirl. The light was weaker with every moment, and Clint had his back to the bright sky. He was becoming an extremely sexy outline of a cowboy, like one of those decorative metal yard ornaments shaped as silhouettes.

I took a step closer. The movement seemed to clear the cobwebs from my brain. I was suddenly glad I couldn't see much of Clint's face. It made talking easier. I said, "I broke up with Ben."

It was Clint's turn to be silent. He made no reaction. He stood as still as an actual yard statue. Ridiculously, I wondered if he'd heard me.

I fumbled on. "I actually was never with Ben, really. The whole thing was kind of a mistake. We'd been dating for a little while and it wasn't going anywhere. It was clear we weren't clicking." Now that I'd gotten going, I couldn't seem to stop. The words came with a reckless, headlong momentum, not stopping at checkpoints to make sure they were authorized. "It probably would have fizzled into nothing, but then I met you, and one night after a date with Ben I...." I stopped, a need to preserve my own dignity stilling my tongue.

But it was too late. Clint took a single step forward, all his focus locked on me. "You what?" The question was quiet, but compelling.

Resigned now to spilling the whole truth, I went on. "I kissed Ben. But I pretended to be kissing you."

Clint came forward another step. He was close enough now that I could see the gentle rise and fall of his chest as he breathed. "And?"

I looked away, my eyes seeking Dots again as if she could help. She returned my gaze with an unsympathetic, matter-of-fact air that seemed to imply she was the sort of dog who believed in personal responsibility. I'd dug myself into this hole. I could find my own way out.

I fumbled on. "Well, it changed everything. He got really interested in me. I thought I could never have you anyway, so I kept pretending. The next thing I knew, he was buying me boots and changing his life around so I could fit into it. But I never wanted that."

Another step. Clint was close enough I could have raised my hand and set it on his forearm. His voice was a thrumming rumble in the half-dark. "What did you want?"

I looked up into the shadowed space under Clint's hat-brim. I could see his eyes, even in the dim light. There was a little spark in them. Humor? Hope? I couldn't tell.

"You." The word caught in my throat. It came out as nothing more than a whisper. But it was loud enough.

Clint heard, and took that last step forward.

Suddenly, he was all around me, one of his warm, gentle hands on my back, the other tipping my jaw up a little. His mouth was on my mouth, and we were kissing.

If I'd thought the kiss in the cottonwood grove had been electric, this was a firestorm. It was as if Clint had been holding himself in check by pure force of will. Now that I'd given him permission, he pulled out all the stops. His lips were warm and firm against mine. I felt the scratch of the stubble on his jaw and tasted the tang of salt on his lips. I ran my hands down his back and encountered the belt of his chinks. I ran them up his neck and they bumped the brim of his hat.

We kissed for a long time. I got lost in the depths of Clint. It felt like he was telling me a secret he'd been keeping half his life—a secret he'd never trusted to anyone.

Finally, the kiss slowed and cooled. Our lips parted.

It was full dark now. Dots had put her head on her paws and gone to sleep, lit by a little solar lamp that glowed next to the door.

Clint ran a hand through my hair, pushing a few stray strands back from my face. "So what now, Erin?" His voice was soft, calculated to carry only to my ears, as if we were in a crowded room and he wanted not to be overheard. I could see that little smile tugging the corners of his mouth.

I had foreseen this moment. I remembered the rest of my plan. "I brought a frozen pizza and a bottle of wine. All I need is an oven, a bottle opener, and some company."

Clint ran a gentle thumb over the soft spot between my eyebrow and hairline. His voice was low and smooth when he said, "I like a woman with a plan. Let's go on inside and see if I can provide those three things."

Exclusive Extended Epilogue

This is the end of Erin and Clint's love story. Although they appear as characters in later books in the series, they're no longer in the spotlight.

There is a 30 page extended epilogue, though! It exists in the form of a story called *Thrown* which reveals a secret link between *A Man Who Rides* and the next book in the series, *A Man Who Starts*.

Thrown is available only to members of my mailing list!

If you want to check it out, please visit:
stefaniwilder.com/clintanderin

About the Author

Growing up in Tucson, Arizona, Stefani always hoped to marry a cowboy. She did not. (Instead she fell in love with a man who turned into a cowboy. But that's a story for another day.) She has always loved to write stories and ride horses. Now she frequently writes stories about riding horses and falling in love.

Stefani Wilder is a pen name for Robin Stephen.

Please visit one of her websites for more details:

- stefaniwilder.com
- robinstephen.com

A Man Who Starts

Tipped Z: Book #2

Stefani Wilder

Nora is determined not to marry a cowboy. But she's also not sure she could ever fall for a man who can't handle himself on horseback.

It's not that Nora doesn't love the Tipped Z. She wouldn't trade her childhood starting colts and driving cattle through sagebrush for anything. But between her close-knit family, the endless work, and the hours in the scorching sun, she feels like she has to fight for the space to be herself. Despite her brother's constant hints that he could use more help, she takes a new job that will mean more travel and less time at the ranch.

As Nora tries to adapt to her new lifestyle, her lifelong crush, Wyatt, agrees to help out at the Tipped Z to make up for her absence. Every time Nora and Wyatt are together, the sparks seem to fly. But Wyatt has a history of leaving. His life as a roving colt starter makes him hard to pin down. Despite his allure and the chemistry between them, Nora knows better than to think she could change him.

So Nora doubles down on her goals to carve out her own space in the world. It never occurs to her that she might not know Wyatt as well as she thinks.

www.ingramcontent.com/pod-product-compliance
Lightning Source LLC
Chambersburg PA
CBHW021028130626
46552CB00005B/1743